'I called you,' he said to her, 'but you did not hear me above the noise of the water.'

'There is no need to lie to me, Rhodri. I understand your position, the loyalties that bind you. I had hoped that leaving me here would be enough, but a warrior's conscience guides a warrior's hand, and I have . . .'

'Wait! Wait!' He flashed his open palm across her eyes as one would across a blind man's face. 'What words are these? They cannot be from the Dena I held so tightly in my arms, the Dena who offered her lips to mine in the darkness of the night.'

Where his incredulous tone could not touch her, his choice of words did. How could he speak of what they had given and shared, when all he wanted was to deny its occurrence?

He rocked back a pace as the full implication of what she had said came to him. 'You think I am going to kill you!'

Since her early teens, Linda Acaster has harboured a love of Dark Age history and adventure fiction. The two are combined in her first novel, *Hostage of the Heart*. She visits ancient sites in England and Wales to inspire her work and aid her research, and spends a great deal of time sifting through post-Norman writings in an effort to glean the true day-to-day lifestyle of pre-Conquest Britain. She lives in a coastal town in the East Riding of Yorkshire, her native county.

Hostage of the Heart is the winner of the 1986 Netta Muskett Award for New Writers presented by the Romantic Novelists' Association.

HOSTAGE OF THE HEART

LINDA ACASTER

MILLS & BOON LIMITED
15–16 BROOK'S MEWS
LONDON W1A 1DR

*First published in Great Britain 1986
by Mills & Boon Limited*

© *Linda Acaster 1986*

*Australian copyright 1986
Philippine copyright 1986
This edition 1986*

ISBN 0 263 75424 3

*Set in 10 on 12 pt Linotron Times
04–0686–69,600*

*Photoset by Rowland Phototypesetting Limited
Bury St Edmunds, Suffolk
Made and printed in Great Britain by
Cox & Wyman Limited, Reading*

To David, Steven and Rex, thanks

Historical Note

BY THE mid-11th century, England was the diamond in the crown of European kingdoms. Its harvests were usually good, its trade advancing. Internal dissenters were few. Yet a current of unease coursed through the land. Edward the Confessor, king for twenty-four years, had no heir to take his place upon the throne. Across the seas, the greedy eyes of Norway and Normandy watched, and waited.

On 5 January 1066 the unthinkable happened. Edward died. Amidst speculation and controversy, Harold Godwineson, the most powerful earl in the country, was offered the crown and enthroned the very next day.

Both Harald Hardrada of Norway and William of Normandy were incensed at what they saw as a flagrant breach of previously sworn promises. Each began building ships ready to take by force of arms what they believed was rightfully theirs.

By September, both fleets were ready. All they needed was a favourable wind. When it came, it came from the north.

Harald Hardrada's distinctive longships were sighted in the Humber, and the English militia, the *fyrd*, was raised and marched towards York to do battle in defence of the kingdom. They came from all parts of northern England, but none answered the call as quickly as the lesser nobility, eager to prove themselves loyal to the new king.

One such man was Edwulf, thegn of a small estate on the borders of northern Wales. What befell his household when he and his men marched eastwards to join the king would not readily be forgotten . . .

CHAPTER
ONE

DENA LOOKED up from her embroidery and out over the dusty yard. Her eyes traced the lane as it wound down the bank, through the palisade and over the defence ditch, towards the little fields beyond. Women, bent double with the weight of corn upon their backs, were shuffling their way towards the wooden hall and its adjacent buildings, their children following behind, each carrying some burden, however small.

She pursed her lips thoughtfully, trying to reconcile the sight before her with her ever-increasing sense of guilt. She stole a glance at the richly dressed woman beside her, but Ethelin had no eyes for the labours of the people. Her attention was fixed upon the partly embroidered banner on her lap, and the girl saw her smile as she fingered the delicate stitches. Dena knew her opinion would get short shrift from her aunt, but she had to voice it.

'We should help with the harvesting,' she said at last. 'With all the able-bodied men gone with Edwulf to rally at the King's standard, there are not enough people left to work in the fields.'

'I have told you before, Dena, it is below your station to harden your hands with such a task. Until you are found a husband, it is your place to be at my side as companion.'

Ethelin did not even raise her eyes from her needlework as she spoke, and Dena let a terse sigh of frustration escape her lips.

'You must learn patience, girl. King Harold will reward our lord when this upstart Norwegian has been routed from our shores, just as the late King Edward did in return for our lord's services. I will ensure that part of it goes towards raising your marriage settlement. Edwulf will gain prestige at court if you marry well. Those puppets are quick to sneer at my lord because his wealth is not inherited, but when the banner rises above the king, Edwulf is first beneath it. Remember that with pride.'

It was well to speak of prestige at court, but Dena felt it had little to do with the matter in hand. 'Edwulf will not be happy if he returns to find that it has rained before the crops are in and the harvest is ruined.'

Ethelin shot her a piercing look, and Dena knew that she should keep her tongue. Edwulf's young wife might not be the best of female company, but she was all that Dena had since she had been forced to seek shelter with her uncle upon her father's death.

She had never met Edwulf before then, or learned a great deal about him from her father. Her only uncle remained a shadowy figure in her thin list of relatives, and although her father would not say, Dena had gained the impression that in their younger days the two brothers had held little love for one another, finally travelling their separate ways long before she had been born.

When the coughing sickness had taken her father from her, Dena had felt desperately alone; with creditors clamouring at the door to the little farmstead, she had been left with no option but to seek the protection of her uncle, or to gain entry to a nunnery.

The first sight of Edwulf had made her wish she had chosen a nunnery. He was short, but powerfully built, with deep-set eyes all but hidden beneath a fierce growth of hair and eyebrows. He growled often and hardly ever seemed in a good humour apart from feast days, but the people did not fear him; since her arrival in the late winter, Dena had come to realise that this was merely his normal manner and not to be taken too seriously.

In such a household she would have felt alone and rejected except for the friendliness shown her by Wybert, Edwulf's steward, who kept the day-to-day routine of the estate running smoothly. He was older than Edwulf, a trusted friend and adviser for many years, she had been told. He was very tall, Dena believed almost a giant, with a great breadth across the shoulders. He had a shock of iron-grey hair and blue eyes that melted like a summer sky. For all his advancing years, his body was still rigid with muscle, for he practised daily with all weapons and did, indeed, live up to his name of Wybert the Bear.

Dena was not allowed the freedom of the estate that she had enjoyed at her father's farmstead. It was dangerous to go out beyond the palisade, Ethelin had told her. The Welsh raided for cattle and sheep and would not be above carrying off a woman, if they were given the chance. Dena remained within the hall's defences, a caged bird yearning for the freedom she could enjoy only in Wybert's company. Under his protection she could go riding, visit the people at the tun, Edwulf's northern outpost, see the spectacular waterfall to the south of the hall, pick mushrooms at the edge of the forest, all the things Edwulf's ceorls could do, but she could not.

Close to tears one day after a particularly cold rebuff from Edwulf, she had confided in Wybert her wish that her uncle could be more like him. The steward had placed a comforting arm round her shoulders.

'You must remember,' he had said, 'that Edwulf is a fighting man in the old tradition. The land, the animals, the people—all this is his wealth, but he is never happier than when he has a sword in his hand.'

That Dena could not deny. When news of the Norwegian invasion had reached the estate, it was as though Edwulf had been bewitched. He gathered all the people into the hall and gave a rousing battle-speech that would have lifted even the faintest of hearts. Before the day was through, he had the freely given allegiance of every man present and ensured that all were equipped with the best weapons available, be it a sword, spear, or plain cudgel. Beneath his banner they had marched eastwards the very next morning, leaving their loved ones tearfully proud, yet fearful, to listen to the dimly echoing drumbeats drifting on the breeze.

'I hope there will be time to get this finished before my lord returns triumphant,' Ethelin mused, inspecting the stitchwork of the banner in her hand. 'He has been gone four days already. Surely that will be time enough to get the men to York?'

Dena did not reply. She did not share Ethelin's enthusiasm for the rigours of the battlefield, or her blinkered view of the prestige and honour to be gained there. Men died. Limbs could be severed in a single blow, skulls crushed beneath the hooves of terrified horses—and these Norwegians, were they not the descendants of the Norsemen who had viciously plundered the land long ago? She recalled the terrifying tales spun by the travelling story-tellers during the long winter evenings of her childhood. Could it all be about to happen again?

'Dena?'

Her thoughts flew back to the reality of the moment, but she could not help blushing as Ethelin peered at her so curiously.

'You looked so pale. Do you fear Edwulf will not return?' The very thought made Ethelin chuckle. 'Poor Dena! He may be your father's brother, but from what I have been told, there could never have been two sons so opposite in temperament. I mean no disrespect to your father's memory, Dena, but Edwulf revels in the chase, in pitting strength against strength. Everything he owns has been gained through force of arms. Was not the land which feeds us wrested from the hands of the barbaric Welsh? Have you never listened to the minstrel's songs?'

Dena turned her face away in embarrassment, and Ethelin laughed at her niece's discomfort.

'Some will die in the battle; no doubt some from this estate, but not Edwulf.'

'No,' admitted Dena. 'I cannot see you in widowhood yet.'

She could see others, though, others Ethelin held no concern for. Ethelin never addressed the people by their individual names, only by their occupations. She even referred to Wybert as 'the Steward', and he was Edwulf's lifelong friend. Dena had seen him cast dark looks in Ethelin's direction after she had arrogantly directed him as though he were her servant, but if he had ever complained to Edwulf, Dena knew nothing of it. Perhaps Wybert realised that his words would fall on stony ground.

For all their difference in age, Edwulf doted on his wife and she on him, though more than once Dena had found herself wondering uncharitably if Ethelin loved the many gifts he bestowed upon her more than the man himself. The attention she paid him in front of guests seemed a little too affected to Dena's untutored eyes, but who was she to judge what passed for love between a man and a woman? She had spent her years in a sad household. Her father had not taken another wife after Dena's mother had died. Dena had always believed that her company had been enough for him, but since coming to live on Edwulf's estate, she could not help thinking that, perhaps, she had been but a shadow in her father's life, a shadow which had constantly reminded him of the dead wife he had loved so much. Whatever she thought of Ethelin, Dena had to agree that compared with Edwulf, her father had been a crushed and desolated man.

Ethelin laid down her embroidery and stretched her slim legs until her slippered feet peeped beneath her green ankle-length kirtle. 'I tire of this,' she groaned, 'and the day is long and hot.' Shielding her eyes with her hands, she looked up into the bright September sky and snorted irritably. 'The sun is at its zenith, yet we sit here without food. Is the cook, too, working in the fields?'

Dena winced at her tone and rose stiffly from her stool. 'I shall go to the kitchen and ask about the delay.'

'It will be I who shall go,' Ethelin retorted. 'With your mild manner, we shall still be waiting when darkness falls.'

Dena returned to her seat with an inaudible sigh. As she watched Ethelin strut forcefully through the open doorway of the hall, she felt sorry for Osyth and the other over-worked women trying to divide their time between harvesting in the fields and feeding the tired workers. She had never sat idly by and watched others toil in her father's household, and she found it hard to do so in Edwulf's.

She tried to direct her attention to her embroidery,

but her concentration had gone and she let her eyes
wander over the countryside which made up Edwulf's
estate. Sitting against the stout log wall of the hall, it
would have been a grand view if the land had looked a
little more hospitable. The hall had been built on the site
of an ancient hillfort, and Edwulf had saved labour by
using the course of the original defences. Although the
ditches had been redug and a new palisade erected, the
old vitrified stonework could still be seen in some quar-
ters. Wybert had taken great pains to point them out to
her when Dena had first arrived. As far as he was
concerned, Edwulf could not have improved upon the
original defensive design, but Wybert was made in the
same mould as his master and admired a keen military
mind. All Dena could see were mass fortifications, the
like of which her father's small farmstead had neither
seen nor needed.

It was a hard land compared with the rolling meadows
of her youth, all high moor and forest-cloaked vales, the
tiny fields hacked from the waste, shining yellow now
through the dark green foliage of tree and thicket. It was
not a land Dena would have willingly chosen to make a
home in, but perhaps she was only seeing it through a
woman's eyes. Besides, her stay would be short. She had
been made welcome by both Ethelin and Edwulf, but
neither hid the fact that they were anxious for her to
make a good match to boost their own standing in the
eyes of their peers. To Ethelin, at least, gaining prestige
at court seemed to be her one goal in life. Dena knew
that she should feel no animosity towards her aunt for
that. Marriage, after all, was a business arrangement. It
was doubtful whether Ethelin had set eyes upon Edwulf
before the pledging papers had been signed, and there
was love between them now. Still, for all his gruff

manner, Edwulf was the sort of man a young woman might warm to. Such considerations could be overlooked in the choosing of her spouse, especially if the matter of prestige ranked so highly.

Dena shrugged such thoughts from her mind. There was no point in fretting over something that might never happen. She turned her eyes towards the women carrying corn towards the hall, expecting to see the same slow toil she had been witnessing all morning. Instead, there was confusion. Burdens were being thrown aside and children swept up into their mothers' protective arms. Everyone was running up the lane towards the hall, some waving their hands above their heads, others shouting an inaudible warning.

Slowly Dena raised herself from her stool, letting the embroidery slip from her lap to lie on the ground at her feet. She stood as if mesmerised by the scene, watching as the women's anxious faces came more clearly into view, waiting, tremulously now, for their words to be carried to her on the breeze.

'Welsh!' the women were crying. 'Welsh!'

Dena furrowed her brow, not understanding; then realisation came like a dagger-blow, making her gasp. She looked up to the land beyond the fields, beyond the enshrouding forest, towards the ridge of wild inhospitable moor where lay the barbarous kingdoms of the Welsh. Edwulf had taken his estate from the hands of the Welsh by bloody conflict, or so the minstrel sang. Now the Welsh were coming to reclaim what was rightfully theirs. And where was Edwulf to hold them back?

She flew into the hall as if on angel's wings, but after the brightness of the sunshine the gloom of the hall reduced her to the state of a blind beggarwoman.

'Wybert!' she cried frantically. 'Wybert! The Welsh are upon us!'

A muffled exclamation came from her right, and she peered in its direction, her eyes gradually regaining their power of sight. Wybert was sitting at the head of a trestle table, Edwulf's huge ledger before him.

'What folly is this?' he demanded.

Dena hurried to his side. 'It is no folly—everyone is running from the fields in panic! Please come, Wybert. Please!'

From the expression on his face, she saw that she was not totally believed, but there was no mistaking the clamouring of high-pitched voices as the people neared the hall. Wybert motioned her aside with a sweep of his arm and strode towards the doorway, Dena at his heel.

They met the fearful throng on the threshold, and for a moment it was all Wybert could do to stop the people from tumbling into the hall. Children cried and women whimpered, some unable to hold back their tears. One old woman even fell on her knees before him, her hands held in supplication as though he were the Saviour.

He stilled them all with a thunderous roar which even the Welsh could have heard. 'What is this noise I hear? Are these the people of our Lord Edwulf or whining curs fit only for the stick?'

Wybert placed his hands on his hips and tossed back his long hair, defying anyone to challenge him. Even Ethelin, who had appeared from the kitchen and knew nothing of their danger, held her peace. He stepped into the open semicircle before him, casting a suspicious eye on anyone who dared to hold his stare.

'Whose ears heard these barbarians? Whose eyes saw them in the flesh?'

There was a shuffle and then a hush, and one by one

the people turned to watch a thin sallow-faced youth step forward and struggle for his words.

'It was I, Radford. I was at the waterfall, hiding from my work in the barley-field. They came past me, not an arm's length away, all armour and weaponry, but very slowly, as if they did not wish to be heard. I ran all the way back, warning everyone I saw.'

Even Wybert looked at him in surprise. Radford might not have been the best worker on the estate, but he was not one for spinning tales.

'You have done well, boy,' the steward said quietly. 'Edwulf shall hear of it.'

The hubbub began almost immediately as the people turned this way and that, putting voice to their fears. Dena risked a glance across the doorway to where Ethelin stood, hoping to gain strength from her aunt's resolute manner, but the news had dented her aloof and arrogant bearing more than Dena could have thought possible. Leaning against the edge of the doorway as if in a faint, she was murmuring quiet prayers of deliverance and crossing herself repeatedly after each short petition.

'Peace!' cried Wybert. 'We can still out-fox these surly Welshmen. It seems to me that they are not planning a main assault, but are intending to encircle the hall and hold us hostage for Edwulf's return. If we act quickly, we can still leave them with shamed faces.' He thought for a moment.

'Into the forest with you all! Women, take your children—take food and clothing, and leave all else. Men, close the palisade to the west. Bring out all the carts. Load them high with food. We will not lose this harvest to those marauding thieves!'

With tasks set them, the people hurried away with a new will. Wybert made no attempt to return to the hall, but marched towards the tight grouping of stores and work-huts, leaving Dena and Ethelin standing alone by the doorway. It was a deflating experience to be ignored in that way. Dena knew every hand would be needed if they were all to escape the ensnaring grasp of the Welsh, and it irked her that she should not be thought fit to be given a task. Wybert considered that she had one, of course, as companion to Ethelin, but Dena looked upon that as being little more than a well-kept maid.

She sighed as she looked at Ethelin, still caught rigidly in her continual evocations of the Holy Trinity. Although the wandering priests may have looked upon her aunt's exultations with pride, at that moment Dena had more faith in the military prowess of men like Wybert. But Ethelin was mistress of the estate, and however much Dena wished she would show a little more defiance, she could not chastise her. Gently she curled an arm about Ethelin's shoulders.

'Come, we must make ready to leave.'

For a moment Ethelin looked as though she did not know where she was; then she gave a little shudder and seemed to pull herself together.

'Yes,' she agreed. 'My Lord Edwulf will expect us to make a stand against these barbarians.'

'He will expect us to escape their clutches so that we shall not be used against him,' Dena corrected.

'Of course,' Ethelin intoned, but Dena was not sure whether she fully understood what was being said.

Ethelin's strange behaviour mystified her, but she knew little of her past life. Perhaps Ethelin had seen with her own eyes what atrocities the Welsh could inflict upon their enemies.

'Come,' Dena gently coaxed, 'we must go to your chamber and make preparations.'

Once surrounded by her personal possessions, Ethelin began to behave more like her usual self, but Dena was uncertain if she preferred her thus.

'I do not think Wybert will take kindly to your wanting to take so much,' Dena offered cautiously.

'Do you think I should leave Edwulf's silver to adorn some peasant hut!'

Dena did not know what to reply as she watched Ethelin pile plates and goblets into the chest containing her gowns. It was large, by any standards, and would need at least three men to carry it to the carts, if a cart were available.

'I will try to find some transport,' she murmured.

As soon as she reached the outside door, she knew that her fears had been realised. The first carts were already moving away, being pulled by lumbering oxen under threat of prodding sticks. The others were being loaded with sacks and earthenware jars. It was as though Wybert intended to take every morsel of food with him.

Dena crossed to the crippled man, Swithun, who was vainly trying to steady the head of a reluctant milk-cow forced between the shafts of a small cart.

'Are there more carts?' she asked. 'Lady Ethelin has a chest to be loaded.'

'I think not, but Steward Wybert has kept some horses back. Perhaps my lady's possessions could be put into saddlebags?'

'It would be best, I think. Where is Steward Wybert?'

'I hear he is in the brewing-house, but I know not the truth of it.'

Dena turned for the brewing-house, but her way was soon impeded by a group of older children driving swine and chickens before them. The air was thick with squawks and squeals as fowl and animal alike fought to escape their drovers. She found it easier to cling to the staves of a wattle fence and let them pass than to try to force a path through them. Everyone but she, it seemed, had a worthwhile task to do.

To her surprise, she did find Wybert in the brewing-house. The potion-woman, Mildthryth, was with him and they were busy crushing freshly-cut herbs with pestle and mortar. Even at this unlikely task Wybert was as if a commander on a battlefield, and several people pushed past Dena as she hovered in the doorway to deliver messages and await instructions.

'Who has been sent to the north tun?' Dena heard him ask of one of the youths. There was an ominous silence. Wybert almost dropped his pestle in his anguish. 'Dear God! Has no one gone to warn them? Take my horse at once.'

'I—I cannot ride such a beast,' came the fearful reply.

'I can!' announced Dena, stepping forward.

Wybert blinked at her in disbelief, but she left him no time for mockery.

'When my father was alive, I bred my own horses and was well known in the district for my skills with them.' She hoped that the good Lord would not strike her down for her exaggeration, but she knew if she were going to be able to do anything worthwhile, this was the task.

'All the horsemen have gone with Edwulf. The boy is as all the people, only used to riding cattle and ass. You have only me to send on this matter.'

Dena said no more. She could tell from Wybert's expression that he was caught between decisions. All she had to do was to hold her tongue and wait until Wybert realised that he had no other choice.

'You cannot go!' he protested. 'I would never forgive myself if anything happened to you.'

'Let her go,' Mildthryth advised. 'Beneath that timid shell, a stout-hearted girl yearns to break free. She will not fail you. There are many lives to be saved at the tun.'

Dena turned to the old woman with a smile on her lips, pleased to have an ally, but her smile faded when she saw the familiar glint in Mildthryth's eye. Some said she was a witch of sorts, living alone in her wattle hut beyond the palisade; but whatever the rumours, everyone—including Edwulf—consulted her for the treatment of ailments and to have bones cast for signs of fate. She was to be neither crossed nor taken lightly, and Dena felt a chill run through her body as her gaze was held for long, curious moments. It was as though Mildthryth was reading the destiny of her soul.

'There is no other way,' mumbled Wybert. 'Any man capable has already left with the carts. Go with care and my blessing, and may the Lord God watch over you.'

Dena's heart rose like a lark. She rushed out into the yard, pulling at her long skirts to draw the hems through her girdle so that she would have a suitable mode of dress for riding astride.

Wybert's mount was a large black war-horse with thick legs and a large head, and he did not take kindly to anyone but his master upon his back. Dena fought with the spirited animal, talking to him continuously until she felt him quieten beneath her; then, with a slap to the flanks, she headed him out of the yard and down the lane to where two youths were making her a way through the closed palisade. Her pulse beat wildly as the great loping horse began to gather speed. If he decided to try and unseat her now, he could do so quite easily, and if she were to land in the dust within sight of Wybert and the estate workers, she would never dare to raise her head again.

The big horse offered no resistance. As his stride lengthened and he gained his wind, Dena found she had to do no more than grip the saddle with her thighs and wind a hand in his flowing mane. He seemed to know he had to keep to the track along the edge of the trees, and with a full heart Dena realised that she would soon be within sight of the massive stone walls of the north tun. It had always surprised her that the tun had been so heavily fortified, when the hall had only a wooden palisade inside its ditches. Not many people lived there— only three families, as she recalled—but Edwulf was as proud of this extension to his domain as he was of the hall itself.

Past the line of the fields worked by the people living at the hall, trees crowded in on either side of the track; to the left the thick forest, to the right thinner woodland already partly cleared under Edwulf's direction and waiting for a plough to break the mossy earth before the onset of the winter frosts. Dena had to keep her head low to stop the reaching branches snatching at her flimsy headcloth. What with the movement of the horse and the height of the closely-packed trees, it was some time before she noticed the pall of grey smoke hanging in the sky.

Fear numbed her senses, freezing all movement in her limbs. Then a different fear filled her mind: fear for her personal safety. She pulled at the mane, and using all her strength, dragged Wybert's great horse to a shuddering standstill. She looked up at the trail of smoke that she knew must come from the burning thatched roof of the tun's dwelling-house. There was no point in going on —she accepted that—but in all conscience could she turn back to the hall and leave the people of the tun to their fate? Perhaps they were already dead—every man, woman and child—but what if they were not? What if one had survived and was making his way along the track towards the hall? What if he was wounded and being chased? He could be just beyond the next curve in the track. Dena knew that she could not turn for the safety of the hall without being certain that no one needed help. She urged the horse onward at a steady walk, all the time keeping alert for sounds and signs which would give her warning of impending danger.

She hardly dared to breathe as she reached the turning. It was a long curve following the stream which fed the tun, and she found she had to take the horse further than she intended in order to gain a view of a sufficient length of track. She saw them before she heard them, men walking on the rough pathway from the tun. She reined in the horse, unsure of what was before her. They looked like Saxons—they were certainly dressed like them—but she had never laid eyes upon a Welshman and did not know what to expect. They saw her and stopped, obviously equally surprised.

One raised his arm and waved, calling a greeting she could not catch, but the other men were moving oddly, shuffling behind one another as if trying to hide. Dena caught her breath as she realised how heavily armed they were. There was no such cache at the tun. These were Welshmen.

She turned Wybert's horse as quickly as she could, pulling at him and desperately digging the heels of her slippered feet into his ribs. The great brute was slow to respond, and before she could get him moving again, the Welshmen were bearing down on her, howling like demons straight from hell.

Dena never looked back to see how close they were or whether they were still running after her. She had not seen any horsemen with them, though it seemed inconceivable that the Welsh force did not have any. Truly the Lord God was watching over her! As long as no more Welshmen, on foot or on horse, blocked the track, she would be able to gain the safety of the palisade round the hall and report the grim news to Wybert. The journey seemed endless, but she never allowed the horse to slacken his pace. At every curve of the track, she expected to see either the hall or the Welsh—or both. She saw neither. Relief flooded through her taut body as she reached the fields and recognised the beginning of the winding lane. She urged the horse on, right up to the outer defence ditch where the lane narrowed to pass through the palisade.

When she called out for help to move the barrier, no one came. As she looked over it, up towards the hall, she saw with a sinking heart that the fortified grounds were deserted. The palisade, which had been made secure against the Welsh, was keeping her from safety.

In desperation, she turned in the saddle to look for another entrance. How she wished she had taken more notice of Wybert's explanations the day he had escorted her round the defences! She dared not try to circle the outer ditch on horseback, as she knew the Welsh were to the north, and Radford had said he had seen them to the south, too. She dared not risk it. The only safe route seemed to be through the grounds surrounding the hall and over the palisade at the eastern side.

Dena drew the horse alongside the rough timber of the palisade, and kicking free of the stirrups, proceeded to climb on to his broad back. To her surprise, he did not mind her shaky attempt to stand on the saddle, and he stood unmoving until she gained her balance.

It still looked a long way from the sharpened tips of

the palisade, and even further to the ground beyond —and Dena was no tumbler. She had watched them often enough, though, at fairs and markets, and knew, or thought she knew, how the feat could be accomplished. She gritted her teeth, determined to try. After all, she could not stand upon the horse's back for ever, no matter how patient he was; the Welsh would not be dallying. She took a deep breath, closed her eyes and launched herself into the air. The flight felt most ungainly, even by her standards, and was accompanied by a loud ripping sound as her skirts were shredded by the deadly tips of the palisade. The heavy landing winded her badly, but she was so relieved to find that she had not broken any bones that she ignored her grazed skin, and struggling to her feet, limped up the lane towards the hall and its outbuildings.

As she came to the brewing-house, she peeped into it. No one was there, as she had expected, and she hurried on to the hall. To her surprise, the great west door had not been made secure, and stood ajar. So quiet now, without a soul inside, the building held a sense of eerie unease that she had not known before. Dena tried not to think of it, and was pleased when she noticed Ethelin's large storage chest slewed at an odd angle across the aisle by the wall. She could imagine the scene as clearly as if she had witnessed it—Ethelin and Wybert locked in a battle of words, as the unfortunate boys ordered to move it stood looking on.

She checked her thoughts: this was no time for idle reverie. She had to cross the open ground on the other side of the hall and climb the eastern palisade. The forest beyond would be her sanctuary, giving her cover until she could catch up with the others from the hall. She hoped Wybert would not be too angry about the loss of his horse, but she knew she had little cause for worry. Unlike Ethelin, he was more concerned with losing people than possessions.

The small door in the eastern wall of the hall was also unlocked—this was a puzzle, but she was pleased to find it so. She would save time by not needing to run round the outside of the building, and she passed through into the open porch. After no more than two steps, she grasped the timber frame for support and flattened herself against the carved wood panelling. Could her eyes be deceiving her? She peeped round the corner of the porch, and bit her lip to stop herself from crying out. Men were cutting at the palisade with axe and sword, men on foot and on horse. They had come not from the north or the south, but from the east, where Wybert had led the people to safety.

Dena re-entered the hall like an apparition slipping between the logs which made up the walls. She had to hide, but where? The hall was so large and airy that it offered no secret places at all. She crossed to the great door, hoping to steal across to one of the outbuildings with their various hay-lofts and grain-bins, but one cautious glance outside told her she was too late. The Welsh were throwing ropes round the barricade across the lane, ready to clear the path. She was trapped. There was nowhere to go.

In a state of near frenzy, she ran to the one private place she had made her own since coming to live in Edwulf's household, her sleeping-chamber. The smallest of the three partitioned cubicles adjoining the south wall, it offered no more comfort than a narrow bed and a storage chest, but the bed was close up against the wall and she slotted herself beneath it, curling into a trembling ball as a small hedgehog might.

She lay there in that cramped position for a near eternity, fighting the ever-present vision of Ethelin crossing and re-crossing herself by the great door at noon that day. It seemed a lifetime ago. Perhaps it would be—when the Welsh found her.

The first noise Dena might have imagined, but then she knew that it was real. They were in the hall, moving stealthily, expecting some sort of ambush. She closed her eyes again as she heard the footsteps gaining strength. There was a pause when she heard nothing, when prying eyes drew back the thick tapestry curtain which served as a door to her chamber.

Go away! she prayed. *Go away!* And she thought they had.

The crack above her head was so sharp and unexpected that she cried out for fear of being crushed by the collapsing bed, and squirmed on to her back in a feeble attempt to use her arms as support for its weight. There was no need. Only one narrow slat had been split, the fibre-like grain tenuously refusing to let it snap completely. Dena's eyes widened as she saw what must have happened. Someone had jumped on to the bed—someone who could not possibly have missed the sound of her cry. She held her breath, not daring to move, her eyes fixed on the shallow gap between the edge of the bed and the stone floor.

First there came a booted foot, then a mass of tangled chestnut hair and a pair of wild brown eyes; next, she saw a grinning mouth, and a hand reached into the tiny space to grab at her.

Dena fought like a fury, kicking and screaming and beating out with her fists, but she was caught like a fish on a hook and hauled from her crevice-like hiding-place. Free from the confined space, she fought more furiously than ever, kicking and biting at anyone who came within her reach, until a pair of strong hands pinned her arms behind her back and bustled her through the chamber doorway into the main room of the hall.

The sight of so many bearded faces jostling to peer at her stole her remaining courage and left her weak-legged. Words were bantered back and forth, words she did not understand, and then slowly, horrifyingly, the barbarous Welshmen advanced upon her.

Dena opened her mouth to cry out. She made a feeble attempt to struggle from her captor's grip, but her resistance was gone. She sagged against him in her helplessness, but he would not let her fall.

A short command rent the stillness of the air in the high-roofed hall. She recognised that it was a command, both by its stern tone and the way the men stood still, almost in unison. She began to take heart as she watched them turn their heads towards the open west door, and when they moved aside to allow the passage of another through their ranks, her relief was complete.

He was a nobleman—she could tell that from his dress and his bearing: a wealthy man skilled in the military arts. Over his pale green tunic he wore a vivid short-sleeved coat of mail which glistened like a lizard's scales as he moved through the shafts of sunlight falling from the high windows. Except for two thin braids which hung down from his cheeks, his dark hair was hidden beneath a low-browed helmet. Coming to a halt before her, he laid a gaudily-ringed hand on the pommel of the sword hanging in its scabbard at his belt. He rested his weight back on one foot, and eyed her curiously.

'Who might you be?' he growled.

Dena swallowed both her surprise and her fright, and

tried to stand as upright as her captor's iron grip would allow.

'I am the Lady Dena, niece of Thegn Edwulf, lord of this hall and accompanying lands.'

The Welsh nobleman bowed a little, raising his hands to grip and push the tight helmet from his head. He drew open fingers through his coarse shoulder-length hair, releasing its dampness from his skull. He looked at her again, lifting an eyebrow in a mocking gesture of disbelief and laughed, full and hearty, as one might at the antics of a Fool worthy of the name. With the laughter still echoing about the rafters above them, the smile upon his lips fell away as though it was a mask.

'Speak the truth of it, woman, or suffer the consequences.'

Dena blinked in stunned astonishment; but as a translation of her words rattled round the hall to the hoots and calls of the assembled men, she realised, with a growing sense of hopelessness, that if she could not convince this Welshman of her identity, she was lost.

CHAPTER
TWO

'I DO SPEAK the truth. I am the Lady Dena.'

The nobleman was neither convinced nor amused. He laid his helmet on the trestle table with a sigh which bode ill, and began to unbuckle his sword-belt.

Desperately she sought for ideas which might assist her, but they seemed so few as to be none at all. She had no proof of who she was, and her dress was in a stained and dishevelled state that no woman of noble birth would tolerate.

She could tell him of the mission she had been entrusted with, but was he likely to believe her? In normal times, such a task would never have been given to a woman, especially one considered a lady. Perhaps if she behaved more in the way that this Welshman expected a Saxon lady to behave, she might be able to sow enough seeds of doubt in his mind to stay his violent hand.

Ethelin's arrogant manner came to her mind. Dena did not know if she had the courage to adopt such an affected bearing with any mark of success, but if her life depended upon it, she had to try.

There was movement in the doorway which gained everyone's attention, and the clustered men parted once more to let someone pass. It was another nobleman, far older than the one who spoke her tongue, with a thick, forked beard which hid most of his face. Dena was surprised how much he resembled her uncle, dressed as he was in the same type of thickened leather jerkin, ringed and studded for protection, that Edwulf had taken with him to York. He was of the same build, too, squat and powerful; much more a brother figure than her own father had been. As she watched the two men speak—about herself, if the gestures were any indication—it became apparent who was subordinate to whom. Were she to address herself to either, it must be to the elder man.

'I am the Lady Dena from the household of Thegn Edwulf, and demand that this oaf release me at once.'

Her icy tone had the desired effect, and both men turned wide-eyed towards her; but having gained their undivided attention, Dena was at a sudden loss as to what to do next, and rising fright made her perspiration stand cold on her skin. Remembering her precarious position, she stiffened her jaw and tilted back her head disdainfully.

'I was told the Welsh were rabble; but even I did not expect them to show such fear before a Saxon lady.'

The expression from the younger nobleman was surprise bordering on rage, but the elder let a smile play across his bearded jowls. After a single command, Dena found herself standing freely before them, and able to massage some life back into her aching arms.

'I thank you.'

She tried to look as though such trials were commonplace, if a little wearisome. This play-acting seemed to be having the desired effect, and she decided she had best sustain it.

'To whom am I addressing myself?'

'Gwylan—as you would say, lord of these lands and, at this moment it seems, this Saxon hall also. My people call me Gwylan the Fearless.'

Dena had heard him called other names by Edwulf,

but prudence told her that this was not the time to reveal them to the Welshman.

'This,' continued Gwylan, 'is Rhodri ap Hywel, and if it is the wife of my adversary, Edwulf, you seek to impersonate, I should inform you that you use the wrong name.'

For a moment Dena was stunned into silence. Gwylan's expression had not changed in the slightest, neither had the softness of his voice, but he was challenging the truth of her words as though he held a dagger at her throat. It seemed that she was not the only one to be play-acting. She smiled as sweetly as she could.

'I am not Ethelin, the wife of Edwulf, but his niece, Dena.'

'We know of no Dena,' came the instant reply.

'Then your spies serve you ill, for I have lived beneath this roof since before the spring sowings.'

The two men looked at each other, but Dena could not tell what passed between them. Gwylan turned back to her as affably as ever, in a manner she was beginning to regard with suspicion.

'Give me your hands, young Dena.'

She held them out for his inspection, realising his motive as she did so. Silently she thanked the heavens for Ethelin's stubborn refusal to allow her to help with the harvesting.

'Well, my Lady Dena, you may not work in the fields, but I have to admit I have touched softer skin.'

'Perhaps the noble ladies of the Welsh prefer to be treated more like babes than do the Saxon,' she retorted.

Gwylan chuckled softly. 'I fear it is the other way about.'

The sudden hostile movement of Rhodri towards her

made Dena take an involuntary step backwards.

'Enough of this foolishness! She is nothing more than a serving-girl dressed in her mistress's rags. A true lady of noble birth would have welcomed us at the door, not cowered beneath a cot. Give her to the men. They have had little enough distraction on this escapade.'

She felt the colour drain from her cheeks and looked to Gwylan for support, but he was stroking his beard thoughtfully, still undecided. 'I am who I say, niece of Edwulf. I came to his care after my father died. I am to stay until I am found a husband. I am companion to Ethelin.' Dena became aware that her aloof and arrogant manner was slipping, that her words were coming in agitated streams—but what could she do to convince them?

Rhodri snorted his contempt. 'A poor relative!'

'But a brave one, perhaps,' Gwylan added softly. 'It was you the men saw on the war-horse we captured?'

They knew of her ride to the north tun, then. A sense of relief threatened to overwhelm her. 'Yes,' she admitted. 'I was the only one who could ride Wybert's horse at speed. Someone had to warn the people.' She looked Gwylan straight in the eye, adding with a fierce edge to her voice, 'Except that I was too late.'

He merely smiled in return. 'And what of Wybert? He moved the people quickly. Where has he taken them?'

Dena looked at him with widening eyes. Did he truly expect her to tell him?

'I have no knowledge,' she said stiffly. 'And if I had, I would not betray them to you.'

'A noblewoman would have the knowledge,' Rhodri asserted.

'And a serving-girl would tell you all manner of lies,'

Dena added quickly. 'Do with me as you will, I shall never reveal their hiding-place.'

She tossed back her head in a defiant gesture, inwardly wishing she had not made it sound as though she did know where Wybert had taken the people. The way in which the younger Welsh nobleman was looking at her left Dena in no doubt that he would find much sport in dragging the truth from her.

'It matters little,' mused Gwylan. 'There is only the forest. With women and children and crippled old men, Wybert will not be able to get far.'

'No,' Dena agreed, almost beneath her breath. 'It is a brave man indeed who attacks another's domain when the defences are at their weakest.'

Gwylan gave her one of those pitying looks she had often received from Wybert.

'Do you know how Edwulf took these lands from me?'

'Through force of arms.'

Gwylan nodded. 'But first he sent a beggar into our midst, a beggar dressed in the robes of a holy man, so that all would welcome him, a beggar suffering from an unknown pestilence. When we were sick, when we were grieving over our old and burying our children, then, and only then, did Edwulf take my lands through force of arms.'

Dena felt her stomach twist. Gwylan's words had been spoken in the same quiet tone he had used since entering the hall. There had been not a sign of anger, but the eyes which held hers had turned to stone. She shuddered to think what form his vengeance would take.

'Lost your tongue?' Rhodri asked pointedly.

The very sound of his sarcastic voice rekindled Dena's indignation, and she turned sharply to face him, the accusation 'Lies!' ready to spring from her lips.

The word was never uttered. Even his scornful expression could not force her to show the defiance she felt in his presence. How could she call Gwylan a liar when the truth of his words was so evident: evident in the fortifications, in the system of lookouts and guards Edwulf insisted upon when the hall was fully occupied. He feared an attack, a reprisal, even after so long. But if that were so, why had he taken all the able men to rally with the king and left the hall so unprotected?

She heard Rhodri snort his derision, and realised that her gaze had fallen guiltily to the stone floor. Try as she might, she could not bring herself to raise it again.

'We have dallied here enough,' growled Rhodri, reaching for his sword-belt. 'Let us be gone from here. We do not want to be scrambling about in the forest in the dark.'

Gwylan lifted his face and gauged the light filtering through the high windows. He muttered something to himself, and then looked about him at the furnishings of the hall.

'That is what Wybert wants us to do. He is a wily old animal. He thinks like a wolf, just as Edwulf does. Even encumbered as he is, he could lead us a dance through those forest trails. He is not one to let the cloak of darkness pass without some benefit, and I have no desire to lose men to an arrow in the back. We shall leave at first light.'

'And this one?' Rhodri murmured.

Dena's eyes were drawn to Gwylan's, but her blood ran cold when she saw the calculating manner in which he regarded her.

'I am not convinced about you,' he announced loftily. 'But if what you say is true, I may well be able to use your captivity to good advantage.'

'Whom shall I use as guard?' Rhodri asked.

'Yourself.'

He almost choked.

'I do not want a repetition of what happened at the tun,' Gwylan warned. 'She is to be your responsibility.'

Rhodri seemed ready to burst with anger. He looked from Dena to Gwylan and launched a vicious tirade in Welsh at his lord. Gwylan responded in like manner, and the young man was stilled. Dena knew who was victor, but was dubious of the outcome. It was Gwylan who spoke to her, in that pleasant, kindly tone which now seemed to fit him so ill.

'Have no fear of my men, Lady Dena. Rhodri will protect you with his life.'

Dena saw him glance at Rhodri, a smile of amusement playing across his lips, then he turned on his heel and left the hall, calling orders to his men as he did so.

As she looked uncertainly towards the younger man, his attention was fixed not upon her but on the figure of Gwylan disappearing through the doorway. With his lord gone, Rhodri turned his brooding eyes on her, and with a softly flowing movement which made his tunic of mail ripple like the waters of a brook, he moved towards Dena with all the malevolence of a viper intent on its prey.

She backed towards the wall without thought of resistance. *Dear God!* she groaned, fear running wildly through her mind. *Who will protect me from Rhodri?*

Her shoulders hit the rough logging and she stood there, trembling like a cornered rabbit awaiting its fate. Rhodri raised a hand and motioned to a stool a little way along the wall.

'Sit.'

Dena moved towards it as quickly as she could, and sat

down with her hands caught anxiously on her lap. She did not want to look up at him, especially now as he towered above her, but she knew from the way he kept shifting his weight that his bitter words were not yet over.

'I have no wish to play the wet-nurse with you, so you will sit like a statue and not utter a word. Should you cause me any concern, I shall be taken short and need to leave this favoured hall of yours. By the time I return, the men will have painted the walls red with your blood. Do you understand me?'

Dena nodded, her eyes fixed on the floor. The time for arrogant retorts had gone.

The Welshmen were not in the highest of spirits. Dena did not need to know the language to appreciate that. Those left in the hall walked about restlessly, kicking at the furniture, pulling down the painted and embroidered banners which hung about the walls. Sometimes they would come and stand a pace away and gawk at her. Sometimes they would pass a remark to Rhodri, and all would laugh lasciviously. He never bade them leave her in peace. He enjoyed her discomfort, watching her like a hawk from his perch on the edge of the table. She loathed him, but no matter how close to tears she felt, she resolved never to show them.

The shadows lengthened. Rush torches were lit and a fire started in the central hearth. The flickering light seemed to improve the men's humour, and one produced a square knee-harp and began to sing to his own accompaniment. All listened to him, even Dena. It reminded her of times in her father's farmstead; peaceful, lazy evenings singing round the fire after the meal. Would she ever know times like those again? She thought she had found something similar in Edwulf's household but there had never been a notion of such a catastrophe as this in the hall of her childhood.

Again and again her mind reeled back to the short argument between Gwylan and Rhodri. *I do not want a repetition of what happened at the tun*, Gwylan had said. Had the walls been painted red with the blood of those people? All those women and children? Dena shuddered as her imagination drew pictures she did not want to see. Why had Edwulf left them like this? Why?

The evening rolled on interminably. Dena found she was losing the feeling in her lower limbs through being forced to sit on the hard stool for so long. She tried to reduce the numbness without drawing attention to herself, but each time she altered her position, Rhodri's head turned towards her. He never chastised her, but his threats were still firmly implanted in her head and she decided it would be foolish to chance his spite.

They were a dour band, these Welshmen, hardly a smile between them. Dena would have expected merriment and rejoicing, considering that they had captured the hall. Perhaps their plans had gone astray. Perhaps Wybert had been correct when he assumed that their goal had been to capture the hall complete with its occupants. She let that musing raise her deflated spirits. Gwylan had no hostages to hold against Edwulf—none but herself, that was. Could he hope to gain the terms he wanted by using her alone? Probably not. That realisation left her with the bitter prospect of being used as a tool of revenge. There could be no end, other than a bloody one, to all this.

The door burst open and more men appeared, some carrying heavy buckets, some pushing barrels before them. There was a good deal of excited chatter, and the doleful Welshmen quickly began to change their humour. Dena sank back against the wall with a sigh. The brewing-house must have been plundered. Contemptuous Welshmen were bad enough: drunken Welshmen would be unbearable.

A man came to Rhodri, spoke a few unintelligible words, and left two rawhide mugs on the table.

'Mardun says there is not a morsel of food to be found,' Rhodri told her. 'It is shameful that Wybert does not think highly of his lord's niece.'

Dena risked a glance in his direction, and found him grinning at her through bared teeth.

'Ah! The lady is not dead! Sitting so still with your head bowed, your face hidden beneath that square of cloth—you look like a toadstool under a tree!'

Glaring at him, she did not rise to the goad. The man was bored and wanted a plaything. She would not give him the pleasure.

'Your face looks pinched. Does the sound of my voice fill you with such dread?'

'I have no cloak. I feel the cold,' she replied sullenly.

'Do you wish to sit closer to the fire?'

Dena looked down the length of the hall to the hearth where the majority of the Welshmen were taking their ease amid the open casks.

'I prefer to remain cold.'

Rhodri chuckled, more softly than she had expected.

'If I were a true nobleman, I would give you the clothes off my back; but I am not, am I? I am a Welshman—a barbarian. That is what you call us, is it not? That is what those prancing fools at Edward's court called me—"our captive barbarian".'

Dena looked up at him in her surprise, and he mocked her expression.

'Does it shock you that such as I have sat with a king of England?' He pushed himself from his seat on the table and stood tall and proud so that she might admire him. Dena drew her lips into a thin line at his conceit.

'You are not impressed?' He sounded truly astounded, and she realised that she had been drawn into this game of his without knowing. And they called Wybert wily, she reflected.

She turned her scornful gaze aside, hoping to end the contest of wills on a winning note, but he pounced on her before she knew it, trapping her between arms of flowing metal as he leaned his weight against the wall. The more she tried to back into the logging, the more he lowered his face to meet hers.

'No? The whores of Edward's court liked the barbarian in me. They vied with each other to buy me with gifts.' He paused as he looked down at her, the taut muscles of his neck relaxing. 'But you are not such a woman. From you, a man would have to steal his kisses.'

He made the slightest of movements, but enough to convince her of his intentions. Her chest heaving with fear and anger, she turned her head and directly looked at him.

'Do so, and I will scratch out your eyes!'

He faltered, a temple braid tracing an arc on her cheek. A smile crept across his face, one of genuine pleasure rather than of teasing, and his dark eyes searched her face for . . . for what, Dena did not know.

'My cowering maid has a fire in her belly. Envied will be the man who beds you,' he tweaked an eyebrow wickedly. 'Or perhaps it will be I.'

She filled her lungs ready to curse him to hell, her colour rising with her fury, but her tongue was stayed by the curious silence of their surroundings. She inclined her head to look beneath his mailed arm, and to her distaste found every Welshman intent on the proceedings. She groaned her shame, wishing the ground would open up and swallow her. Rhodri played to his audience, bantering with them in his own tongue and gaining much uproarious laughter.

'What did you say to them?' Dena demanded hotly.

'That the lady does not appreciate my advances— more or less.' But she could see by the sparkle in his eyes that the truth of it was far more than less.

He pushed his weight off the wall, and turning to the table behind him, picked up the mugs and handed one to her.

'Here, with no cloak and no fire, it is all the warmth you will feel this night.' He drained his mug in one draught, tilting his head like some coarse pedlar so that he might not miss a drop. He wiped his mouth on the back of his hand and smacked his lips appreciatively.

'At least you Saxons know how to make ale!' He turned to the men, calling for more.

Although Dena thought hard for some cutting reply, the image which flickered unbidden into her mind froze the breath in her lungs. She could see them working in the brewing-house as clearly as if she were standing in the doorway—Wybert and Mildthryth pounding herbs with pestle and mortar. They had been poisoning the ale. That was why Wybert was so adamant about taking all the food: the poison would work faster on an empty stomach.

Dena looked at the mug cradled in her hands, into the ominously dark liquid within. She could not drink it, she could not! But she had to, and she knew she had to, or the Welshman would suspect, and Wybert's plans would fail. Her people would be caught in the forest and murdered.

'What is wrong with your ale?'

At Rhodri's question, she sprang upright as though she had been pierced by an arrow.

'Nothing,' she snapped back, far too quickly.

'Then drink.'

'I cannot.' Her voice quaked as she spoke. With an inner heave, she pulled her scattered wits together. 'I have a weak stomach. I have had it since birth. Ale makes me ill. I can drink only mead or clear spring water.'

Rhodri threw back his head and guffawed. Dena took heart and strengthened her jaw as though she were merely rebuffing another of his gibes. He could laugh all he liked, as long as he believed her!

He gave her a low mocking bow. 'Well, my lady, there is no mead for your sweet lips, and I shall not act the servant to bring you water from the well, so you will either drink the ale or go thirsty.'

Dena could not help giving him a deprecating smile, knowing that she had spoken the same line about the fire. 'Then I prefer to be thirsty.'

Rhodri saw the humour, too, but his reply twinkled unspoken in his eyes. He drained his own mug and took hers for himself.

'An odd maid,' he mused, swirling the liquid about its container. 'Wears rags, rides war-horses, but is made ill by ale.'

He chuckled to himself and looked deeply into the mug as though it were a seer's vessel. Dena's chest was gripped with cramp as she watched his expression change. Even in the dim light she could see the colour drain from his cheeks. He raised his eyes to look at her, and a coldness reached out from the pit of her stomach, running along each fibre of her body until all she could feel was her own heart beating in the hollowness of her chest. He knew. *He knew!*

Slowly he extended his arm, pushing the mug towards her. His voice was hardly above a whisper, but it held the hatred of centuries.

'Drink.'

She swallowed down her rising bile. 'I cannot. I have told you.'

'That it will make you ill? Will it make me ill, too?'

He grabbed at her throat with his free hand, but she moved quickly and he missed, taking her headcloth and one of her braids in his crushing grip. Dena cried out with the pain to her scalp and tried to force his hand open with her fingers, but he was far too strong for her.

'It will! Deny it! You whore! You have poisoned the ale!'

In his fury he threw her aside, turning to the men to call a warning. Bruised and shaken, she scrambled to the end of the hall to crouch in the corner by the cubicle wall. Close to tears now and trembling with fear, she looked back to see Rhodri kicking over buckets and attacking barrels with a huge battle-axe, its polished blade glinting in the torchlight as he raised it. She shuddered each time it splintered the wood, knowing it would splinter her skull just as easily, but she could not shut her eyes to the scene.

With every cask asunder and ale flowing freely about the floor, a deathly hush fell upon the inhabitants of the hall. It was soon dispelled. First they scowled at her, muttering among themselves, then they began to shake their fists, baying for blood. In the midst of the furore, Rhodri gradually advanced upon her, tight-lipped and hostile, weighing the solidity of the axe in his hands.

Dena shrank further into the corner of the wall, curling into a tight ball, but her eyes were drawn to his as though she were under a spell.

The angry Welshman glanced at the heavy blade and tossed the axe on to the table with a clatter.

'It is too quick a death for you,' he spat.

He lunged out, laying heavy hands upon her shoulders, and dragged her to her feet, twisting her round so that she faced the yelling mob. She looked from face to face for a sign of pity, but there was none, and the faces became a blur—all except one, to which Dena clung out of hope. Gwylan was fighting his way through the crush, shouting to make himself heard. Dena had never been so thankful to see anyone in her life.

The noise eventually subsided enough for him and Rhodri to exchange short phrases in Welsh. By the way Rhodri kept shaking her, she knew the gist of what was being said. The older man scowled at her, his face dark as thunderclouds.

'I did not poison the ale!' Dena cried hysterically. 'It was not I.'

'What was used, and what is the cure?'

'I do not know.'

She cried out as Rhodri squeezed her arms more tightly.

'I do *not* know,' she insisted. 'Wybert was working with the potion-woman in the brewing-house when I went inside. He told me to take his horse and ride to the tun. I tell the truth. Believe me!'

Gwylan grunted in disgust. 'And I was worrying about tricks in the forest! The trick was here. No wonder he took all the food with him.' He narrowed his eyes, nodding grudgingly as he peered at her. 'Wybert did well to chose you to act the lady. You can die knowing that you were very convincing.'

She felt her legs go weak. 'But I am the Lady Dena. I am!'

Rhodri again shook her roughly, bringing pain surging up her arms and neck.

'The Lady Dena would know the poison. She would have been party to the plan.'

'You waste your time, Rhodri. Give her to my men.'

Gwylan turned away, wanting no more of her.

'No! Wait!' she cried in alarm. 'It is not a poison which is fatal, only one to make you ill—that is all I know. It was meant to check your advance, to slow you and your men down so that Wybert had enough time to be sure that the people escaped.'

Her words sounded hollow to her ears, as though someone else were speaking. How easily the lies tripped off her tongue in her desperation; how effortlessly she damned her soul with them! Dena took strength again as Gwylan turned back to her. Better that she damn her soul to an everlasting hell than let them send it to heaven by their chosen path!

'The truth?'

'The truth,' she swore without a flinch.

Rhodri shook her once more, not convinced.

'Give her to me. Within the blinking of an eye I shall break her, and then we shall hear the genuine truth.'

'There is no point to it. If she is a servant, she will not know what the poison is, and if she is the lady she claims to be, Wybert will not have told her for fear of this very moment.'

He chortled derisively into her face. 'Did you realise you had been sent on a fool's errand, my lady? That ride to the tun that no one else could undertake.'

Dena knitted her brows, not understanding what Gwylan was taking so much pleasure in telling her.

'If we had not found you here, like as not I would have ordered the men on into the forest while they still yearned for glory. There would have been no stopping here the night, no time to drain the brewing-house; but Wybert was cleverer than I. He dangled you here as bait, and I took it like a fish to a hook, fearing non-existent traps in the darkness of the forest.'

Dena began to shake her head, paling by the second. 'No,' she murmured. 'No, Wybert would never do such a thing to the niece of his lord. He is an honourable man.'

'Honour?' Gwylan blustered. 'This is not a song some simple-minded poet sings, this is *war*. There is no honour here. I have little doubt that Edwulf was a party to your sacrifice. The poisoning of the ale, the taking of the food—it was all too smooth and quick for it not to have been planned many days ago.'

Dena flopped against Rhodri like a rag doll, her head spinning as she became aware of the magnitude of her betrayal.

'Yes, my lady. Think on it well while you await your lot! When the first of my men dies, I shall bind you to your own fire-dogs and roast you alive. Take her away!'

CHAPTER
THREE

DENA WAS bundled through the cubicle doorway and thrown on to the stone floor of her own chamber. Beyond hope, beyond reason, she crawled to the narrow bed and lay on the soft covering. She ached with the weight of her misery, and at last she buried her face in the pillow and let the sobs rack her body.

Somehow she slept. She did not know for how long, but when she stirred she did so with a jolt and anxiously looked round for her gloating captors. Rhodri was the only man in the room with her, leaning against the wall by the doorway, his fingers caught in the edge of the tapestry curtain that made a window into the hall beyond. He turned weary eyes towards her as she made to sit up on the bed.

'Did you sleep well?' he sneered.

His bitter words stung her cheeks, and she drew her hands across her face in her confusion. How could she have slept at such a time?

When she dared to glance at him again, she found that his attention had returned to beyond the curtain. Peculiar sounds were coming from the other side: moans of pain, groans of retching. The poisoned ale was beginning to have its effect.

Dena shuddered. She had lied so easily about the deadly potion, but to what end? She had only postponed the inevitable. She had not the slightest idea of the plants used, no matter how often she tried to picture them lying on the table in the brewing-house. Neither could she deny the hatred that Gwylan bore her uncle and his household. Despite the light and boastful nature of the songs and stories she had heard since her arrival at the hall, she realised now just how ruthless Edwulf could be in obtaining what he desired. Any poison he used would not merely make men ill—it would be designed to be fatal.

But had he betrayed her? That was the question that preoccupied her. Had Edwulf plotted with Wybert to use her as some kind of scapegoat, as Gwylan believed? No, she would not accept that! Yet, in the far reaches of her mind, nagging doubts manifested themselves like grinning devils bent on her destruction. Once given their orders, the people had moved very quickly, almost as though each had remembered a specific duty allotted to him—duties of which she had no knowledge. And Wybert's instruction to take all the food—that had been no idle decision. It had been his first command—and whence had he issued it? From the brewing-house.

Dena held her head in her despair. Every action fitted the puzzle, just as Gwylan had maintained. She had been so blinded by her own frustrations that she had not seen how she had been used. The boys on her father's farmstead could ride the most obstinate of horses. They stole their chance to practise at every opportunity; surely the boys on Edwulf's estate were the same? None might ride with the flair and dignity of his master, but at least one could have handled Wybert's great horse. He had acted very obediently to her touch.

The poor occupants of the north tun came to her thoughts. Had they, too, been pitilessly sacrificed to assist Edwulf's plan? It seemed so. How certain of its success Edwulf must have been to lead all the able-bodied men east to swell the army of the King! she reflected bitterly. How little he valued the lives of his loyal household!

'You look like a pod shelled of its peas.'

Dena had almost forgotten Rhodri's presence in her chamber, and the sound of his voice startled her. Still he was at his post in the doorway, but he had let the curtain drop and now stood with his arms folded across his chest, his back leaning against the wall. He seemed to have been quietly regarding her for some time. As he gave a low, sardonic chuckle, Dena looked down, but she raised her eyes again immediately, reasoning that in the flickering light her face would be only a shadow to him. Now, he was not even looking at her. Indeed, his irony seemed aimed at some inner, secret thought, rather than at her.

There was time for her to study him while his mind was elsewhere. He was taller than the other Welshmen, though his bearing could, perhaps, account for that. He certainly held himself straight, as she would have expected any nobleman to, Welsh or English. He had a slim, angular face, but the lack of facial hair surprised her. She had seen cleanshaven men before, but accustomed to a male populace which considered a full beard a mark of manhood, it still seemed odd to her, if not unpleasing. Obviously he did not mind being ridiculed by his contemporaries, or perhaps his social position was such that none dared.

Dena gave thought to that. Gwylan had introduced him as, what was it? Rhodri ap Hywel? A longer name —or was it a title—than by which he had introduced himself. He had certainly not introduced him as 'my son', though their difference in age had pointed to a possible kinship. No, it was beyond her understanding. He looked the born nobleman, used to a life of quality, whereas Gwylan, like Edwulf, had that air of brusque unease about him, as though he had needed to fight all his life for what he called his own. Yet, for all the younger man's manner: his quickness to argue, his costly armour, it was Gwylan who gave the orders, Gwylan who called the men 'his'. A curious affair.

Rhodri flicked back the curtain to peer into the hall. The sounds of pain and vomiting were still drifting over the top of the partition as, now, was the pungent stench of bile.

While Dena was thankful that she did not have to share the hall with the Welshmen, at the same time the hidden scene held a dreaded fascination for her. How feeble were the men? How close to death? How close was *her* death? Surely poisons worked faster than this? She reproached herself for her train of thought. It would be much more in her interest to pray for the men's deliverance. She placed her hands together and bowed her head, but Rhodri's words interrupted her appeal.

'Beyond this doorway the men lie pale and weak, gripping their bellies and retching up their empty stomachs; yet I stand here quite untouched by the infirmity. Why do you think this is so?'

Dena felt fear crawling across her skin. 'I did not poison the ale,' she stated with steadily rising emphasis.

He let the curtain fall and turned to look at her. 'I believe you. The sacrificial lamb is always innocent of the plot to kill it; but my belief will be of no comfort if one of the men should die. Gwylan will tie you to the fire-dogs as he threatened. And I shall help him.'

It was like staring into the face of death itself. There was no mockery, no anger, no emotion at all, only the certainty of his quietly-spoken words. Dena could feel his steady gaze peeling away her flesh, revealing her

bones, as though she had already lain in her grave for a
decade or more.

There was a tightness in Dena's chest, a tightness
which burned until it hurt. Only when the pain became
too great to bear did she realise that she had been
holding her breath in awe of this Welshman. She inhaled
the sour air. Again and again she filled her lungs with the
sickening odour, and slowly the chilling numbness in her
limbs receded. Pulling her eyes away from his, she eased
herself the short distance back to the corner of the bed.
Here, the thin partition met the logging of the outer
wall. She rested her head against the roughly-hewn
wood and put her arms about her knees.

There was no comfort in the vastness of the hall,
neither sympathy nor pity for her predicament. A sacrificial lamb, Rhodri had called her, sacrificed by Edwulf,
her only kin, and Wybert, her only friend. They had
planned this together, knowing the outcome, knowing
how grotesque would be her death. And she had trusted
them. She had trusted them.

Dena tensed as she heard a movement beside her: the
gentle clinking of the Welshman's mailed coat. Rhodri
had stayed still so long that she had drifted into a
semi-trance, and it took a great deal of effort to force her
woolly mind to act with any speed. She turned her head
slightly so that she could see him. He was prowling the
narrow space between the doorway and the logging wall,
contorting his face in different masks in an attempt to rid
himself of his weariness. She watched him stretch his
arms above his head, watched the heavy coat of mail
ripple across his body, each scaly link sparkling like a
sinking evening sun.

'Is that a well out in the yard?'

Dena could do no more than nod. He turned and drew

back the curtain, to leave her in that shrinking cell, alone. Her eyes widened without blinking. They felt as large as her face. He had gone. He had left her. The power of his threat screamed in her head '. . . painted the walls red with your blood.'

She stared at the gently swaying curtain, hardly daring to breathe. A dagger-wielding hand would fling it aside at any moment, she was sure. She buried her head in her hands, waiting, waiting . . .

The nauseating sounds from the other side of the partition became amplified beyond endurance. She felt alone, exposed. She feared the Welshman, Rhodri, feared the slowly burning menace behind his voice and the violence of his hand. So why did she feel so vulnerable without his presence?

She paced the floor, her arms clasped to her chilly shoulders, in an attempt to make the time pass. If only she knew what was happening. Dare she look? With an effort, she took a deep breath to awaken her courage. There seemed no other way to calm her mind.

Her heart wildly beating, she tiptoed towards the curtain and peeped round one edge. It was worse than she had expected. Men were sprawled on the stone floor, some as still as corpses, others rocking gently in an effort to find ease for their pain. More men sat on benches beside the wall, their heads laid upon the trestle tables, cushioned by their arms. Among the broken casks and the slurried floor all manner of discarded clothing, armour and weaponry lay strewn. It was a dreadful sight, one straight from the teachings of hell.

A lone figure moved between the prostrate men at the other end of the hall, tending each with the gentle patience she had once seen monks use many years before. She had given the man no more than a cursory

glance as her eyes took in the repelling scene, but as he
slowly wound his way towards her, further into the weak
pools of light the flickering torches offered, she saw that
it was Rhodri. With a pail in one hand and a cloth in the
other, he was washing the face of each man in turn with
all the humility of a lowly ceorl. His compassion surprised Dena, touched her. She stayed by the doorway
watching each caring movement, listening to the quiet
murmur of his voice as he spoke words of comfort in a
tongue she could not understand.

Even as he approached the tiny bedchamber, she did
not shy away. It was as though she, too, had been helped
by the calm he exuded. He drew back the curtain, but
caught his stride on seeing her so close, his tranquil
expression changing to one of fierce mistrust.

Dena's lips parted. She was trembling. She wanted to
speak words which would reassure him of her intentions,
but what words could she use to an enemy of her people,
to a man who held her life upon a whim? She backed to
the bed and sat upon the edge, lowering her head until
all she could see of him were his dark boots bound to his
calves with narrow strips of braided leather. How stupid
she had been to stand there by the doorway; how stupid
even to move from the bed! What devious notion did he
believe she held in her heart? What was he going to do to
her?

She stared at those boots of his, expecting them to
move, to come closer, expecting him to strike her.

'The men look a little better. At least, they do not look
any worse.'

His words were spoken softly, tentatively, as if he
were testing her reactions. He had not moved towards
her. Perhaps he realised that she had meant him no
harm. Cautiously she looked up until she could see his

face. His head was tilted towards one shoulder, his searching eyes peering through the gloom. He lifted his head when their gaze met, blinking sharply as though drawing across a shield to protect himself. He altered his stance and leaned against the wall.

'You may have been right when you said the poison was not designed to kill.' Rhodri looked at her again, his dark eyes as impenetrable as before. 'The truth of it is that you do not know, do you?'

Put so baldly, without anger or threat, Dena could not bring herself to lie again. She shook her head and lowered her eyes dejectedly.

'So, your life is as much in the balance as anyone's. Take heart. There are no ravings and no fever. It is a good sign. Here . . .'

She took the jug of water he held out and lifted it to her lips, but somehow her thirst had left her.

'Drink. Even Edwulf would not have poisoned his own well. He means to return to this hall triumphant, and he cannot do that if the water is fouled.' Rhodri allowed a deep sigh of concern to escape him. 'I hope he does not return too quickly, though. It would need only six strong men to render this hall knee-deep in blood.'

Was that the plan? Was Wybert going to return and put the Welsh to the sword while they were incapable of defending themselves? It was a ghastly prospect, but Dena clung to it, clung to the hope of rescue.

'Do not rally your spirits,' he snarled. 'Should so much as a Saxon mouse cross the threshold, I will cut you in two.'

Dena clutched the jug to her breast as if it could offer her the protection she craved. What dark powers did he hold to be able to read her mind so easily; or had it been merely the power of sight that he had used? How could she have let her thoughts stand so plainly in her face?

She sank back upon the narrow bed, edging away into the corner of the walls. He offered no more conversation, and Dena feared to look in his direction in case she met his gaze.

The night dragged on. Dena dozed fitfully, but Rhodri seemed to need no sleep at all. Occasionally he left his post by the doorway to tend the men in the hall, but otherwise he was there, watching her.

She was startled from her shallow slumber by a jolt to the bed. When she opened her eyes, Rhodri was leaning over her. In her terror she pushed wildly at his shoulders, trying to fend him off, but instead of fighting her he rolled on to his back and slipped off the narrow bed to slump to the floor. Apart from straightening one leg, he remained there, unmoving. Dena stared at his still form, unable to grasp the situation. She could hear him breathing. Each lungful of air was being dragged unwillingly, painfully, into his body.

Fearing some trickery, she carefully inched her way to the edge of the mattress. He said something she did not catch, and she faltered a moment before moving closer.

'Rhodri!'

The gasp came unbidden to her lips. The young Welshman was ill. He was very ill.

Had he been wrong? Had the well water been poisoned, too? Dena anxiously searched for signs of sickness in herself, but there was nothing except an aching hollowness in her stomach that was obviously due to lack of food. She looked at Rhodri again. He kept murmuring, blinking rapidly and screwing up his eyes as though trying to bring his sight into focus. It was the ale, Dena realised. He was not to be free of its effects, after all.

With a shuddering effort he raised an arm to clasp the edge of the bed, and slowly hauled himself to a kneeling position on the floor. Exhausted, he rested his head on the mattress by Dena's leg. Perspiration ran in rivulets into his eyes and down his neck. His sodden hair was caked, black, to his head. He did not seem to notice her existence.

She watched as he clawed at the wide neckline of his coat of mail. He was trying to free himself of it, and was desperately struggling to pull it over his head. She reached out to help him, but stilled her hand. He was a Welshman, her enemy. He had threatened her life and caused her to fear. She tried hard to concentrate on the ill he had done her, but all she could remember was the tender way he had cared for his sick countrymen. He needed assistance now, but there was no one to give it—no one except herself.

Dena swung her feet to the floor to stand beside him, but was unsure what to do. Never had she helped a man with his armour before, and there seemed to be no ties or buckles to loosen the heavy garment. He was trying to pull it over his head, so perhaps that was the only way to get it off.

She took a firm grasp of the neckline and tugged with all her might. For a moment there was no give at all, and then it slid over his shoulders and head with such speed that she could not contain it in her arms, and it slithered to the stone floor, jangling like a thousand silver coins.

Now that he was unencumbered, Rhodri managed to stand upright, but he was too feeble to keep his balance and tottered backwards until his flailing arms met with the wall behind him. He stood there, shaking slightly, rasping with each breath he took.

In a stride Dena was beside him, feeding her head and

neck beneath his arm to take his weight upon her slim shoulders.

'Come,' she coaxed. 'You must lie upon the bed.'

She eased him away from the wall, and in three faltering steps was lowering him to her pillow, but try as she might, she could not get him to lie down. He was telling her something, but the tongue he used was Welsh, and she could not understand.

He began pulling unsuccessfully at the leather belt about his waist. She unbuckled it and helped him out of his padded jerkin and the fine woollen tunic beneath. He was becoming weaker by the moment, almost like a babe in his lack of control over his limbs. When he clutched at the neck of his linen smock as though it was strangling him, she undid the ties so it fell open down his sticky chest. Even that did not seem to be enough for him.

'No,' Dena told him. 'You must keep it on. The chamber is cool. If your body is chilled, it may be entered by the coughing sickness.'

The coughing sickness! Spectral images of her dying father overwhelmed her. Rhodri was far too hot. Indeed, he was fever-like. She took his shoulders and laid him on the bed. This time he did not resist. She draped the coverlet over his shaking body and sat on the edge of the straw-filled mattress, looking down into his pallid face.

The likeness between the young Welshman and her dying father was horrifying; his grey-rimmed, sunken eyes, his hollow, rasping breaths, the ungodly way his skin had paled to stretch waxenly across the protruding bones of his skull-like face. How many days had she sat by her father's bedside, holding his hand, trying to bring comfort to a man who did not know she was there? She had fed him broths and potions, had prayers chanted over him, ancient charms recited. None of it had slowed his inevitable deterioration.

Rhodri grew worse. Perspiration flowed from him, and his gentle shaking turned to convulsive shudders. Dena removed her headcloth and used it to mop his brow and neck. There was still some water left in the jug, and she raised his head and poured a little into his mouth, but he would not drink. He began to toss and turn most violently, growling and crying out as if living a dream. He was starting to rave, and there was nothing, nothing she could do.

'Take heart. There are no ravings and no fever. It is a good sign.'

But there *was* raving and there *was* fever, just as there had been with her father. And her father had died.

She pushed herself to her feet and hurried across to the doorway. Without fear of drawing attention to herself, she flung back the tapestry curtain and peered out into the hall. It was more gloomy than ever, with several of the rush torches having flickered their last long ago, but the fire had been kept fuelled and many of the men were sitting round it with hunched shoulders, trying to keep warm. Others leaned against the walls, their heads held heavily in their hands. Hardly anyone was lying on the floor, and those that were seemed to have chosen the position out of comfort rather than pain. The time of sickness had passed, though the air was still heavy with the stench of it.

The sickness was the key, Dena realised. Rhodri had not vomited as the other men had. If he did, it might herald the turning-point towards recovery.

She dropped the curtain and moved back across the tiny cubicle. She stood over him, wondering how to go about the task, but as she compared his state with the

men in the hall, she began to fear that he had already
held the deadly liquor in his body far too long. Perhaps
the only paths open to him were to heaven or hell.

What would cause him to vomit? A solution of salt and
water would have been ideal, but there was no point in
wishing for items that were not to hand. Something long
and slender, which was not sharp . . .

She heaved up the lid of the oak chest by the bed,
praying that it had not been rifled, and found its familiar
contents staring up at her. Beneath her spare kirtles and
smock, beneath the heavy winter bedding, towels and
tiny bags of sweet-smelling herbs, she found them—
the long iridescent tail-feathers of a magpie. She had
plucked them from a thicket in a moment of idle fancy
not long before the onset of the harvest, when she had
escaped the eagle eyes of Ethelin and joined the women
from the kitchen on a berry-picking foray.

Dena selected the leanest and most supple and
dropped the others back in the chest. She did not relish
pushing the feather down Rhodri's throat—the very
thought made her shudder—but she knew it had to be
done. Gritting her teeth, she forced open his mouth and
began to insert it.

'Woman! What are you doing?'

In her fright, her heart tried to leap out of her chest.
Before she had a chance to turn and explain, Gwylan
had caught her about the waist and thrown her against
the wall. She landed in a heap on the floor, more
shocked than harmed.

'God's teeth, woman! What have you done to him?'

She struggled to her feet, anxious to explain before
she received another blow, one more likely to come
from a blade than from a hand.

'He will not vomit up the poison!' she cried. 'He

showed no signs of suffering when the other men suc-
cumbed. He believed he was free from its effects, but he
became hot and dizzy, and . . .' She looked down at
Rhodri, so pale and wraith-like. 'I was only trying to
help him.'

'How much did he drink?'

Dena cast her mind back. 'Two, three mugs, but that
is all.'

'It is enough,' Gwylan grunted.

Taking Rhodri forcefully by the shoulders, he pulled
him to a sitting position. Within a moment Gwylan had
pushed back his head and was unceremoniously feeding
his fingers down his countryman's throat. Dena closed
her eyes and grimaced, trying to keep her own stomach
under control as Rhodri began to cough and choke
beneath the onslaught. Gwylan's brutal remedy soon
had the desired effect, and Rhodri slumped to one side,
spilling the bilious liquid on to the floor and splattering it
in all directions. He kept on and on until there was no
more to be drawn from him. The stench was unbelievable, and she turned away to fight the nausea rising in
her own throat.

When she looked back, she found Gwylan sitting by
Rhodri's head, gently massaging the young man's pul-
sating neck muscles with the tips of his fingers. It was not
a task undertaken out of duty, or even compassion, but
more, she thought, out of love.

Gwylan raised his brooding eyes to her. 'Fill the pail,'
he snapped.

Dena made her way to the doorway on unsteady legs.
Drawing back the curtain, she picked up the pail Rhodri
had left by the partition wall. It was only then that she
remembered the men sitting round the fire. She lifted
her head cautiously and looked down the hall. Already

she had been noticed and was becoming the centre of every man's attention. No one uttered a word, but the silence was undeniably hostile.

Would they harm her? Would she dare to re-enter the cubicle and ask for Gwylan's protection? She knew that she could not. Gwylan's mind was fully occupied with Rhodri's comfort and recovery. He would not take kindly to his ministrations being interrupted by a frightened Saxon maid he had little time for in any event. Whatever happened, she would far rather face the men's wrath than Gwylan's.

With her only weapon, the heavy wooden pail, grasped firmly in her hand, she started the long walk to the west door. She tried not to look direct at any of the men, but they all kept a steady eye upon her. She could feel their gaze burning through every muscle in her body. As the door loomed large and beckoningly before her, Dena found she hardly dared to breathe in case she suddenly found her way blocked. What would she do? Stand aloof and proud and await their next move, or hit out with the pail, and run?

The choice never had to be made. She stepped through the door and out into the yard, pausing a moment to fill her lungs with the crisp, clear air. The sky was much lighter than she had expected, the dawn chorus well under way. A new day was at hand.

The pail filled, the walk back through the hall seemed half as long as the outward journey. Dena cared little, now, whether the men watched her or not, even if they tried to stop her. She would have rebuked them sternly within a moment, whether they could understand her words or not. Seeing the new day, appreciating the hope it brought, had hardened her resolve and put flight to her female frailties. Whatever would be, would be, and no amount of anxious tears or fearful cowering would change it.

She pulled back the tapestry curtain and set the pail down by Gwylan's feet. He had already stripped Rhodri of his sweat-laden smock and immediately began to wash the drying perspiration from his skin. She produced a towel from the chest, and helped to rub him down.

'Do you think he will live?' she asked.

Gwylan shot her a mortifying look of disgust. 'Do not fret about your own life. If the time comes to cut you down, I shall give you warning!'

Dena was hurt by his rebuke. She had not been thinking about his threat of death at all, only of Rhodri's health. Her hurt turned to annoyance, and she stood back and gazed upon the pair with new eyes. She had seen only the suffering and the despair that night, her compassion heightened by the vile and cowardly act of poisoning the ale; but she must remember that they were Welshmen and she English, one of the hated Saxons. Any compassion might be better spent on herself.

'I will see if I can find another smock,' she murmured, and was thankful to leave the stinking cubicle.

The central chamber of the three partitioned sleeping compartments belonged to Ethelin and Edwulf, and was a much grander affair than her own box, with wall-hangings, a brazier for winter nights and a feather-filled mattress upon the wide, curtained bed. None of it had survived the Welshmen's onslaught. The rush-covered floor was buried beneath a sea of curling down which swirled about her ankles as she lifted the tattered decorations, searching for a smock among the discarded clothing. Ethelin had been right to insist on taking

Edwulf's silverware. Better to weigh down an ass with it than the backs of these wretches who took such pleasure in destroying another man's property!

A smock found, she stalked back into her own chamber and tossed it on to Rhodri's legs without a word. Gwylan turned his head to glance at her, but she averted her eyes, standing woodenly in the corner like a soulless carving.

'Give me a hand here,' he ordered. 'And do not act so surly in my presence, or you will feel the weight of my cuff.'

Dena glared at him, but realised that she was in no position to do much else. She was a battle-prisoner, to be used as a hostage if the time presented itself. As such, she had no more standing than a common slave, her treatment dependent on the discretion of her captor. It might be most unwise to rile the likes of Gwylan!

She let her forced pique subside and stepped across the slurried floor to help to dress Rhodri. One touch of his skin with her cool hand told her that his fever had dropped substantially. And he was no longer raving. There was a good chance that he would not die as her father had, and for that she was thankful, but as the feeling began to stir in her breast she crushed it most brutally, with a reminder that she needed her compassion for herself.

Once dressed in his apple-green tunic, Rhodri was laid back upon the mattress, and the enveloping coverlet drawn about his neck. Gwylan stood and surveyed him for several moments without speaking.

'He needs to be close to the fire,' Dena advised. 'Should his blood become chilled while he is weak . . .' She left the rest unsaid, not wishing her intentions to be misconstrued a second time.

'Ay,' Gwylan murmured, 'but only until we can make ready to leave this forsaken hole.'

'*Leave?* He is in no condition to leave! Surely you cannot expect your men to comb the forest for Wybert and the people now? The ale may have had little effect upon you, but it has weakened your men terribly. Even I can see they are in no state to take up arms against anyone.'

Gwylan watched her with steadily rising eyebrows until she remembered her place and fell silent.

'I shall be still.'

'No, no,' he mocked. 'Let us hear your thoughts. If we had heard them a little earlier this night, none of my men would have drunk the poisoned ale.'

She blushed in her discomfort, wishing she had never opened her unguarded mouth.

'Like you, I never drank the ale, though it was more by turn of fate than good judgment. It was most perceptive of you, a mere woman unskilled in the military arts, to show such reasoning in the strategies of war. Does that mind of yours hold other information that it would be best for me to know—or, perhaps, not know?'

A sudden foreboding coursed through her as she noted the change in his tone. She raised her eyes slowly, choosing her words with care in case he read more into them than was actually there.

'Other information?'

'Ay,' he purred, but the look in his eyes told of his true attitude towards her, and Dena felt her pulse begin to quicken as she realised what he might do if he believed she was withholding further information from him.

'I have none. My thoughts were only for the condition of Rhodri. He cannot ride a horse.' She tried to sound convincing, but it was having little effect on Gwylan. 'You are fearing another trap,' she added.

He cocked his head to one side and narrowed his eyes. 'And what makes you say that?'

Again, she wished she had said nothing, but she could not keep silent now.

'Rhodri believed the ale might have had a double intention. He was worried in case a few strong men might infiltrate the defences and put your followers to the sword while they were too ill to defend themselves.'

Gwylan eased his stance a little. 'A good plan, except that Wybert did not have the men to carry it out.'

Dena could not understand his reasoning. 'Then why do you fear him now? Your men grow stronger by the hour.'

'It is not *him* I have concern for. It is those he has ridden to for assistance.'

She looked at him incredulously. 'But the next estate is a full day's journey hence . . .'

Gwylan shook his head in open-mouthed astonishment. 'I apologise. I had endowed you with quicker wits than you obviously own! Wybert will have sent his fastest horseman, like as not well before you were set upon your false errand to the tun. Baldric is no poor thegn needing to ingratiate himself with the new English king. He is himself of royal blood—not a ceorl like Edwulf, who has raised himself above his born station. There will be plenty of fighting men left within his defences for Wybert to call upon. And all of them will be riding hard for here, hoping to trap us in this accursed hall!'

Dena was stunned. There was hope of rescue, after all. She kept her face as still as a mask, but within her being her spirit was cheering at the news. She watched

Gwylan pace back and forth across the floor, the burden of his predicament weighing heavily upon his shoulders. He had made his plans, waited for his moment and endeavoured to regain his lost lands. None of it had gone right for him, and now he was in jeopardy of losing even his men. She could find little compassion for him, but neither could she find it within herself to glory in his misfortune.

He came to a halt facing the curtained doorway, his hands caught tensely behind his back. Without warning, he straightened his stance, pulled at the lower edges of his heavily ringed jerkin and flattened down his unruly hair. He was making himself ready to speak to his men, Dena realised, to tell them—to tell them what? That there was no hope of success now, that they were about to be over-run by a horde of Saxons who would slaughter them to a man?

Dena could not help her eyes wandering to the still form of Rhodri lying on the bed. Would he, too, be killed? Even as he lay unconscious? The answer which slowly filtered through her numbing brain was 'Yes', such was the way of this warfare. Forgiveness and mercy were only for the songs the poets sang, just as Gwylan had said.

She saw Gwylan falter as he raised his hand to draw aside the curtain, and sat expectantly as he turned to look at her.

'I shall send two men to carry the cot to the fire. You seem versed in the art of tending the sick. You will care for him.' He disappeared through the curtain.

Care for him! She looked down at Rhodri, so still beside her. She had cared for her father, cared for him out of love; but this Welshman, this enemy . . .

Who was her enemy, truly her enemy? Was it Rhodri

who wielded his weapons on the battlefields of his people? Or was it her kin who had plotted her demise?

She reached out with her fingertips, slowly, tentatively, in case Rhodri should suddenly blink open his eyes and glare at her. His forehead was damp to her touch; cold, like death.

She brushed aside a wisp of his dark hair that was threatening to fall into his closed eyes. He needed her care—someone's care—and she had to prove, to Gwylan at least, that she was worth keeping alive.

She wiped Rhodri's brow again with her headcloth. How different he looked, lying there so serene, from the moment she had first seen him, striding through the ranks of Welshmen, the fading light rippling over his coat of mail. Which was the true Rhodri? Where did the trained warrior end, and the feeling man begin?

CHAPTER
FOUR

IT WAS not long before two burly Welshmen entered the sleeping-chamber and carried Rhodri and the narrow bed through to the main part of the hall. The combined weight proved no obstacle to them, even in their weakened state, for the bed was no larger or more elaborate than an uncovered horse-litter. Dena stood against the logging wall to give them room to manoeuvre, and followed them through the doorway with the pail.

Gwylan had already left, as had most of the men. Those remaining were donning armour and helmet as if they had no time to lose. Only three sat round the central fire, their sunken eyes and curious pallor telling much about their state of health. One was shivering most violently and kept offering his hands to the heat of the flames as though he could not feel their warmth. Dena watched him for a while as she sat by Rhodri's head. This man's condition worried her. Even in the dim light, the scorch-marks on the knees of his loose woollen braies were plain for her to see. He had spent a good deal of time by that fire, very close to it, but it seemed to have had little, if any, effect. He needed a covering as much as Rhodri did, and there were two on the bed.

It took no time to release the rough blanket on the mattress from his weight; Rhodri did not even murmur as she moved him, but the shivering man was both surprised and grateful when Dena placed it about his shoulders. It pleased her that she could do some small thing for one of the Welshmen. It might help to dispel the hostility they felt for her, the guilt she herself felt for being a party, however unwitting, to the poisoning of the ale.

She walked about the hall quite freely as men came and went around her. She carried wood in from the store outside the west door and rebuilt the fire. She found new rush lights among the broken pottery in the devastated kitchen area and replaced the spent torches on the walls, bringing bright pools of light to the gloomy corners of the hall. She even fetched clean water from the well and offered it to the men sitting about the fire, though none would touch the rawhide mug she held until she had drunk from it. It lifted her spirits to have a purpose to her time after so long spent idly sitting, waiting, letting her imagination heighten her fears. In an odd sort of way it reminded her of the harvest feasts in her father's home when she had wandered among the workers, filling horns and mugs with ale and mead. Was it only the turning of a year? It seemed such a long, long time ago.

The thought of harvest feasts brought back the pangs of hunger she had been trying to keep at bay. Already her belt was loose around her waist, the tattered blue kirtle hanging more than ever like a sack over her slim frame. There was no food to be had, she reminded herself resentfully. Wybert had taken every last crust with him when the people had fled, so that the effect of the poisoned ale would be that much worse. She wondered what he was doing now, that grey-haired old bear. Was he toasting his triumph with others of his kind? Was he giving a single thought to the predicament in which he had placed her? Or had she served his purpose and was dead to him now, dead and forgotten . . .

She heaved a sigh and brushed away an emerging tear.

She had never meant to dwell on such melancholy, to pity herself. Edwulf had taken her into his household only because of the favourable marriage she might make in his name, she knew that. She should have expected no better than to be used to further his advancement in time of war. Her father would never have dreamed of doing either, but, as Ethelin had so condescendingly reminded her, no two brothers could have been such opposites. Little wonder that her father had acted as though Edwulf had not existed. No doubt he, too, had suffered at his brother's hands.

Dena balled her fists and brought them thudding down on to her thighs in her agitation. Rhodri stirred. She was leaning over him in a moment, anxiously peering into his pale face for signs of renewed raving. His eyelids flickered as if he was dreaming, and then an unearthly sound rattled deep in his throat. She laid her hand upon his brow to test for fever, and was relieved to find none. She drew her fingers along his high-boned cheeks, and softly called his name.

At first there was no response; then his breathing became noticeably deeper and his limbs moved tentatively as though seeking the level of their strength.

'Rhodri?' she whispered.

His eyes finally opened and she gazed down at him, a smile lighting her face, as she waited for him to pull his sight into focus.

'What is this?' he murmured. 'I am at the mercy of a Saxon maid, and yet my throat remains intact.'

Her smile broadened at his jest, but as his eyes swivelled in her direction, she realised he was deadly serious. That he should think such ill of her hurt more than she cared to admit. She pushed the cover further up to his neck and lifted a disparaging eyebrow.

'You must have known some very peculiar women.'

He said nothing, though his eyes remained constantly on hers. Dena was determined not to be the first to break away, and held his gaze until he spoke.

'You are alive, so the men must be, too.'

'They are all well.' She glanced at the men beside her and quickly reconsidered such a comprehensive reply. 'Some have taken it better than others, but the worst affected share the fire.' Her irritation began to subside.

'Gwylan?'

'He did not taste the ale.'

A weak smile played across Rhodri's thin lips. 'I always knew a saint watched over him. Is it day yet?'

She knew what was in his mind. Even in such poor health as this, he was calculating the moves and strengths of the Saxons.

'The new day dawned long ago. The sun is up and rising.'

It was as though a tired ox had been jabbed by a pointed stick.

'Then we must be gone from this hole.'

He flung the cover aside and wrapped his fingers round her wrist, fighting to pull himself to a sitting position, using her as a lever.

'No,' she countered, pushing him backwards. 'You must rest. I have not tended you this long night for you to slump to the floor and crack your head open on the stone. Gwylan is making arrangements for the men at this very moment. He has no need of your help. Your duty is to be strong enough to ride a horse when the time arrives.'

To Dena's surprise he slumped back on the pillow without argument, closing his eyes with a tired, dispirited sigh. She dipped her headcloth in the pail and wiped his brow and lips. He opened his eyes again and looked at her.

'Could you take a drink?'

He nodded, and lifted himself on one elbow as she brought the mug to his lips. He sipped cautiously and lifted his hand when he had drunk enough. He did not lie down again, but painfully pulled himself round to a sitting position before the fire and cradled his head in his hands as the other men had. He looked grey.

There was a rattle of hooves on the courtyard, which caught everyone's attention. When the door burst open, spilling men inside, Dena held her breath, believing, for a moment, that the Welsh were under attack, but although the men moved with great speed, no one seemed to be unduly afraid. In their wake strode Gwylan, snapping orders in quick succession. Rhodri raised his head at the older man's approach, but did not attempt to stand.

'I see your wits have returned. That will be the last ale you will drink for a while, I have no doubt.' Gwylan smiled broadly, pulling and separating the two points of his thick beard as he cast an appraising eye over him. 'Can you ride?'

Rhodri gave him an ironic chuckle. 'If I do not ride, I shall fall.'

'I shall sit behind the saddle and guide him,' Dena interjected. 'He will not fall.'

Both men turned their heads to look at her. There was a curious state of unease in the air, as though she had said something she ought not to have done.

'You are being left for Wybert to find,' Gwylan stated flatly.

She could hardly believe her ears. She had expected to be taken along as a hostage, not to be set free so quickly.

'No,' Rhodri snapped. 'I want her to come.'

Dena looked at him aghast, but his eyes were not for her. They were fixed squarely on the uncompromising features of Gwylan.

'I have decided,' he said, and turned on his heel. Rhodri was up in a moment, rocking dangerously on his unsteady legs, his face full of fury which erupted in a tirade of Welsh.

Dena watched in silence as the two battled out their vehement words. At last Gwylan took a step backward. The contest seemed to be over, leaving Rhodri the winner, but not until Gwylan had fired a quip which brought a smirk from every man in the hall. Rhodri turned blood-red, and muttered something low and malevolent beneath his breath. He turned to Dena with hatred in his eyes, and called her to his side as though she were a dog. Incensed, she did his bidding. There seemed little point in risking the violence she knew was lurking only surface deep in this angry Welshman, but even so, her tongue would not be entirely still.

'Do not shout at me!' she hissed. 'It is not for my pleasure that you wish to drag me round after you.'

Rhodri laid a heavy hand on her arm, and Dena automatically took his weight as he leant against her for support, but the act was twofold, and his slender fingers gripped vice-like about her upper arm, threatening to tear flesh from bone. She gasped with the pain and desperately tried to break his grasp, but Rhodri did not even notice. He bent his head close to hers, his hot and rancid breath pouring down her neck.

'This is no time for you to voice your protests! If you value your life, stay close by my side and do not utter a word.'

He pushed her away from him, staggering back himself to fall gracelessly to the bed, and sprawled there to regain his breath.

Dena drew her lips into a thin line and glowered down at him. If he wanted silence, he would get silence, she vowed angrily. All her life she had played the cringing shadow, first with her father, who had wanted only peace to dwell within his memories, and then with Ethelin, who wished to act the queen. It would be no hardship at all.

The Welshmen began to file out of the west door. One stopped to offer Rhodri his arm. Dena picked up the heavy coat of mail and followed like the dutiful servant, only the defiant blaze of her eyes telling of her true feelings.

The waiting horses were nothing like she thought they would be. After seeing the great war-horses owned by Edwulf and Wybert, she had expected every nobleman to ride one, but the shaggy mounts standing in the yard looked pitifully small in comparison. Her dismay lessened as she stood besides Rhodri's black mare. These horses might have been short in leg, but they were broad in back and shoulder.

The saddle was already on, if it had ever been taken off. Behind it, over the double carrying-bags, lay a thick wolf-fur cloak. She would, at least, have something comfortable to sit on during this journey into the Welsh mountains. She should be thankful for small mercies.

Rhodri's sword had been strapped along one side of the saddle. His shield hung loosely from the other, as Dena found to her cost when she struggled up behind him and banged her knee into it. She soon discovered where his helmet had been stowed, too, in one of the pockets of the saddlebags. It stuck uncomfortably into the back of her thigh, no matter how she tried to cushion it with the edge of the fur cloak.

As if her discomfort was not enough, she found that the hem of her kirtle was too narrow for her to sit astride a horse without showing a good deal of bare leg. She had not worn hose since the beginning of the summer, but how she wished for some now! Already the Welshmen were passing whispered remarks. There seemed no other solution. She reached for the hem, and ripped the length of the cloth to give herself more freedom.

Rhodri turned on hearing the sound, and looked down at the bare leg she was vainly trying to conceal.

'Would it not have been easier to cover yourself with the fur? Or, better still, to sit sideways as a true-born lady would?'

Dena glared at him. Even though she knew he was right, she was not going to give him the satisfaction of agreeing with him—nor to receive more of his sarcastic comments.

'And how am I to hold you on this mule-horse if I am sitting sideways?' she demanded. 'The first jolt would bounce us both to the ground.'

Rhodri's hollow eyes narrowed until only a shard of cold hatred glinted through the sunken apertures.

'I will give my soul to the Devil before I fall off my horse this day.'

She shrank back in alarm. He spoke his words so quietly, hardly above a breath, yet there was this seething rage within him—she could feel it. It was like the trembling of the earth during a storm. How could anyone so ill hold such power within him? It was not natural.

The horses moved forward, the milling group turning into an untidy line as they reached the lane and began the descent to the defences and down into the fields. It had been a long time since she had ridden behind a saddle. It was not at all like riding with the reins in her hands, and Dena felt vulnerable as she swayed unsteadily on the haunches of the shaggy little animal. When Rhodri kicked her into a trot, she found she had no alternative but to slot her hands about his waist to maintain her seat.

'So much for her keeping *him* on the horse's back,' she muttered to herself.

She glanced at him uncertainly, but if he had heard her, he gave no sign. His head was held high, his dark hair flowing behind him like feathered tendrils reaching out to flick and brush her face. They were just too short to touch her skin. Dena watched the tantalising dance of his sweat-woven locks, and wondered how they would feel when they were washed and brushed and as glossy as a raven's wing. What did he look like in the hall of his lord? Were his tunics embroidered with gold? He wore rings. Had they been given to him by the princes of his realm? Was he admired by men—and by women?

Dena sat back with a start. What was she doing, letting her thoughts roam like this? What was the matter with her? One moment her heart ached for the suffering he endured, the next her blood roared in anger for the contemptuous way he treated her. It was as if she had been tied to a see-saw as a prank during a feast day. Up and down her emotions went, up and down like a girl of twelve caught in the first anxious throes of womanhood.

Her condemnations weighed heavily on her flagging spirits, constricting her throat, filling her chest. She had never thrilled to the shyly exchanged glance, never entwined fingers with a loved one, never tasted the sweetness of a kiss stolen beneath the eyes of a watching grandmother. Her childhood friends from the wattle

huts had grown and wed before her eyes. Motherhood
had replaced their girlish laughter, and Dena had felt
alienated and alone, no matter how they had tried to
ease the change.

No carter's boy for you, they had said. *No smith's
labourer or ploughman's boy. You shall wed a thegn's
son, and he will carry you to his father's hall on the back
of a great white steed.*

They had foretold it, but it had never happened; and
she had grown older, more lonely and more dispassion-
ate, surrounded by her elders, cocooned by the repeti-
tive cycle of the farm. She had never rebelled. She had
never known how to. Ethelin had laughed when she had
told her. 'Worse than a nunnery,' she had said, but Dena
had not seen that, not until Gwylan and Rhodri had
burst into her life.

Gwylan. In a way, she admired him for his refusal to
accept the loss of his lands, even after all these years.
Her father would have held up his hands in despair and
bowed to his fate, saying that it was the will of God; but
not Gwylan. He was determined to regain what was
rightfully his. And Rhodri—she sighed as she looked
bleakly at his square shoulders—if only her feelings for
him were as straightforward as those for the elder man.
It was as though Rhodri had unlocked a door within her,
a door barred since the wedding-days of her childhood
friends. All those emotions she had never experienced,
years of them, had come spilling out in a cacophany of
sight and sound and confusion. Was she equating Rhodri
with the thegn's son those young mothers had promised
her? Was she seeing him in the love-songs of the poets,
inserting his name in the old hero stories of battle-
winners and gentle wooers of maids?

A solitary ironic chuckle nearly burst forth. How

stupid! How childish! Why had she dressed him with attributes he had never even heard of? Why could she not see him for what he was—a battle-winner? Yes, he probably was a battle-winner. No timid man would own such armour, but where was the honour that went hand in hand with the prestige? Where was the gallantry? The honesty? Gwylan had wanted to leave her at the hall, but Rhodri . . . What did he want with her?

Even as the question came into her mind, she knew the answer. Her eyes burned hatred into his back, fired by the revulsion of having to touch him, having to hold him about the waist to keep herself upon the shaggy mare. After she had satisfied his lust, would she be given to the men? She screwed up her eyes as tightly as she could, trying to banish every emotion from her heart, every thought from her mind, but still one teardrop managed to find a way through to roll down her cheek. She bit back the rest and swallowed the pain choking her throat. Tears would not help her now, but prayers might.

Pitiful God, she began, but she reached no further. Her mind had filled with the memory of Ethelin clinging to the west doorway of the hall, her eyes staring blindly as she repeated, again and again, prayers of deliverance from the hands of the Welshmen. Ethelin had known how it would be. Ethelin had known.

Dena did not look back as the riders left the lane and followed the track by the side of the forest. Edwulf's hall had not been a home for her, it was true, but it had been a place to rest her head and watch one season pass into another. She would never see it again, she was certain, but there was no great pull to turn round and impress its solid façade upon her memory. This was her ride to the tun, the ride of her betrayal. It was difficult to think of anything else, but she tried to close her mind to it, staring hard at Rhodri's back, trying to see nothing on either side of her which would mark the path.

When they reached the partly-cleared ground beyond the last field, the horses were reined in and made to walk. The men without mounts were already waiting there, lying amid the bracken, partly concealed, partly resting. All rose with their packs and weapons ready for the next stretch of the march. Dena saw some of them point to her in surprise, and she felt her cheeks begin to colour. She wished they would go instead of standing there, even if it was into the depths of the wild Welsh valleys. She looked for Gwylan at the head of the column. He was taking advice from two of his men, who were eagerly pointing this way and that.

Dena slowly brought her gaze to Rhodri. He was still sitting upright in his saddle, as stiff with anger and resentment as when they had left the hall. She could not tell for certain, but his eyes did not seem to rest upon Gwylan, neither did they guardedly search the country-side around them. Strange, too, that he was not a party to the discussions of their route. Could more have been said during that argument at the hall than could easily be forgiven? Rhodri had gained his victory, so why was he hanging back so churlishly? It made no sense for a warrior of his standing to refuse to help his comrades-in-arms. Or was he in disgrace? Was that the reason? It would certainly account for his odd behaviour. She studied him again, as well as she could from so close behind, but the ways of fighting men were a mystery to her and it was a fruitless exercise to try to read their minds.

Suddenly they were moving again, a great flank of

men and horses as they headed further along the track, closer to the north tun. Dena felt a hollowness swell within her. Was that where they were going? To the tun? She feared so. What would she find there? What devastation of dismembered limbs and torn flesh?

Shame flooded through her. She wished for revenge against Edwulf and Wybert for her betrayal, but there were others, innocents caught in this nightmarish trap of fighting lords. Had she given a thought to the children driving the swine, chasing the fowl? Had she placed herself in the position of those mothers with babes on their backs who toiled in Edwulf's fields; of Swithun, the crippled man with his milk cow, leaving all his poor but priceless possessions to be ravaged by the Welsh so that his lord's silver might escape intact? Had she grieved for the people at the tun, hacked to death or locked in their burning dwelling? No, she had shuddered and forgotten them. Her pain, Wybert's treachery, had been all that had filled her thoughts. Her compassion had been for the poisoned Welshmen. It should have been for the people of the estate, but she had not spared them a drop. Dena hung her head and wished herself in hell.

The trees crowded in on the column, branches snatching at them as they passed. The pall of smoke was no longer visible in the hazy morning sky, but the acrid after-stench of burning cloaked the leafy track, unable to escape the tight mantle of leaves. All of a sudden they were upon the wide clearing of the tun, and a great weight dropped leadenly in Dena's stomach as she saw it.

Surprisingly, there was hardly anything to be seen outside the walls. The wattle swine-pens were down, the vegetable-patch trampled, but that was all. Tentatively she raised her eyes to the stone fortifications, but again there was nothing, although there should have been

—there should have been the thatched roof of the dwelling-house visible above. It had gone, totally. Not even a charred end-wall had survived to stand like a monument to the people who had died there. Onward they rode, coming closer to the open gateway, closer to the one window on to the devastation the stone walls enclosed.

It was a penance, Dena told herself, that she should be made to see this, a punishment for her selfish thoughts —but she could not bring herself to look and turned away her head, closing her eyes, holding her breath.

Then the horses were trotting again, past the open gateway, past the stone walls, leaving the lonely tun behind for the encroaching forest and its nocturnal scavengers. Dena's arms clung to Rhodri's waist. She did not care, now, what he thought of her, how he treated her; she needed someone to hold, someone's back to cry upon.

The horses slowed. The track narrowed to a deer run. There was no space for wide-leafed bracken to grow. Not enough sunlight reached the springy earth to sustain the smallest green shoot. Only gorse flourished in wild profusion, its razor-sharp thorns catching at their legs, ripping Dena's shredded kirtle even more. Low branches, more dead than alive, fingered her hair with brittle twigs, pulling at her scalp, mocking her despair.

As they continued on, following wolf-trails and boar-runs, twisting and turning, the ribbon of sky above them clouded first white and then grey until no shadows at all were cast. No birds sang. No man spoke. The tortuous forest corridor felt like the very bowels of the earth.

Sometimes they stopped, but not to rest. Silently they waited while men scouted ahead. Rhodri's mare was near the back of the column. Dena hardly ever saw the front. It was a tiring, monotonous journey. It could have been in circles for all she knew. Half awake, half asleep, she swayed dangerously, perched high on the mare's rump. Even Rhodri no longer sat upright in his saddle, but was slumped over her neck. He never complained, though, when Dena leaned against him to close her eyes.

The tracks grew worse, and they had to walk. Dena was so stiff that she could hardly move. Rhodri was little better, but on they plodded, man and beast alike.

The natural clearings were sent from heaven as far as Dena was concerned. Like a bumpy, knee-deep mantle, bracken cloaked the ground, burying and protecting the late summer flowers. It would have been such luxury just to lie back in it, to let it carry her weight, to let the sweetness of its scent fill her nostrils and act as a cooling balm to her aching head, but they never stopped in a clearing, always on the narrow track; and once, just once, they lingered at the crossing of a brook.

Falling to her knees on its soft, mossy bank, Dena cupped her hands to drink the chill water, but instead of refreshing her, the coldness bit painfully into her lips and she opened her hands with a gasp and it fell to wet her grubby kirtle.

'You have been too long without a drink,' she heard Rhodri say. 'Your lips are cracked and split. You should have told me. I have a water-pouch tied to the front of the saddle.'

Dena looked up at him as she cautiously examined her lips with wetted fingers. He was sitting on the opposite bank, his arms caught about his upward-thrusting knees as if it was the only position he could manage without tumbling over. His colouring, if anything, had grown even worse, a pale grey tinged with hints of purple about his sunken eyes.

'You must be hungry, too,' he added. 'There is a little venison in the saddlebags and some bread, though that is probably stale now. You are welcome to it.'

Welcome to it? She looked at him, perplexed, not able to accept this change in his mood. One moment he wanted her as his whore, the next he was giving her his food.

'You should eat, too,' she murmured across the gurgling water. 'You look ill.'

He nodded. 'Perhaps, when we stop. It should not be long. The air grows heavy. We shall have rain. Night will be upon us before we know.'

'Will we reach our destination tonight?'

He furrowed his brow quizzically. 'Our destination?'

'The home of Gwylan.'

'We do not ride to Gwylan's vale. What gave you that notion?'

Dena was lost for words. 'I thought . . . Where are we going?'

A bemused smile crept hesitantly across his pale features. 'Nowhere,' he said.

Dena sat back on her haunches, completely confused. Rhodri's gentle chuckle rippled over the bubbling surface of the brook towards her, but she could not see the joke.

'Poor Dena! Where do you think we are? Only a quarter-day, perhaps less, from Edwulf's hall, as the raven flies; but, alas, we are not ravens and neither, praise God, are the Saxons who hunt us. Did you not see the men laying false trails? Did you not notice the sun circle us three times?'

She looked about her as though seeing her surroundings for the first time. Each tree had blurred in her mind into an exact replica of the last, each twist and turn in the path they followed. Had they been travelling in circles?

'Poor Dena,' he repeated. 'No. It is not sympathy you warrant. It is—' he shrugged his shoulders '—admiration. No faints, no temper, no complaints. Truly a strong-hearted girl.' He smiled at her, an odd kind of smile which left her pink about the cheeks.

A call caught their attention. The men were assembling themselves for the continued march.

'We must go.'

They rose together and walked either side of the brook to where the mare was lazily grazing.

'Do you wish to ride?'

Dena shook her head. She had ridden enough, and ached with it. Rhodri gathered up the reins, but did not mount. Instead, he fell into step with Dena, leading the mare behind him.

It was difficult walking two abreast along the narrow track, and they had to bob and weave through a multitude of overhanging branches and creeping thorn. Dena did not like to wonder why he kept so close, but the question drifted through her mind where, for once, no other thoughts scurried back and forth. He was looking at her, too, she could see through the corner of her eye, stolen glances, like . . .

He wrapped his hand round hers, and she caught her breath, uncertain if the tingling sensation rushing up her arm was really there or a figment of her imagination. She turned her face to look at his, and found him smiling down at her like a fresh-faced boy half his years.

What was this? More deceit? More mockery? Dena could not tell. Rhodri would not hold her eyes with his, but cast his gaze ahead, the smile still lighting the greyness of his face.

This is folly, she thought, pure folly. She should

wrench her hand free from his, denounce this cruel joke in temper and indignation . . . but she did nothing. And as they walked along the track she felt him gently push his fingers through her own, scarcely entwined, yet locked so tightly that nothing but a poleaxe could break the bond.

Folly, a voice clamoured inside her head, but she could not deny the stirrings of her heart, or the glow which blossomed and spread within her as skin brushed skin and melted into one.

CHAPTER
FIVE

THE TANGIBLE proof of their new-found harmony was short-lived, broken not by spite or weapon, but by the precipitous bank of a trickling stream. Rhodri went first, leading the mare. Despite her load, she seemed to negotiate the crumbling shale better than Dena, who followed behind. The girl slipped and slithered and lost her footing several times, but Rhodri waited at the bottom, and offered his hand to steady her.

There was no reluctance in taking it this time. She smiled her thanks shyly, not wishing to damage their fragile rapport by appearing too aloof, yet afraid to show more than the merest hint of her inner thoughts and feelings lest she found them held to ridicule at some future time. She wanted Rhodri to like her, to show friendship and understanding, but she was wary of placing all her trust in the warm smile of a man whose nature was so quick to change. Perhaps he thought the same of her, she reflected guiltily. She had hardly been constant herself.

They wandered along the boulder-strewn stream bed, Rhodri walking in the water, Dena stepping from rock to rock, until they reached the place designated for clambering up the further bank. Once it was reached, they discovered to their relief that Gwylan had finally called a halt in an undisturbed glade high above the watercourse. Dena was not certain whether it was the odd way the daylight dappled through the gently dancing leaves or the culmination of her hunger and fatigue, but the place had a strangely unreal quality about it, as though it had been sculpted from a hundred dreams and fantasies. Young trees of hazel and birch sprouted from a carpet of dark green grass, fine-leaved and so luxuriantly thick that she felt she was walking on a feather-filled mattress. Everywhere men were stretched out in their exhaustion, some already asleep and snoring.

Rhodri led the mare away from the main group to a fallen ash, whose roots had long since overcome the shock of a winter gale and had thrown up a host of new shoots which acted like a screen, towering above the height of a man. He dropped his heavy coat of mail to the ground and proceeded to untie the rest of his accoutrements from the saddle. Realising she was soon to be free of her load, the shaggy little animal tossed back her head and stamped a hoof as if chastising him for taking so long.

Dena watched him smile as he rubbed the mare's neck in return, and she helped to unload the animal by lifting off the saddlebags and the thick wolf-fur cloak. She noticed Gwylan walking through the ranks of men, stopping at nearly every stride to exchange some word or gibe with them. It heartened her to see him walking towards them, his face so full of smiles. The animosity of the early morning had evaporated during the long march, and she was grateful. Gwylan and Rhodri were the only two Welshmen she could converse with, the only two who understood her tongue. It made her feel more secure if they were on friendly terms with each other. She turned to Rhodri.

'Gwylan comes.'

'I have eyes.'

The guttural loathing barely suppressed in his voice started shrill alarm-bells jangling in her head. She had no wish to believe what she was hearing, but as he looked round at her, she knew there had been no mistake. She could see the dark light of anger flaring in his eyes.

'You will not speak to him,' Rhodri ordered. 'Sit by the tree, and lay out the food.'

Dena did as she was told, too numb to harbour rebellious thoughts. She cast out the wolfskin cloak and sat upon it, clutching the saddlebags to her. What had she done that his mood should change so suddenly? Had everything changed between them now? Could she count on nothing?

She watched Gwylan make his way across to them, smiling at one man, playfully jeering at another, but when he turned his attention to Rhodri, his face became serious, even hard. With a deepening sense of dread, she looked to Rhodri for his reaction, but he was blatantly ignoring his lord, acting as though Gwylan did not even exist.

What was happening? Where were the concern and the love she had seen pass between these two?

She forced a finger between her parched lips, anxiously biting on it, as if by doing so she could avert this confrontation and return the men's normal equanimity.

Gwylan stopped not six paces away and thoughtfully curled a finger round his beard as he assessed Rhodri's mood. When he spoke, it was in short, clipped phrases of Welsh. Dena wished she could have understood the language, but wishing, she knew, would not bring comprehension, and she watched and listened for telling changes in tone and expression.

The older man might have mellowed during the journey, but Rhodri definitely had not. He released the bridle from the mare's head, and with a sharp slap to her rump, sent her freely on her way. Now there was nothing in the space between them, nothing but the breeze which had suddenly sprung from nowhere, chill and ominous, catching and lifting tendrils of the men's hair like battle-pennants. A low rumbling echoed through the darkening trees as though the earth itself was churning.

The contest never took place. With a defiant toss of his head, Rhodri turned his back on Gwylan and stepped on to the wolfskin cloak, lowering himself beside Dena, the air round him bristling with antagonism. Carefully, she began to edge away from him, astutely aware that any act might provoke him further.

'Where is the food?' he snapped.

Dena recoiled, grappling with the heavy saddlebags, trying to find their openings. Her eyes registered a movement before her, and with a sinking heart she glanced up to see Gwylan striding away. She struggled with the fastenings on the saddlebags, her trembling fingers seemingly unable to do what her mind intended. She could feel Rhodri's stern eyes upon her, watching each clumsy movement. She could sense his mounting exasperation, almost hear his sharp retort as she imagined him tearing the saddlebags from her hands. All at once her throat was choked with rising tears which brimmed up in her eyes, blurring her vision so that she could see even less of what she was doing. Her chest was cut by a searing pain and she bowed her head, letting her tousled braids fall across her face so that he might not witness her first tears.

The straps holding the saddlebags gave at last, and she fumbled inside, blindly searching the pouches for the bread and venison and laid them on the cloak between them.

She started at the touch of Rhodri's hand. She had not seen him raise it, and she was uncertain if it bode fair or ill for her as he drew a dangling braid aside.

'Why do you cry?' he breathed, his face a study of incredulous incomprehension.

Why did she cry? Was he so unfeeling that he truly had no idea? She was tired. She ached. She was frightened. She had no understanding of what was happening any more, not to her, not inside her. That frightened her. That frightened her more than anything. If only one thing had been stable, had been constant enough for her to rely on no matter what else happened, she could have coped, she knew she could. She had half-believed she had found that stability in her relationship with Rhodri; perhaps it had only been wishful thinking, but that was gone now, shattered, leaving her with nothing but this frailty, this deep, echoing loneliness. It was like waking from a dream and finding herself in a never-ending nightmare.

The tears trickled down her cheeks, faster now that she did not try to hide them, but still without a sound. How could she tell him why she cried? How could she make him understand when she herself did not understand? She turned her head away, pulling her long hair from his open hand.

'You are tired,' he told her quickly. 'You have been too long without food.'

She heard him break the bread, saw his hand holding it above her shoulder, but she shook her head. She was past the need for food now, too exhausted and distraught even to curl up and sleep.

Sleep. How wonderful it would be to wipe this wretchedness from her mind with blissful sleep!

'Dena!'

She heard him call her name, but he seemed very far away, and she was sinking, down, down, into a bed of warm grey fur, cushioned from the world and from people and from life itself.

'Dena!'

The voice was more insistent, closer, and she was being tossed like a leaf in the wind. She could feel her arms lifting, the lifting wings of a bird, but uselessly, uselessly. Something was in her mouth—water—and she swallowed it down. There was more, and she choked on it, coughing and gasping and forcing her heavy eyelids to part.

'Dena . . .'

She could hear relief in the voice now, and could see the figure of Rhodri swimming before her eyes like a reflection in a rippling stream. Her world rocked again, and she realised that he held her in his arms.

'You are ill,' she heard him say, but she knew she was not ill, only tired, and she laid a hand on his chest and rolled her head against him.

The ground trembled beneath the wolfskin cloak, the shock-waves tearing though Dena's body like a stampeding animal. It sounded as though every tree in the forest was splitting and falling around her, threatening to pound her body into the earth. A hand clutched at her shoulder, and she caught her breath.

'You are well. Be still. It is only the storm. It will be gone soon.'

The unseen hand glided down her arm to her waist and curled itself round her middle, pulling her backwards, nestling her body against his like silver spoons on a salver. Dena's senses rippled and exploded at Rhodri's touch, but she could not make the distinction between pleasure and apprehension. She tightened the muscles of her hollow stomach, but he did not remove his gently draped hand.

She became aware of a good many things at the same time. The wolfskin cloak was not just beneath them as they lay, but above them also, sheltering them from the worst of the rain. Her legs and feet were wet, her slippers and the bottom part of her kirtle sodden, and she could see nothing, nothing at all.

There was a flash of white light which hung for long moments about their canopy, trying to force itself through each chink above their heads. Then it was gone, leaving a ghostly silence in its place.

When it came, the rolling thunder cracked like a thousand rawhide ox-whips, and Dena shuddered in fright. Rhodri's still hand suddenly came to life, clutching her to him so tightly that she could feel his solid chest against her shoulderblades, his knees against her legs. His long fingers, spreading out from his open palm, radiated in all directions; over her hips, her abdomen, her midriff, her lower ribcage, so close to her raging heart and the sweeping curve of her breasts.

'Are you cold? Come closer.'

He pulled her to him again, altering his own position so that his head was level with hers, his mouth bent close to her neck so she could feel his warm breath upon her skin.

'No,' she said quickly—perhaps too quickly, she was not sure. 'I am not cold,' she added, though she was. The tiny hairs on her skin were rising all along her arms.

'You are afraid of the storm? There is no need. I shall keep you safe.' His hand pressed into her stomach, gently stroking, soothing her, stimulating her, raising a dread and a desire.

Was her mind playing tricks on her? Was she seeking fears which did not exist? Were his actions innocent or calculated? How did lovers begin their play?

Dena felt a softness brush her neck. At first she thought she had imagined it, but no, it came again, like a downy feather tracing an arc, warm and moist across her skin. A caress . . .

She held her breath, unable to move, unable to think. His hand was moving now, his fingers searching, curling beneath her hip, forcing themselves between her kirtle and the wolfskin cloak they lay upon. He was trying to turn her to him!

The alarm screamed in her head, but still she did nothing. His touch was warm and gentle, soothing . . . beautiful . . . Her body was her own no longer. It responded, not to her will, but to Rhodri's touch.

Desire was rising fast now, forcing itself through her limbs like sap in a young spring tree, denied the zest of life throughout the winter of her years. He prised her body from the cloak and she turned to him, her cracked lips parting, needing the moisture only his could give.

Her arms braced against his chest and held. Recollections of where they were, what they were, the Welshmen lying so close around them . . . it was like being woken by a pailful of water from an icy brook.

'No!' she gasped. 'No, I am chaste.'

For a moment she thought he had not heard her, but he must have done, she reasoned. He was as still as stone.

'No?' he breathed. 'No! You took your time deciding that!'

He shook her roughly, pushing her away from him with an oath she could not catch and did not wish to hear. He was right. She had taken her time to refuse him. She had wanted him—wanted him out of wedlock, without a promise, without even one word of love; wanted his body to take hers with the base instincts of the animals of the forest in which they hid. She felt cheapened, ashamed, angry with herself for her lack of strength, angry with Rhodri for taking advantage of their situation. She did not want to be so close to him any longer, did not even want to be within sight of him. She wanted to be away, away by herself, away from all these Welshmen. It was still raining. Even though the lightning had stopped and the thunder was no more than a low rumbling far across the tree-tops, she dared not leave the safety of the heavy wolfskin cloak. The storm might return, the vivid, awesome lightning that killed.

Rhodri moved. Dena did not wait to see what he had in mind. Denying her fears, she flung up her arms, fighting with the sodden cloak to find its edge and make her escape.

'Dena!'

She felt his hand grasp for her, but she slithered free, the cold rain acting like oil upon her skin.

Her heart raced as she padded across the wet grass. It was difficult to see where she was going. The brush and trees melted into one dark shadow before her, and her stomach churned as she remembered the men who would be taking shelter beneath them. She could so easily fall over one. One might even be able to see her coming towards him, be hunched there waiting for her. She could expect no better treatment at their hands than at Rhodri's.

Her mind filled with their jeering faces. Their lascivious laughter echoed in her ears. She twisted her head left and right, anxiously trying to peer through the gloom. She strained her ears trying to listen for the

gurgling stream below the bank, but all she could hear
was the steadily falling rain splattering on the unseen
leaves around her.

Which way was the safe way? Which way?

An arm wrapped itself round her waist and lifted her
clear off the ground, turning her in mid-air and hoisting
her across a bony shoulder. Dena cried out in terror. She
kicked with her feet, beat with her fists, but her assailant
would not drop her.

'Quiet!' Rhodri muttered. 'You will wake the men.'

The power left Dena's limbs as a wave of relief swept
through her body, but it was short-lived. It seemed he
had no intention of allowing her to walk beside him, no
matter how hard she tried to prise herself free. She hung
there like a screaming youngster retrieved by its ex-
asperated mother, and the fierce heat of humiliation
burnt her face.

When he did drop her to her feet, it was with a tight
grip on her wrist. They stood facing each other in the dim
light, rain trickling down their faces, bonding their hair
to their heads.

'You must never do that again,' he rasped.

Dena's eyebrows rose with her indignation. 'No, my
lord,' she spat back in the most scathing tone she could
muster. 'I can see now that you do not like your slaves to
show any will of their own, no matter how high born.'

Rhodri jerked her hand awkwardly. 'Do not play
games. I am in deadly earnest. If you do not stay by my
side at all times, your life will be forfeit.'

'And if I do stay at your side, my honour will be forfeit
before the sun has chance to rise!'

He muttered something low under his breath, and
pulled her close enough to him so that he could grip her
shoulder with his other hand.

'Why do you insist on acting as if all this were a tale to be repeated over an evening meal? I am with a group of Welshmen fighting the Saxons for our very existence. You are *Saxon*. You mean nothing to these men, *nothing*—except a body of a woman to be used for their pleasure, either willingly or held to the ground screaming. Why can you not understand that?'

The mocking retort she had held ready for instant reply fled from her, leaving a hollowness she could not account for. He was exaggerating, she told herself, making his words as frightening as he could so that she would cling to him and be his willingly. It was nothing but a ruse.

'Do not try to convince me of your fancies. I have no doubt that your men are as vile as you paint them, but Gwylan bears higher standards of conduct and would soon put them—and you—in their place.'

She stood her ground, bristling with indignation, awaiting his reply. To her surprise, there was none. His shadowy figure seemed to go limp before her. His hand slipped from her shoulder to dangle uselessly by his side, and the grip on her wrist lessened until he was merely holding her.

'Oh, Dena . . .' he sighed. 'If you leave me, the men will take you, hold me back and make me watch. Those were the orders Gwylan gave after our argument at the hall.'

Dena stared at the shadowy outline that was Rhodri, unable to accept any truth in his words.

'You lie! It was you who wished to feed me to the men. It was almost your first word. Gwylan was going to leave me at the hall. It was you who insisted on dragging me behind you like some possession!'

He renewed his grip on her arm, pulling her towards

him, but she had one hand free and she pummelled his chest, his face, anything of him her hand could contact in the consuming darkness, until he caught that, too, and twisted her arms behind her back, hugging her body to his.

'Dena . . . Dena . . . He was going to leave you dead, butchered like an animal from the fields, hung from the rafters for Wybert to find.'

She stopped struggling, the horror of the imagined spectacle making her shudder, but still she would not accept what he told her.

'No! Gwylan was going to hold me as a hostage.'

'The plan changed, Dena; the ale saw to that. The tide of war turned against him. He was no longer the hunter, but the hunted. He did not need a hostage any more. He needed a defiant gesture to show that he was still a force to be reckoned with. You are Edwulf's own family. What better gesture did he have?'

He shook her, not hard, not to hurt her, but to try to make her understand by actions that which she would not believe by words alone.

And she did believe him, now. She saw the awful, gruesome sense of it, if there was any sense to be gained from these bloody rivalries. Gwylan, himself, had spoken the words which bound Rhodri's earnest explanations. 'There is no honour in war,' he had said, and she realised that like a playing-piece on a game-board, she was expendable to both sides in the conflict.

Dena ached with the terrible knowledge of her worthlessness. Her body creased with the pain of her suffering. She wanted to fall to the sodden grass and weep there, letting her tears mingle with the rain in the puddles on the ground, but Rhodri held her, and she was grateful. She laid her forehead against his chest, and sobbed.

He released her hands and put his arms round her waist and shoulders, comforting, as best he could, someone who could not be comforted.

'Why?' she cried in her desolation. 'Why?'

She had not asked for an answer, had not expected or desired one, but he hugged her to him more tightly than ever, burying his face in her neck as though living her suffering.

'I have known this sorrow, this hollowness. I was hailed by men who called me brother, or son, even; given rings and made gifts of fine horses. There was a pact with the Saxon King and I was sent to Edward's court as truth of this pact. A Welsh prince, they called me. I was given an honoured place on Edward's table, treated like . . .' His body shuddered against Dena's, and he drew a deep, cleansing breath.

'Within two months those who had called me brother had betrayed my trust. They left me in that hell without a thought, without a hope, while they torched Saxon-held lands all along the border country.'

He pushed Dena from him, holding her shoulders, looking into her face which would be no clearer to him than his was to her, and she wanted her face to be clear to him, for him to see the sympathy, the understanding, held there.

'I could not stand back and let that fate take you. I could not.'

His hands left her shoulders and gently cupped her face. 'Stay with me, Dena. Please, stay with me.'

Tears choked her throat so that she could not speak, filled her eyes and ran down her cheeks so that she could not see, but she could touch, like Rhodri, blinded by the rain and the starless night, she could touch.

She raised her hands and laid them on top of his. They were cold hands, cold and wet, but bonded to his they filled with a fire, burning as her cheeks were burning, and she held his hands tightly and pulled them together, pulled them to her cracked and broken lips, and she kissed them.

'Dena.' He breathed her name like the whisper of a butterfly's wing. 'Dena, forgive me. I should not have looked upon you as a wanton inn girl, I know, especially after you cared for me in my sickness. I . . .'

She gently put her fingers to his lips, and he could say no more.

She had no wish to hear his apologies, no wish that he should even tend them. Perhaps, if it had been another place, another time . . . but for now it was enough to stand and feel the warmth of him through their rain-soaked clothes, relax in the security of his arms, thrill to the touch of his rich, warm lips.

CHAPTER
SIX

THE GREY mist hung damply about the trees like garlands on a revered prayer-bush. It swirled around the men's legs as they moved, seeming to ooze unnoticed from the ground on which they trod. Most of all it was cold, so bone-chillingly cold that Dena could easily have believed the winter snows were already on their way.

Men stood or sat in groups, huddled in their sodden cloaks, forcing down what little there was to eat without the benefit of a warming fire. She had witnessed Gwylan stamping out the first flickering flames of one, watched him change the disgruntled, scowling faces of his men to expressions of long-suffering compliance. She did not need to understand the language to know that Gwylan still feared the Saxons were close enough to snap at his heels.

'Eat this,' Rhodri said, holding out a piece of venison on top of a chunk of bread.

Dena took it from his hands, her jaws clasped so tightly together to stop her teeth from chattering that she could neither speak nor raise a smile. At least, that was the more obvious excuse. In truth she did not know how to react to him. He was distant and very cool towards her. He had been ever since she had woken, and, to her horror, had found herself alone. He had returned almost immediately with his little shaggy mare, but after all he had said to her the previous night, his action had still stunned her. How long she had been left unguarded while she slept, she dared not guess. There had been no word for her, no smile, nothing to indicate that what they had shared in the darkness and the rain had been anything but a vivid dream which she, alone, had seen.

She had thought that, perhaps, the effects of the poisoned ale were telling on him again, but his colour was returning, that weatherbeaten glow she had seen in his face when he had first removed his helmet in the dimness of Edwulf's hall. She sat and watched him eat a good amount of the meat and bread from the saddlebags and had slowly come to realise that the change in him stemmed not from his sickness but from his clearing head. He saw things differently now, saw her not as a lover, either wanton or companionable, but as a heavy millstone round his neck.

If she had given thought to all that had happened to her, she could have seen this coming, but she had been blinkered by the constant rise and fall of her emotions, giving so much concern to the unfolding events of the present that there had been no time for looking to the future.

And now the future was here. Rhodri had thought better of the pit he had dug himself, of the fierce argument he had had with Gwylan in front of all the men. She was astute enough to be able to see his point of view, which surprised her a little. Rhodri had been ostracised, pushed to the rear of the marching column, laughed at, jeered—and for what? For protecting a Saxon lady, an enemy of his people, someone whose only family would not even pay a ransom for her.

Dena sighed as she watched him begin to saddle the mare. She was a responsibility he no longer wanted—a liability, in fact. Was that why Gwylan had come to talk before the onset of the night, to ask if Rhodri had changed his mind, to ask if he now saw their predicament through Gwylan's eyes? It seemed likely . . . more than likely.

A throb rippled through her chest, filling her throat with rising tears. Determinedly she swallowed them. Crying would not help. Rhodri would be looking for excuses to rid himself of her, to regain favour with Gwylan, to regain his prestige among the men. She would not help him. Whatever he decided her fate would be, it would be on his conscience alone.

Rhodri had almost finished loading the mare. The Welshmen, too, were readying themselves for the day's march. Some were tying their packs, others relieving themselves. Dena cast her gaze aside, knowing how they felt, but she had no intention of doing the same before their eyes. A little privacy was what she needed, but she dared not take it, not on her own. She would have to ask Rhodri to go with her. She was loath to do so, but there seemed no alternative. She rose stiffly and crossed the squelching grass to stand at his shoulder.

'I need to go to the stream. Would you escort me?'

She waited long moments while he tightened the strap holding his shield to the saddle. She became more and more tense, wondering if he was going to ignore her request altogether, but at last he turned and nodded for her to lead the way.

In her relief she was not aware of the significance of this, not until the path she had taken thickened with gorse and brush. It should have been he who bent back the low-hanging branches, he who trampled down the thorn so it did not tear at the skirts of her kirtle. She was not even certain that she was heading for the stream-bank. Perhaps he was allowing her to lead them into the mist of the forbidding forest so that he might turn quickly and leave her there. Perhaps he was even considering stabbing her with the dagger he kept at his belt.

She turned, almost expecting to see the weapon in his hand.

'A little further, I think,' he said. 'I can hear the water rushing over the stones.'

Off-balance now, Dena could only look into his dark, haunting eyes and wonder what thoughts lay behind them. She carried on, careful to hold the brush back for him until he took it from her hand, careful to glance at him each time she did so.

Concentrating more on what was behind her than in front, she was upon the crumbling bank before she realised it. She stood teetering on the edge, looking down the wall of dark grey shale, through the rising mist, to the white water tearing along the stream-bed below her, so far below her that it would need only one gentle push.

She stepped aside, her eyes wide with fear and accusation, and waited for Rhodri to make his move.

'That way, I think.' He pointed to a narrow deer-track cut neatly in the precipitous face. Dena held back a moment. 'I shall wait here if you wish,' he added.

She wrung her hands, unsure of how to answer. Did he really think it was her wish for privacy that held her back? Did he believe she was unaware of his thoughts, that she had not noticed the change in him? Although she drew a deep breath to calm herself, the words still would not come, so she nodded her head and passed by him to begin the tortuous descent to the stream.

There had been no need to walk such a distance, she thought as she slipped and slid down the track. They had been far enough from the little encampment before they had even reached the bank. The undergrowth had offered enough privacy for the most fastidious of high-born ladies. Why had she carried on? Why had he let her?

Her relief in reaching the stream-bed was matching only by her fear of his desertion, but she was determined not to show her worries by searching the shrouded skyline for him. She went about her toilet as if nothing untoward had entered her mind, finally pausing at the edge of the surging torrent to wash her hands and face.

The chilled water refreshed her more than she could have believed possible. It seemed to add new zest, new hope, to her inner being. Even if Rhodri did leave her, it did not matter. She was alive. She was cold, she was hungry, her kirtle was tattered and soaked, but she was alive. She could give praise to the Lord for that. But she had to look! She had to know for sure. So she stood, erect and defiant, and gazed upwards along the wall of shale to the highest point of the deer-track. Cloaked in the morning mist, the rain-laden trees hung heavy and silent as though embroidered on a flat wall-hanging. Of Rhodri, there was no sign.

She turned quickly, biting back the tears that pricked her eyes. What use was there to cry over men, she chided herself. Edwulf and Wybert had sacrificed her, Gwylan would have done the same if Rhodri had not interceded, and Rhodri . . . but she could not damn him. Like her, he was a victim of his own people, caught in the spiral of his own fate. She had felt a bond with him. Amid the terror and the tyranny, he had touched her heart. She would never forget that.

Dena walked along the muddy bank, the rushing water roaring in her ears louder than the thunderstorm that had created it. How long should she stay in the little ravine? How long would it take for the Welshmen to break their camp? Wandering further, she faltered by a

small pool as unruffled as a mirror which had been left by
the first wave of the slowly decreasing flood. She bent
her head over it, peering down to see what ravages had
befallen her. Only her long hair looked worse than she
had imagined it would. Without thinking, she untied the
sheepskin ribbons which bound her braids and drew her
fingers through the dishevelled waist-length locks which
clung strand to strand still damp from the previous
night's rain. Her attention was pulled to a ripple in
the dark stillness of the water, and her heart missed
a beat when she saw a shadowy face beside her own
reflection.

She spun round, her hair flying out behind her like an
undulating cloak. Rhodri stood there, his dark eyes
wary, his arms frozen awkwardly a little way from his
sides as though he had been caught in the midst of some
guilt-ridden action.

Dena felt her heart turn to stone. *Dear God, her
instincts had been right. He had come to kill her.* Her
leaden heart began to slip from its appointed place,
dragging muscle and fibre, flesh and bone, deep into the
wastes of her echoing belly, subduing terror and fight
before either had gained a chance to be born inside her.
Yet, from within the crushing desolation, an inner peace
flickered into life. It grew at a rate beyond human
understanding, gaining strength and power, filling her
body, her limbs, the very tendrils of her loosened hair. It
was the calming power the holy men spoke of, the power
of angels, and of martyrs.

She looked at Rhodri anew, watched him swallow
down his consternation, and rub his palms along his
thighs. His lips quivered as they parted, and when
he spoke, the sound was nothing more than a hoarse
whisper.

'I called you,' he said, 'but you did not hear me above the noise of the water.'

'There is no need to lie to me, Rhodri. I understand your position, the loyalties that bind you. I had hoped that leaving me here would be enough, but a warrior's conscience guides a warrior's hand, and I have . . .'

'Wait! Wait!' He flashed his open palm across her eyes as one would across a blind man's face. 'What words are these? They cannot be from the Dena I held so tightly in my arms, the Dena who offered her lips to mine in the darkness of the night.'

Where his incredulous tone could not touch her, his choice of words punctured her protective sheath of inner tranquillity. How could he speak of what they had given and shared, when all he wanted was to deny its occurrence?

He rocked back a pace as the full implication of what she had said came to him. 'You think I am going to kill you!'

Dena's inner strength was ebbing fast now, pouring from the chink he had created. Her hands began to tremble. She clasped them together before her, willing herself to remain in control of her resurgent emotions.

'Can you deny that I am the cause of bad blood between you and Gwylan, that your esteem has diminished in the eyes of your men because of me?'

Rhodri raised his arms in a gesture of hopeless assent. 'No. No, I cannot deny that.'

'And can you deny that if I were dead, all would return to the way it was?'

She hardly saw his hand reach for his sword. The movement was so swift, so fluid, as to be almost invisible. One moment his dark eyes were staring into hers, the next the singing blade was slicing the air between them. It arched high above her head to be plunged, blade first, into the soft ground at her feet. He withdrew his grip with a flourish, leaving the hilt to rock back and forth under its own momentum. Dena gasped, releasing the breath caught in her lungs, but before she could drag her widened eyes from the swinging hilt, Rhodri reached for it again, not as a man would a sword, but as a priest would a blessed crucifix. His voice was full of fury.

'As the Lord God is my witness, I have not come to kill you, Dena!' His tone and stance eased a little. 'Though hell, alone, knows what torments you are putting me through.'

He unlocked his fingers from the cross-guards of his sword and retreated a pace, looking this way and that in agitation before he stared at Dena's face.

'If I did not know better, I would swear you had bound a charm round me!'

He turned away from her, lowering his head and lifting his hands to push his fingers through his damp raven hair.

'Of all the maids who crave my heart, I allow it to be stolen by a *Saxon*! It is unthinkable.'

An excitement began to bubble up inside Dena, lifting her own heart, filling it afresh with all the surging emotions she had experienced in Rhodri's arms during the long, rain-soaked night. She edged towards him, cautiously at first, then with a determination born of truly-held beliefs.

'Is it so unthinkable?' she asked.

His startled eyes darted towards her. His expression softened, and a smile crept across his lips. He even raised a chuckle. 'Oh, Dena! You know nothing of me. A bitterness for all Saxons has torn at my soul for longer than I care to remember, and yet . . .' He reached out and wound a finger about a wispy tendril of her hair. 'And yet, being close to you dispels it all.'

'I think I love you, Rhodri.'

'Love me?' His voice was almost a croak.

'Yes,' she said. 'I know no other word to describe the way I feel.'

She lifted her arms to slip her hands round his neck. The heat of his skin burned her fingertips, sending rivulets of tingling expectancy racing towards her heart. His arms about her waist drew her closer, ever closer, his nails clawing at her flesh through the kirtle she wore. His misty breath seared into the skin of her jawline, and she angled her head to offer her neck to his searching lips. His mouth enveloped hers, hot and demanding, burgeoning with a pressure that she felt would suffocate her. And then his mouth left hers to run rampant and wild over her cheeks, her ears, her neck. His lips, his tongue, his teeth swept over her with an appetite she had not known a man could possess. It was all she could do to twist her fingers into his long, dark hair as her passion rose and sang.

His onslaught slackened. His touch became more tender. He bent his head to place his cheek against her own and let out a long, trembling sigh.

'What I would not give to have half a day in this glade with you!'

Dena smiled with the warmth she held for him, and felt his cheek welcome a smile for her, but he laughed then and drew his face away.

'Gwylan would take both our heads to see this foolery.'

She sensed a chill rush between them, and the smile faded from her lips. 'I feel no foolery,' she said. 'I love you, Rhodri. I know it plainly.'

A pulsing consternation flickered across his face that was unmistakable to Dena's eyes. She even felt the disquiet rippling through his muscles as he held her in his arms. Although his feet stood solid on the ground, it was as though he had stepped back a pace.

And then all doubt was swept away as a brilliant smile lit his face. He drank deeply of the morning air, filling his chest until his body threatened to break through the green tunic enclosing it. In a surge of enveloping power he lifted her off her feet to hold her high above him.

'I love *you*, Dena, and it is indeed no foolery which I speak.'

Those simple words, that had been so hard for him to say, thrilled her more than any others could have done. She lowered her head towards his and sought his reaching lips. Their kiss was as soft a caress as the stroking of a butterfly's wing, but held so much that she did not feel her feet touch the ground again. Rhodri drew his fingers across her brow and pushed them deep into her tangled locks.

'I have something for you,' he whispered.

From a hip-pouch on his belt he withdrew a flat, yellow object as large as his palm, and offered it to her. A bronze comb-case.

'There is no time now, we have dallied here too long, but perhaps you could use it later in the day.'

Dena took it from his outstretched hand and marvelled at its workmanship. One side was highly polished like a mirror, the other covered in delicate carvings of twisting serpents. It held a comb of finely sculptured bone, the twin rows of pointed teeth fanning from a central spine, itself etched with matching decoration. Dena had never seen anything like it in her life.

'It is beautiful,' she breathed.

'Beautiful hair should have a beautiful comb.' He smiled again, savouring the moment, and then curled an arm about her shoulders. 'Come! We must go now, or we shall be left behind.'

Arm in arm they walked together until they reached the deer-track that climbed the bank. Rhodri led the way, his strong hand gripping hers tightly so that she did not fall. They ploughed through the dripping undergrowth towards the cramped encampment, and although he held back the screening branches, twigs and leaves tore relentlessly at Dena's loosened hair. All she could do was to twist it into a spiral over one shoulder and secure it with the sheepskin ribbons as she walked.

When they reached the clearing that had been the night's encampment, they found it already deserted. Dena felt a twinge of dismay that Gwylan should leave without them. Perhaps Rhodri's remark about him taking both their heads was not such a jest as he had tried to make it. His own exuberance had fled, too, when he found only his laden mare tethered to a bush. As if to underline their rising unease, the animal stamped a hoof in irritation. Rhodri let his hand slip from Dena's, and began to jog towards her, calling to the girl over his shoulder and pointing into the trees.

'That way,' he said. 'Go quickly. It is dangerous for us to be away from the rest of the men.'

Dena turned at his bidding and headed for the track he had indicated, but she had gone no more than three paces before an ear-splitting scream froze her to the spot. On every side armed men were mushrooming out of the undergrowth.

'Run, Dena! Run!' Rhodri shouted desperately.

She turned her head to see him mount his mare, sword

in hand, and throw his heavy mail coat from the animal's neck. It arched in the air between them, the breaking sunlight catching each polished link. Dena never heard the expected thud as it landed on the ground. Individual sounds were drowned in a rising sea of howls and whoops and screams as the attacking men converged upon them.

Rhodri's words finally hit their intended mark, and she turned to flee—but something stopped her short. Who was she fleeing from? These were not outlaws. These were Saxons; they had to be. These were the men Gwylan feared, the men of Lord Baldric. They had come to rescue her.

She wheeled about, her thoughts a confusion of relief and anxiety. No one seemed to notice her standing at the edge of the clearing. They were too intent in trying to unhorse Rhodri, surging about his prancing, wide-eyed mare, their long spear-like weapons catching in the overhanging trees.

Dena felt her colour drain as she watched, dread filling her pounding heart. The men were trying to kill Rhodri. He was fighting for his life in their midst, swinging his long-bladed sword about his body in an effort to fend off the slashing weapons of his foes. Without thinking, Dena raised her hands to her cheeks, wanting to hide her eyes from the horror of the inevitable, but she was so inextricably caught in Rhodri's struggle for life that she could not bring herself to desert him in even the smallest way.

A man in front of the mare stumbled. The shaggy animal leapt into the narrow space before it, and suddenly Rhodri was free from the bellowing mob which screamed for his blood. He urged his mount on without a backward glance, his eyes wide and wild as he searched for a route of escape. They rested, not on a beckoning boar-run, but on Dena.

The look of horror which swept across the dark hollows of his face made her catch her breath, and then, unbelievingly, he reined in the mare and turned her head towards Dena, right across the path of his pursuers. She tried to shout a warning, but there was no air in her lungs to carry the sound. She ran forward, waving her arms, but she got no further than a step before a Saxon spear swung behind Rhodri, arching his back as if it had been cleaved in two. His dark hair whipped across his face as his head rolled on his shoulders, and the reins slipped from his opening hands as he fell sideways from the saddle.

Dena kept running, her eyes seeing nothing but Rhodri hitting the hard earth, his limbs bouncing awkwardly like a rag doll thrown aside in temper. She bobbed between the milling Saxons, oblivious to their reaching arms, their swords, their cries. She had to reach Rhodri. She *had* to.

He lay there so still, face down in the grass. Dena chanted his name as if it was a charm, silently at first, and then, as her lungs filled with air and her voice regained its power, louder and louder until she saw him stir and raise his head. A Saxon foot kicked him back down and a sword rose to strike him dead.

Dena flung herself across his prostrate body, beneath the booted feet, beneath the swinging blade.

'No!' she cried. 'No!'

She clung to Rhodri, her fingers digging into his arms, her head pushed into his neck. She closed her eyes so tightly that no flicker of light could penetrate, and she held her breath as though she were able to hold time itself. The noise of men and animals, the vibrations of the ground on which she lay with Rhodri, all became muffled to her ears.

Suddenly the world turned over and she was being hoisted to her feet. Someone was shaking her, calling her name. She opened her eyes and found herself staring at Wybert.

'Dena . . . Oh, my Lady Dena, you are alive!'

She looked at the familiar iron-grey hair falling lankly over his shoulders and gazed into his eyes, moist with tears of joy. It could not be he. It was impossible!

'Dena . . .' He whispered her name softly, as though he could not believe he held her, and she found herself pulled against him, her head forced into the bulk of his massive chest as he wrapped his arms round her body and hugged her to him.

'It is Edwulf's niece,' she heard him call. 'The Lady Dena.'

'What of this one?' another voice asked. 'Do we put him to the sword?'

Dena's wits returned instinctively, and she fought against Wybert's encircling arms so that she could turn and speak for Rhodri.

'No! He must live!'

She caught her breath at the sight of him. With a boot across his neck and one arm twisted upright from the shoulder, he was as immobile as a hog tied for the slaughter.

'Who is he?' Wybert asked her. 'Someone of standing?'

'Yes,' she cried, catching desperately at the idea the steward offered.

She turned to him, her arms reaching for his to make him understand, but the lined face, which a moment before had been swept with relief and joy, held a more familiar determination. His eyes were narrow with the cold callousness of the man who had sent her on a false errand to the north tun and sacrificed her in order that the poisoned ale might work its deadly trickery in the hall of his lord.

She stared at him, reliving moments of her terror, remembering all the ill she had wished upon him. Could she forget that now, put aside her betrayal, act as though it had never happened? Yes, she breathed, yes. If it could save Rhodri's life, she would do anything.

'He is a man of noble birth,' she began. 'His name is Rhodri. He is second in command only to Gwylan.'

Wybert raised a disparaging eyebrow. 'Second to Gwylan, eh? Turn him over. Let us have a look at this Welshman.'

Rhodri's arm was released and he was none too gently turned with a foot, the point of a sword quickly at his throat forcing him flat again in the wet grass. Dena winced at his treatment, but more disturbing was his show of defiance. His gritted teeth shone white between his thinly drawn lips, and hatred shot from his eyes like arrows of death.

'A young upstart,' Wybert grunted. 'His face means nothing, like his name. These Welshmen are as leaves upon a tree.'

Dena realised that Rhodri's life was slowly slipping from her grasp, and turned plaintively to Wybert.

'No, you do not understand. He must be of high rank. He has been in the court of King Edward. He has a double name.' She sought it in the reaches of her mind. 'Rhodri ap Hywel.'

Wybert's eyes widened a little, and he turned from Dena to exchange a glance with the man whose sword lay against Rhodri's neck. A quiet murmur rippled through the growing crowd as both men looked down at their captive.

'Do you know the name?' Dena asked.

'Yes. If this Welshman is the true owner of it, he will make an excellent hostage. You have done well, Lady Dena, very well indeed.' He patted her shoulder and proudly smiled down at her before turning his attention to those around him.

'Secure him for travelling. We must leave this place before Gwylan discovers that we are so few and rallies his men. This is a prize we must not lose.'

The weight of Dena's relief made her droop at the shoulders. Rhodri was safe. She could give thanks for that.

'My lady?'

She turned to the youth at her shoulder. He gave her a short bow.

'Wybert asked that I escort you to his horse, my lady.'

Dena looked at Rhodri. She had no wish to leave his side, but could not think of an excuse which would allow her to stay with him.

'I am to refresh you with food and ale, my lady.'

Dena turned back to the youth. 'You have brought ale?' It seemed incongruous to their situation.

'Ay, my lady, and though it is not my place, I must say you look in need of it. It is barbarous the way these Welshmen have treated you.'

Dena shook her head. 'They treated me very well. I am merely wet and tired.'

'Yes, my lady.' But the look the lad gave her from the corner of his eye belied his acceptance of her explanation.

She became aware of other eyes, too, carefully watching her as she followed him to Wybert's waiting horse.

The men were gazing at her with grim faces, passing guarded comments in tones too low for her to hear. What did they believe had happened to her? She glanced down at her kirtle, torn and muddied to the thigh. She rubbed her hands together, but it made no difference to the ingrained dirt. Her ragged hair was caught loosely over one shoulder, her headcloth non-existent. These men called the Welsh 'barbarians' in the same breath as they would call a leaf green. What might they do to Rhodri if she were to say that she had given him her heart? What might they do to her?

The youth gave her meat and ale from the saddlebags of Wybert's allotted horse, and she ate, more to pacify him than because of any hunger she felt.

'You must wait here,' the youth instructed. 'We shall be leaving soon.'

Dena nodded, and he left her to her meal. At first she was reluctant to look at the men about her for fear of the expressions she might meet in return, but slowly her courage grew and she searched the faces for friends she had made among Edwulf's people. There seemed to be none, and she realised that these men must all be from Lord Baldric's estate.

As her gaze wondered over the glade, her eyes fell on Rhodri. She could hardly see him for the men clustered round him, but could tell from the line of his legs that he was now sitting on the grass. She watched for a moment as the men moved about, and caught a glimpse of a raised hand and the edge of a bound stick. Her mouth fell open in horror, and she ran across to him, forcing an opening through his guards.

Rhodri's hands were held at shoulder height, tied by the wrists to two freshly-cut sticks which were bent at either side of his neck, threatening to throttle him.

'What are you doing?' Dena gasped. 'Set him free at once!'

The men looked at her, but paid no attention to her words.

'Wybert's orders, my lady. We do not want him darting off into the undergrowth. We would never find him, would we?'

She would grasp at anything in an attempt to change their minds! 'He is a nobleman,' she persisted.

'A Welshman,' the man corrected. 'They would kill you as soon as look at you. You did well to escape with your life.'

Appalled, she watched as he slipped a noose over Rhodri's head and tightened the knot to within a finger's breadth of his throat. She turned to the others, trying to find one who was willing to listen to her pleas, but in vain.

She looked down at Rhodri, wondering what she could say to give him comfort, but his eyes were not on her. They were gazing straight ahead as though he were sightless. It was then she noticed the trickle of blood drying on his cheek, the bruise turning yellow and purple at his temple. She could not believe what her eyes were telling her.

'Oh, Rhodri . . .' she breathed.

She fell to her knees and lifted her hand to draw aside the dark curtain of his hair, but before she had even touched him, he jolted back his head and glared at her.

'Lay not a finger on me, woman!' he hissed. 'I have no need of your solace.'

Dena shrank away in alarm, not understanding his sudden hostility.

'I believed you! I believed every word you said, and you betrayed me!'

'*Betrayed* you?' She let the word sink into her mind. What Wybert had done to her was betrayal. She had not betrayed Rhodri. She had not!

'I saved your life. They were going to kill you.'

'*I wanted to die*: to die by the sword, to die like a man. You have condemned me to a life of torture, of hell, the plaything of women!'

As his voice rose, so did his despair. Dena could do nothing but look at him and shake her head.

'I curse you, you Saxon witch! May your tongue wither in your . . .'

Someone dragged hard on the noose-line about his neck, and Rhodri was jerked sideways, to be sent sprawling across the grass, choking and gasping for breath.

'Enough of that,' his guard murmured. He handed the noose-line to a companion, and gently took Dena's arm. 'Your compassion is wasted here, my lady. Come, let me get you away.'

Too stunned to resist, Dena let the man escort her to the horses.

CHAPTER
SEVEN

DENA SAT behind Wybert's saddle, forcing the harsh events of the morning through her numbed mind.

Had she truly betrayed Rhodri? Had she, even inadvertently, put his life at risk? He believed she had, of that there was no doubt. Never would she have expected such an outburst from him. He had cursed her, called her a Saxon witch. She had tried only to save his life. Surely he could not condemn her for that? But he had, and the more she dwelt on what had happened the more she saw the truth in his accusation.

If only she had not dallied at the stream. If only she had turned and run when he first told her to. If only he had not turned his horse towards her when he had escaped his encircling attackers. Was that what he had meant by her betrayal, or was it, as she now feared, something she had said?

Rhodri ap Hywel. She repeated his name until it filled her body, burst from her every pore, but still it meant nothing to her. It had meant something to Wybert, though. It had meant something to all of Lord Baldric's men. She could vividly recall the murmur which had passed amongst them. Yes, vividly. Even then she had known she had said something amiss. She had tried to mask her rising apprehension, but she could not deny the way Rhodri had been treated, tied like a runaway slave, dragged behind a horse, the noose cutting into his throat, choking his breath. He was ill, still weakened from the poisoned ale, but none of the men cared. They had harried him, jeered and prodded him and laughed —and Wybert had smiled down at her and told her she had done well. That was the worst of it. That great bear of a man had patted her on the shoulder and told her she had done well.

Dena felt tired and confused. She closed her eyes as if that might stem the torment she felt, but it only made her aware of how close she was to Wybert as they shared the horse. She turned her head to gaze at the width of his broad shoulders, the slight bowing of his back as he guided his mount after the one in front. His iron-grey hair sparkled as the sun's rays cut through the last of the mist to touch his head, sparkled like the smile he had given her when he had held her in his arms, like the unshed tears of joy caught in his eyes at finding her alive and unharmed.

It was inconceivable to Dena how he could have felt those emotions. It had been he who had poisoned the ale, he who had sent her to the north tun knowing what the outcome would be, and yet those emotions had been genuine. She had no doubt that he had truly felt them. Had his conscience troubled him so much that his relief at her safe return had clouded his mind? Did he not realise that she could point her finger and accuse him of her betrayal before his peers, before Lord Baldric, before the men here? But she had not pointed her finger. She had placed Rhodri's life before her honour, and perhaps, now, it was too late to save either.

No, she must not think in that way. She had been right to put Rhodri's life before her own anger, before her thirst for personal vengeance. Wybert had done what he had for the good of the people, she had to believe that, and to keep it in her mind. Rhodri's well-being was all that mattered. She had to discover who he was, and why he was considered so dangerous as to warrant such treatment. She had to speak on his behalf, but not to Wybert—no, not Wybert. He was a fighting man who saw people only in terms of military strategy. She would have to speak to Lord Baldric, as he was a nobleman by birth, part of a royal line. He would see things differently. He would ensure that Rhodri was treated with the respect due to his station. The day suddenly looked brighter. All was not lost. Dena would show Rhodri that she had not betrayed him! She would speak to Lord Baldric as soon as the party arrived at his hall.

The morning dragged through till noon. The sun dropped to hide behind the tree-tops, cloaking the narrow track with fingers of cold shadow. The column rarely stopped for rest. It plodded onwards at the same monotonous pace Gwylan's men had used the day before. Often Dena glanced back to seek a sign of Rhodri, but the track wound in tight curves between the dense foliage, and the horsemen were so close one upon another that it was difficult to see what lay behind. She hoped, she prayed, that someone had been merciful enough to share his horse with him.

Dark clouds covered the ribbon of blue above Dena's head, and a new gloom descended to mingle with the shadows. Her back ached, her seat was numb, her slippered feet so cold she could not feel them. Respite was what she needed, respite from the continual swaying of the horse so that her heavy eyelids might stay open. But the party kept moving, and she had to rest against Wybert's wide back to stop herself from slipping off the horse. She hardly noticed the darkness grow around her. She never saw the path widen as the trees fell back, or the welcomir.g light filtering through the windows of the hall.

The noise startled her to wakefulness: men's voices giving orders, calls and answers across the night, sounds the silence of the forest never knew. She blinked at the brazier standing by the gateway, its yellow flames being whipped away by the night breeze. They were there at last. They had arrived.

Dena groaned her relief as they passed through the defences and plodded on to the hall. People pressed towards them, calling for news, but she could see no faces in the darkness. She tried to remember the look of the space before the main buildings, but her muddled mind could recall no details, only that it was large, much larger than the surroundings of Edwulf's hall, yet everywhere torches flickered, small fires crackled red sparks high into the air. It seemed that a whole army was encamped there.

They drew up alongside the stone buttresses which formed a porch to the main doorway of the hall, and an unseen arm encircled Dena's waist and pulled her off the horse's back. She clung to the man's arm, desperately trying to regain her balance as her useless feet were racked with the pain of a thousand needles.

'This is the Lady Dena,' she heard Wybert say. 'Niece to Lord Edwulf. Take her to Lady Ethelin's chamber.' She felt a hand touch her shoulder. 'Go with this man, Dena, and sleep without fear tonight. I shall come to see you on the morrow.'

Dena could do little more than nod and allow herself to be helped along the porch and through the open doorway. The brightness of the torches clustered about the walls made her narrow her eyes against the sudden glare. The acrid smell of sweat and burning oakwood vied with the sweet fragrance of roasted beef to fill her nostrils and envelop her senses, while the heat of the vast chamber threatened to overwhelm her more completely than the rigours of the journey. She leaned heavily on her escort as they made their way through the couches and prostrate forms trying to sleep.

'Not far now,' the man whispered. 'We are nearly to the steps.'

'It is the Lady Dena!' she heard someone cry. 'She lives!'

Others took up the call, and then one voice rang loudly across the multitude stilling all the rest.

'Dearest Lord, look at her . . . What have those heathens done to her?'

A gasp rent the pungent air, followed by a babble so loud that Dena could not hear what was being said by anyone, but she could guess!

She pulled on the arm of her escort, making him pause. 'I must speak to them,' she begged. 'They are the people from my uncle's estate. They think I have been harmed.'

The man forced her onward. 'Later,' he said. 'In the morning. You are too faint now. Here, we are at the steps. Lady Ethelin's chamber is aloft.'

She saw him draw aside the curtain and felt the first step with her foot.

'No, I must speak to them,' she insisted, turning her head towards the crowd, but the curtain dropped across her face and the moment was lost.

The man almost carried her up the steep flight of steps. The corridor at the top was lined with sleeping-pallets, nearly all of them occupied. It left only a narrow walkway, and they had to stop their progress several times to allow others to pass in the opposite direction.

At last he banged his fist hard on one of the iron-braced doors. It was opened by a young girl Dena recognised from the hall of her uncle. The girl's timid expression changed to one of wonder, and she turned away into the room.

'It is the Lady Dena!'

The man did not wait to be asked inside. He kicked open the door and carried Dena to the voluminous bed which almost took up one wall.

'The lady faints. Bring water, girl,' she heard him rasp.

Until he put it into words, Dena had not realised the severity of her condition. She could not stand without his help, nor could she distinguish how far the bed was from her outstretched hand. The coverlets, the woman sitting upon the pillows at the further end, all swam back and forth before her eyes like a rushing tide. And then she was floating on it, the softness of the woollen sheets caressing her cheeks, easing her limbs, calling her to sleep.

'Dena! You are filthy!'

The agitated tones of Ethelin made her smile, and knowing there was no further to go, Dena let slip her grasp on the real world in favour of a more comfortable place.

It was light when she awoke. The shutter had been removed from the small window and the day flooded into the room, making it appear far larger than it had the previous night.

Dena shrugged back the coverlets and sat up, partly relieved, partly disappointed, to find herself alone. She was wearing only her thin woollen smock. Her tattered kirtle and broken slippers were nowhere in sight. Laid across the top of a nearby chest she could see a complete set of clean clothing, including a kirtle of palest green. It reminded her of Rhodri's embroidered tunic, and she wondered anxiously how he had spent the night. The sooner she was suitably attired to be presented to Lord Baldric, the better.

She was about to swing her legs out of the bed when the door opened and the young girl she had recognised the night before struggled into the room carrying two heavy pails.

'Oh, my lady, you are awake.' She stood the pails beside a cut-down barrel behind the door and turned to Dena full of smiles. 'Do you feel well now? You looked deathly white when you were brought in last night.'

'Yes, thank you.'

Dena padded across the bare floorboards to where the girl was standing, and peered into the barrel already a quarter filled with water.

'The Lady Ethelin insisted that you bathe before meeting the other ladies, but I could not find a tub. Do you think you can manage?' Her nervous expression showed the sort of answer she expected. Dena could well imagine the criticisms levelled at her by Ethelin's cutting tongue. Her aunt was apt to make a drama out of the slightest discomfort.

'Of course,' Dena smiled. 'It was good of you to go to so much trouble. I could easily have made do with a pail.' The girl visibly relaxed. 'I am sorry, though,' Dena continued. 'I have forgotten your name.'

'It matters little,' the girl replied wearily. 'I am becoming used to answering to "maid". My name is Elma.'

'Then I, at least, shall call you by it,' and the two women smiled at one another, each pleased to have found a friend.

Dena stripped off her smock and climbed into the

barrel, luxuriating in the tepid water. Elma poured a pailful over her head, and between them they washed from her hair and skin the mud and dross the forest had deposited. Dressed in the clean smock, Dena sat in the shaft of sunlight as it poured in through the open window, and allowed Elma to towel her hair dry and comb out its tangles. But it all took time, too much time, and Dena grew anxious to be away.

'Do you know where I shall be able to find Lord Baldric at this hour?'

'Lord Baldric? He is not here, my lady. He is with King Harold to the east.'

Dena turned to her in dismay. 'With the King?' Of course, she reasoned. What a fool she had been to think otherwise. Those of royal blood would be the first to rally to the king's banner.

'Then who is running the estate in his absence?'

'His wife, Lady Nearra. Who else?'

Who else, indeed! It was, after all, the wife's place, and not all were like Ethelin, content to leave the day-to-day business to a steward. But what if she were like Ethelin in other respects? What if the very thought of a Welshman on her lands brought on a fit of rage—or even blood-lust?

To Elma's astonishment, Dena rose from her stool and darted across the chamber to the chest by the wall and began to drag the clean kirtle over her head.

'I must speak to her at once, Elma. Where shall I find her?'

Elma spread her hands in desperation. 'In any number of places. She may still be in her bower. She has broken her fast there with the other ladies since we came.'

Dena adjusted the long, tight sleeves of the kirtle so that they lay in folds from her elbow to her wrist, and slotted the small belt pouch containing Rhodri's comb-case on to the beaded girdle that accompanied the gown.

'You must show me this bower, Elma. There is no time to be lost.'

'But, my lady, your hair is not dry yet! I have to braid it with ribbon. The Lady Ethelin stipulated that I . . .'

'Forget what Ethelin commanded! I have no time for the fripperies she delights in. Find me a headcloth. I must speak to the Lady Nearra *now*.'

Elma gave up all hope of dissuading her, and the two women made their way along the busy upper passage-way and down the steps to the lower chamber. A few people, mostly old or crippled, were sitting on the sleeping-benches built into the stone wall, but hardly a one raised his head to see who passed along the rush-strewn aisle. The tall double doors had been flung open to let the crisp morning air replace the stuffiness of the previous night, and outside, crammed in the space be-tween the hall and the manned defences, were people too numerous to count, their meagre belongings piled beside them as they sat round their cooking-fires. Ani-mals seemed to be tethered everywhere Dena looked, oxen and sheep and milk-cows and goats, all bellowing their cries of fear at being confined. Dena winced at all the noise.

'Surely all these people cannot just be from the two estates?'

'No, my lady. News spreads fast. People have come from the smaller estates all along the land. With our fighting men away with the King and these Welsh hordes trying to murder us as we sleep, it is better we all stay together.'

Dena looked at her in utter disbelief. Elma spoke with a conviction born of listening to other people's conversations. If she truly believed the whole of Wales was rising against the Saxon English, how many more believed the same? Did the Lady Nearra?

The girl continued to lead the way onward, and they wove between the groups of people round the side of the hall and into the bright sunlight of the south-facing area. A number of circular low-roofed bowers interspaced with cobbled paths occupied this space, and Elma had no difficulty in deciding which would contain the gathering of ladies. She had obviously been here many times before.

Sitting outside the doorway were three girls of Elma's age, maids taking their ease in the sunshine away from their mistresses' eyes.

'It is not my place to enter unless asked,' Elma offered humbly.

Dena nodded her understanding and turned to face the door, her heart suddenly in her mouth. Should she knock, or boldly walk inside? She could hear the soft banter of conversation through the thin walls. She had expected to find the ladies in a quiet, pensive mood. Perhaps it was a good sign.

Lifting the latch, she passed inside, the tinkling of women's laughter suddenly stifled on her entrance. Dena felt every eye upon her, appraising, speculating. She could feel her colour beginning to rise, and quickly looked about the bower, seeing not the faces but the decorative tapestries hanging on all the walls.

'Dena! Oh, how well you look! I am so pleased.' Ethelin dropped her embroidery upon her stool and crossed to the door to give Dena an unexpected hug. She turned to the group, her face full of smiles.

'Lady Nearra, Ladies, may I present my Lord Edwulf's niece, the Lady Dena.'

It sounded rather formal, and then, with a sinking feeling, Dena realised that this was the intention. Ethelin would not miss any opportunity of furthering her own prestige.

'Step forward, my dear,' instructed Lady Nearra in a quiet tone. 'I am so relieved to see that you are in good health. We have been hearing such blood-curdling tales of the ravages of the Welsh.'

Dena gave Ethelin a quizzical sideways glance. If she had been spinning tales for the ladies, the saints alone knew what had been seeded in their minds. Dena had grave doubts that her aunt had seen even one of Gwylan's men.

'I was treated with every kindness and consideration, my lady.' It might have been smoothing over the truth somewhat, but Dena decided that it was justified, considering the magnitude of the falsehoods being circulated about the Welsh.

She took another step forward, away from Ethelin's suffocating protection.

'Lady Nearra, it is most urgent that I speak with you on the matter of the Welsh nobleman who was brought to this estate last night under the most dire conditions.'

'Dena!' Ethelin's reproof got no further, for the Lady Nearra waved her aside.

'Of course, my dear. Your bravery astounds me. The steward Wybert gave me a full account of how you captured him. My praise knows no bounds.'

Dena looked at her in open-mouthed astonishment. '*Captured* him? I did not capture him. I saved his life. Your men were about to cleave him in two!'

The indulgent smile on Lady Nearra's ageing face remained steadfast. All the women in the bower were silent, even Ethelin.

'He is a nobleman of rank, but he was treated like a runaway slave. His hands were bound to stakes and he was dragged behind a horse with a noose round his neck.'

Dena looked from one unresponsive face to another. Nobody seemed in the least perturbed about Rhodri's treatment. Perhaps she should try another route to their compassion.

'The Welsh leader, Gwylan, held me as hostage against Edwulf. If I am correct in assuming that Rhodri will make an excellent hostage for Edwulf's cause, surely his treatment and well-being will be of the utmost importance?'

Lady Nearra murmured to herself reflectively. 'Yes, of course, but there are other considerations. With this uprising all along the border . . .'

Dena could not contain herself. 'There is no uprising. It is only the Welsh Lord Gwylan who wishes to reclaim by force those lands taken *from* him by force!'

Lady Nearra's face suddenly turned cold towards her, and Dena realised that her attitude had been her undoing.

'I can see no use in furthering this conversation,' the Lady Nearra remarked pointedly. 'I think you had better speak to the steward Wybert personally on this matter. As my own Master of Arms is away with my husband, and the steward Wybert is more than accomplished in this area, I have given him full authority to secure the lands about the hall. I believe this prisoner you speak of falls within his jurisdiction.'

The two women looked at one another until Dena found she could no longer hold the other's eyes. Dispirited, she let her gaze fall to the ground.

'I apologise for my outburst,' she murmured.

The Lady Nearra made no mention of accepting it. 'You may leave us,' she said.

Dena gave a short curtsy and turned to the door, the stinging silence matched only by the flash of Ethelin's furious eyes.

Outside, Dena was thankful for a breeze to cool her perspiring skin. What a fool she had been to let her emotions run away with her like that. She had offended the one woman who could have interceded on her behalf, who, in far outranking Wybert, could have demanded that Rhodri be treated in the manner his station deserved.

Wybert. His name kept cropping up with alarming regularity. Had he truly told Lady Nearra that she had *captured* Rhodri? He must have done. Lady Nearra was not so old as to be suffering confusions of the mind. Why had he said it? What had he hoped it would gain him?

This false rumour about a mass Welsh incursion worried her more than anything, though. Lady Nearra had been correct when she had said there were considerations other than Rhodri's treatment while a hostage in Saxon hands. With every man, woman and child expecting to be over-run and massacred at any moment, common decency would be the last thing on their minds, especially for a prisoner, nobleman or otherwise. The sooner she spoke to Wybert and found out what was planned for Rhodri, the less anxious she would feel.

Elma was not with the maids waiting outside the bower, and Dena felt too exposed to question the girls about Wybert's movements. Maids were apt to listen at doors, and she had endured enough cutting glances for one day. She walked round to the front of the hall, hoping to see a familiar face from Edwulf's estate. His people would be certain to know where Wybert could be found.

The area before the hall's main doors was as tightly packed with people as before. The heavy gates built into the stone defence wall lay wide open, the narrow harvested fields beyond beckoning better grazing than ever could be scratched within the enclosure, but the people were so afraid for their safety that hardly any had taken advantage of it. It was madness to think Gwylan might even consider attacking such a stronghold.

Dena mingled with the people, seeking faces she knew among the crowd. Everyone seemed to be a stranger. Regardless, she asked for Wybert among them, but few knew the name. None knew where Edwulf's people sat. It was a discouraging task, but she was determined to find someone who knew where Wybert could be found, even if it took her all day.

'Is it me you are searching for?'

Dena turned at the familiar voice, and found herself looking into the wild eyes of Mildthryth. She stepped back with a start, her mind filling with images of the brewing-house where she had last seen the old woman pounding the poisonous herbs to be added to the ale-barrels. Mildthryth had known the plan. Mildthryth had advised Wybert to send her to the north tun, knowing what would happen.

'Is it me you are searching for?'

Dena remembered herself and stood straight-backed and aloof. The old woman was of no standing and she should not feel intimidated by her presence, no matter what rumours surrounded her.

'No.'

Mildthryth seemed disappointed.

'I need to see Wybert. Do you know where he can be found?'

Mildthryth shook her head, as an indulgent nurse might to a wilful child.

'You do not wish to see Wybert. What use would it serve?'

'I must speak to him. Do you know where he is?'

'No,' she answered at last. 'But I know where he is not.'

Dena looked at her in bewilderment, hardly able to believe that the old woman should choose such a time to play with riddles. Mildthryth cocked her head to one side in a strangely tantalising manner and grinned widely to show the remnants of her dark and broken teeth.

Dena forced down her rising irritation. 'I have no mind for these games. Where is he not?'

'He is not with the Welshman.'

'Rhodri?' His name slipped between Dena's lips like a breath of night air. 'Do you know where he is being held?'

Mildthryth nodded. 'I can take you, but I cannot gain you entrance. Only you can do that, if you care to. I have my bag.'

She pointed to a battered rawhide case at her feet. The yellow paint upon its surface had almost faded, as had the runic lettering round the base. It was said to have been bestowed upon her by her dying grandmother, and contained all manner of charms to ward off illness, as well as jars and bottles of medicinal potions for man and beast alike. Dena paled as the inference became apparent.

'Have you seen him?'

Mildthryth shook her head and bent to pick up the bag. 'No, but I heard him. All night I heard him.'

Dena shuddered and closed her eyes, catching her hands together before her breast. 'Most merciful God . . .'

'Prayers be no use,' scolded Mildthryth. 'Come.'

She led Dena along the wall of the vast hall to the further end, where the adjacent kitchen opened to a beaten earth courtyard and numerous fires burned beneath steaming kettles. They crossed it, passing through the gate of the waist-high wattle fencing erected to keep stray animals from wandering in and fouling the food. Boys were busy grooming horses by the stables, and an over-worked smith toiled with anvil and hammer. Dena held her nose as they passed a pile of steaming dung, but Mildthryth did not seem to notice it.

The old woman became more stealthy in her movements, pausing at the edge of each closely-packed wattle and daub hut to gaze carefully beyond before venturing further. Dena realised that they must be close to where Rhodri was being held, and her heart began to beat wildly in fear of meeting a challenge.

'There,' Mildthryth whispered, indicating diagonally across the narrow path.

Dena peeped round the corner of the wall to see a man lounging in the doorway of a small hut, an evil-looking cudgel resting by his knee. She did not recognise him as one of Edwulf's men, but he was obviously some sort of guard.

'There is only him to pass,' Mildthryth told her. 'But he takes his orders from Wybert, so you will have to be strong-minded.'

Without waiting for Dena to gather her wits, she pushed her on to the path and followed on her heel. The guard saw them immediately and stood to attention, his hand tentatively feeling for his weapon as his eyes scanned the way behind them. He gave a short, nervous bow of his head as Dena drew level with him.

'I wish to see the prisoner.'

The man looked blankly, first at her and then at Mildthryth.

'Do not stand gaping. Open the door!' Dena snapped.

'I cannot do that, my lady. No one must enter. It is the Lord Wybert's orders.'

'He is not a lord,' Dena corrected icily. 'He is steward of my uncle's estate. I am the niece of Lord Edwulf, and I demand to be allowed inside.'

The man shuffled uneasily. 'Steward Wybert's instructions were clear. No one is to be allowed inside.'

'I am the one who *captured* him!' Dena stormed. 'Do you think such an order applies to me?'

The guard looked at his feet and began to shuffle back towards the door. 'No, no, of course not, my lady. I did not realise . . .'

He lifted the latch and swung open the door. Dena gave the man a look which would have withered crops, and stepped across the raised threshold.

It was a sunken-floored hut without the benefit of windows, and the stifling atmosphere held a pungent edge to it which caught in Dena's throat. The only illumination came from a narrow shaft of sunlight filtering through the smoke-hole, not enough to reach the furthermost recesses, and she had to peer awkwardly about her until her eyes became accustomed to the gloom. The dark shape of a brazier was recognisable, and she reached out to it to steady her footing on the cluttered and uneven floor. She gasped as the iron bindings burned her hand.

'Oh, no!' she cried. 'Please, God, no . . .'

'Here.'

Mildthryth's quiet voice broke into her mounting fears, and Dena carefully made her way across to the old woman's shadowy figure. There was a spark, and the sound of Mildthryth's gentle breath easing the flame to life, then the naked wick caught and a crescent of yellow light flooded the battered body slumped against the wall.

Dena shrank back, her hands clasped over her mouth in an attempt to stifle a rising cry of horror.

'Rhodri . . . Oh, Rhodri . . .'

CHAPTER
EIGHT

ONCE, MANY years before, Dena had seen one of her father's men after he had been set upon by outlaws. His condition had so appalled her that images of his bloodied face had haunted her dreams; but Rhodri . . .

He had been stripped of his tunic and smock, which lay in tatters beside him. The noose was gone, but his wrists were still bound to the two sticks on either side of his throat. The one behind his neck had split, the white fibres of the wood showing through the darker bark. Dena gave her thanks for that small mercy, until she realised what strength had been needed to break it, strength he must have been using against his torturers . . .

She put out her fingers to touch his brow, but her hand was shaking so much that she drew it back in case she might cause him more pain.

'Here.' The blade of the knife Mildthryth offered glinted in the flickering light, and Dena took hold of its leather handle, grateful to be following someone's instructions.

'Free his legs and then his hands.'

Rhodri's ankles had been lashed to a securing pin hammered into the earthen floor of the hut, but Mildthryth's knife had a good edge to it and it was not long before Dena was sawing through the twisted rawhide rope that bound his wrists. Freed from the stakes, his body flopped like a child's doll. Dena lifted his head from the hard floor and laid his cheek upon the softness of her thighs, carefully brushing away the loose dirt pitted into his skin with the edge of her kirtle. He did not make a murmur.

'Are his hands warm or cold?' Mildthryth asked.

'Cold. As cold as water from a winter brook.'

'Rub them. Rub them hard to stir the blood.'

Dena rubbed with all her might, frantically trying to recall the charm sung over her dying father. Desperately she fought for it, but the words would not come, and finally, as despair overtook her, she had to admit that, just as her father had left this world, the charm might not be strong enough to save Rhodri, either.

She watched Mildthryth work with the ointments and the herb potions in the dim yellow light until her vision turned glassy and opaque. She had not meant to cry, had not wanted to shed futile tears when Rhodri needed so much help, but of what use was she? She did not share one-hundredth of Mildthryth's knowledge. It was the old woman he needed, the old woman dressed in rags who lived aside from all others in a little wattle and daub hut no bigger than the hell-hole in which they now knelt.

A warm tear slipped from her cheek to land upon Rhodri's. Another followed it. Dena brushed them from his cool skin, making a cleansing streak amid the grime. Wonderfully, magically, he opened his eyes.

Dena held her breath, hardly daring to speak in case she broke the spell.

'Rhodri?' she whispered. 'Rhodri? Can you hear me?'

His eyes stared dully through slitted lids, and Dena took his hand in hers and pressed it to her damp cheek.

'Rhodri . . . Oh, Rhodri, my love, be well!'

Mildthryth cackled to herself, and Dena glared at her for finding humour in such a situation.

'You choose a fine man to call "my love",' the old

woman cruelly imitated. 'Rhodri ap Hywel? He needs no prayers for strength. He has strength enough, given from his father's loins. Move the light closer. My eyes are older than my aching bones.'

Dena lifted the little jar of melting tallow, making the dancing flame cast strangely grotesque shadows on the wall. Pictures of the future, some people called them. Pictures of fate. Dena drew her eyes away and moistened her drying lips. She did not want Mildthryth to laugh again, only to answer her question.

'You know of his father?'

The old woman's eyes darted across the space between them, and her mouth opened in a mischievous grin showing all of her decaying teeth.

'You do not? You do not know whose head lies on your knee?' She laughed again, and shook her head in irony.

'Tell me!'

Mildthryth pushed her face close to Dena's, her sparkling eyes tainted with madness.

'A prince,' she hissed. 'A prince!'

Dena sat back in open-mouthed disbelief as Mildthryth cackled on again.

Then the old woman stopped abruptly, and sighed. 'At least, he would be, had his mother been of a royal line and not some serving-maid! Ignore the name he stands by now. It is a blind that fools no one. The bastard son of Gruffydd, that is whose head lies on your knee.'

Her eyes turned misty in the glimmering light, as though she were recalling a special memory to mind. 'Gruffydd was a sight to see. Men trembled at his name. He united the kingdoms against the Saxon English. He had a presence, a power . . .'

She shook her head wearily and turned her attention back to Rhodri, but Dena wanted to hear more.

'Is Gruffydd dead?'

Mildthryth nodded sadly. 'His own men sent his head to Earl Harold two, no three, years ago.'

Dena's eyes widened. '*Earl* Harold? The king Lord Edwulf rides to serve?'

Mildthryth smiled absently. 'Ay, but he will not see the coming of the snows with such a mighty title. I have read the signs.'

Dena let her eyes fall to Rhodri's pale face. A prince —of sorts—it was hard to believe. She stroked his cheek, but his eyes had closed again and they did not re-open.

'Do you understand now, why he has been treated so?'

Dena looked up into Mildthryth's lined, enquiring face. 'No,' she said. 'No. I do not understand.'

A sudden brilliance filled the hovel, making both women shade their eyes. Dena turned to find Wybert's huge frame blocking the open doorway, a giant of a torch blazing in his hand.

'Then you are as witless as you are meddlesome,' Wybert spat. He took the steps to the sunken floor in one angry stride.

Dena laid Rhodri's head upon the ground and struggled to her feet, determined that he would come to no more harm at Wybert's hands.

'Take care with that torch!' she warned. 'Set the thatch of this hut alight, and every building within these defences will burn.' Realising what she had said, Dena stood defiantly to her fullest height and met Wybert eye to eye.

'Perhaps that is what you want, *Lord* Wybert! It

would give you the evidence you need to support this false rumour of a Welsh uprising you have been peddling before the Lady Nearra. You could tell her how you single-handedly beat back twenty Welshmen to save her life! No doubt she would be so grateful that she would grant you the lands to go with your self-appointed title!'

Dena's tirade surprised even herself. In her anger she had let her tongue run away with her, accusing her uncle's closest friend of the most dire treasons. She stood breathlessly waiting for some harsh rebuke, but none came. Wybert appeared mortified by her outburst.

Taking heart, she continued in the same tone. 'I want him carried from this hovel of torture to a place of cleanliness and light where he can recover from these hideous wounds.'

Wybert glanced down at Rhodri's slumped body, and his stance visibly relaxed. He lifted his eyes to Dena again and snorted his derision, curling his lips at her as he spoke.

'He can give me no more information. Do as you wish. I praised God for your safe deliverance, but I can see now that it had nothing to do with His good works.'

With an arrogant toss of his grey hair, Wybert turned on his heel and stepped out into the sunshine. He threw the wicker door into its place, forcing the women back into the realms of deepest gloom. Dena clenched her fists in frenzied indignation, and would have ripped the door from its ties had not Mildthryth caught her arm.

'Later,' she whispered. 'Later. Let us move our prince while we have the chance. I know a place.'

The door opened again, sending a bolt of light across the floor of the hut. At first Dena thought it was Wybert returning with a changed mind, but the guard who had opposed their entry timidly peered into the gloom, his head slightly bowed.

'I have been told to carry out all instructions, my lady. Is—is there anything you need?'

Dena glanced down at Mildthryth, hardly believing their good fortune. 'Yes,' she answered. 'Fetch a cloak and a pallet and another man to help you to carry it. We are moving this nobleman immediately.'

The place Mildthryth had in mind was a narrow storeroom built into the stone wall of the hall, next to the busy kitchen archway. It was so small that it hardly took the pallet as a bed for Rhodri, and left just enough room at the side for Dena to stand. They had aroused no opposition or ill-feeling among the people as he had been carried through the open encampment outside the main doors, for no one knew who he was; but now that he was placed in the tiny store, Dena began to worry about whether he would be safe. His arrival had not gone unnoticed by the kitchen workers, and already questions were being asked outside the thin planked door.

'This place is not suitable. There are no windows, only the one door. We cannot barricade it. It is a ready-built tomb!'

Mildthryth lowered herself down the wall and sat cross-legged by Rhodri's head. She pulled her faded rawhide bag closer, and began to untie its neck.

'Where do you suggest? Your chamber? Do you think the Lady Ethelin will accept him with arms out-stretched?'

An image of Ethelin's furious eyes came to Dena's mind. 'Perhaps not,' she admitted.

'This is a good place. Only one person brings un-wanted attention to it—you. It is you they whisper about

out there, not our prince. You, in your green kirtle of finest spun wool. Only high-born ladies wear such clothes, and high-born ladies do not secrete themselves in kitchen stores. You must go.'

'Go? Leave him here, alone?'

'I shall stay by his side.' She nodded beyond the wall to the kitchen. 'They will not come. They know who I am, and what I can do.'

Dena watched her unload her bag and place the pouches, jars and tiny blue glass bottles in a line beneath Rhodri's pallet. Mildthryth was not speaking of healing now, but spell-binding, ill-wishing, cursing charms. Dena had been taught since childhood that such things were false and not to be believed, but after spending time with Mildthryth she knew she would not want to displease the old woman. Like the workers of the kitchen, Dena believed.

'What of Wybert?' she whispered.

'Wybert has no more need of our prince, and he knows better than to seek vengeance at my door for any loss of honour he might feel. It is you who will have to be on your guard.' She gazed strangely at Dena, as if reaching out with her mind, touching, searching . . . It made her quiver.

'I am not certain, but all is not at peace within his breast. I think he has a madness.' Her old eyes cleared and she squinted ominously at Dena. 'Beware,' she said. 'Beware.'

Dena felt it was the hardest thing she had ever done, to close the door on that little store, to turn her back on Rhodri. He had opened his eyes only the once, in that hovel where he had cried out in pain, but he had not seen her, he had not heard her call his name. In all his torment he would have held tightly to one vision, to the memory of her betrayal. It would be with him still, as he slept. When he awoke, as she knew he would awake, it would not be her face he would see smiling down at him, nor her hand upon his brow. He would still believe she had betrayed him.

'Lady Dena! Oh, Lady Dena, I have looked everywhere for you.'

She heard Elma's anxious voice, and dragged herself out of her despair to wait until the girl could make her way through the trestle tables raised for the midday meal.

'Lady Ethelin has had me looking everywhere for you. She wishes to see you in her chamber at once.'

Dena looked into her flushed and plaintive face, knowing exactly what would meet her in Ethelin's chamber.

'I have no wish to see her,' she murmured wearily, and began to turn away.

Elma caught her arm. 'Oh, my lady, please . . .'

Dena looked back, catching a glimpse of a bruise on the side of Elma's temple.

'Has she cuffed you?'

Elma shrank away, pulling her coarse headcloth further across her forehead. 'It is nothing.'

Dena's rage erupted. There was brutality on every side. She stormed down the aisle to the stairs and ran up the steps, striding along the upper passageway so quickly that everyone she met stepped aside to give her room. She did not knock at the heavy oak door but burst inside, slamming it noisily behind her.

Ethelin, gazing out of the open window, turned in alarm, but when she saw who had entered, her startled expression changed to one of calculated displeasure.

'How dare you shame me by your . . .!'

'You hit Elma!' Dena accused. 'You hit a poor serving-girl because you could not vent your anger on me. Well I am here now, so let your fury have its head. I am more than ready!'

Ethelin seemed incapable of uttering a word. Her face had turned ashen, and Dena could see that her lips were trembling. After a moment, she clasped her hands together and lifted her chin haughtily.

'Your eyes are as large as broth-bowls, niece. I trust this monstrous mood of yours will not be shown to the Lady Nearra during the meal.'

'Your food would choke me!'

'Then I hope an hour of your own counsel will help to curb this excessive show of temper.'

Ethelin gathered the skirt of her heavily embroidered kirtle and swept past Dena out of the chamber. The resultant draught seemed to pull all fight from Dena's heaving chest, and she slumped limply on to the bed to hold her head in her hands. She had accused Ethelin of cuffing Elma out of sheer frustration, yet what had that flood of rage been for if not to make Ethelin feel the pain that she, herself, was suffering?

She closed her eyes, but could not keep back the tears which bubbled up from the depths of her soul. She ached for the power to right the wrongs of the world, to help those too lowly or sick to help themselves. She ached to help Rhodri, to show him how much she cared.

Dena awoke, without realising she had been asleep, and turned on to her back to look about the room. From the light at the window she guessed evening was close at hand. She pulled herself to a sitting position, feeling strangely light-headed, yet free from the heavy despair of midday.

How had Rhodri spent the time? Was he still asleep? There was little point in wondering and worrying. She did not know, and she could not go and enquire. It would be hard to keep away from the store, to be without word of his progress, but she knew she had to comply with Mildthryth's wishes. Rhodri's safety was paramount.

Dena crossed to the window and gazed out over the thatched roofs of the circular bowers below. Armed men patrolled the stone defence wall; and beyond, in the creeping darkness of the forest, Gwylan lay.

Did he think Rhodri was dead? Did he care? Yes, Dena knew he would care. Their argument would have been forgotten. She had glimpsed the love of kin pass between them, though it seemed they were not kin at all. Gwylan would be wrought with grief and despair, but would he try to set Rhodri free? It seemed unlikely. Too many of his own followers would die in the attempt. No, Gwylan would pray and keep his distance. It was up to Dena to see that Rhodri came to no more harm.

She patted her stomach and wondered how long it would be before the bell was rung to gather the people for the evening meal. She had missed so many meals that she was beginning to feel as thin as a beggar. It would be foolish for her to act like a fasting penitent. She did not know when she might need her strength.

A pail had been set behind the door, and she found that it contained sweet-smelling petals floating on clear water. She cupped her hands and splashed her face, rubbing it well to bring some colour back into her cheeks, then dabbed her skin with a towel and arched her neck, feeling much invigorated.

Ethelin was right. She had to show a more decorous face to Lady Nearra and the other noblewomen. Her role was not that of a military man like Gwylan, or a healer like Mildthryth. Hers was a role of diplomacy, of quiet words and listening ears, of watchful eyes and a mind quick to sense deceit. She *was* of use to Rhodri, and she would see that she did not let him down.

She took off her headcloth and delved into her belt-pouch for the comb Rhodri had given her. She held the case in her hand for a moment, gently caressing the intricately etched design. She liked to think it had been given as a gift and not just lent for its use. It was something of his to hold and to treasure, something that could bring her closer to him when she could not be by his side.

She removed the bone comb and began to draw it through her hair. The tangles had returned since it had been washed by Elma that morning, making the task take longer than she had expected. Only one side was braided when the door opened behind her. Expecting it to be the maid, Dena turned with a smile, only to find Ethelin standing there.

'Ah, good, you are awake. Are you feeling refreshed?'

It was difficult to determine what was in Ethelin's mind from the tone she used. Perhaps she wished for the episode at noon to be forgotten. Dena hoped so. It would serve neither of them any purpose to allow tempers to flare again.

'Yes,' she said at last. 'I am feeling much better now.'

Ethelin seemed genuinely relieved.

'Good. The Lady Nearra asked why you did not dine with us. I told her that the strain of the last few days had been too much for you, and you were resting. I said I hoped you would join us for the evening meal. Will you be strong enough?'

Dena turned her head aside and grimaced. So that was it. Ethelin was afraid of losing face again.

'Yes,' she rasped tersely. 'If you wish me to walk down with you, I shall be ready as soon as I have braided my hair.'

Ethelin moved forward, her skirts rustling about her ankles. 'You should have called for Elma.'

'There was no need.'

Her hands full of twisting hair, Dena watched in horror as Ethelin's fingers darted to lift the comb-case from her lap.

'What is this? I have never seen it before.' She turned it in her hand, inspecting it closely.

'It was a gift.'

'A gift? From whom?'

She swooped down before Dena so that their faces were level, her eyes widening in delight and excitement.

'Not that barbarian!'

'He is not a barbarian! He is a Welsh nobleman of the highest rank.'

Ethelin smiled knowingly. 'Some say a prince. Is that what you think you have caught yourself, Dena? A prince?'

Dena felt her cheeks begin to flush. 'I could not be so conniving.'

'No? Then how did he come to give you a gold comb-case?'

'Gold?' she breathed.

'Of course it is gold. Did you believe it was made of bronze?'

She laughed, and Dena snatched the comb-case from her hand.

'Oh, Dena! You should not take so much to heart. You are very naïve in these matters. Men of his rank often play with the affections of unworldly girls. It is merely a diversion for them.'

Dena's heart stopped in her breast. No, Rhodri had not been playing with her affections. He had not!

Ethelin did not seem to notice the consternation she had seeded within her niece, and rose to re-pin the brooches holding her kirtle tightly across her slim waist.

'Come, Dena. Let us hurry. I wish to claim a good seat near to the fire. That hall is magnificent in its decoration, but more draughty even than Edwulf's.'

It was not the thought of draughts which drove Ethelin to seek an early seat at the tables, but the thought of another woman sitting closer to the Lady Nearra than herself. It was more than obvious that there was some sort of rivalry between the noblewomen. Each was decked in her finest clothing and glittered with more jewels and gold than Dena had ever hoped to see in her life. Maids scurried back and forth bringing cloaks of fine pelts for their respective ladies to sit upon, even though an embroidered cushion was provided for each.

Lady Nearra was escorted to the table not by one of her own men, but, to Dena's surprise, by Wybert, who was dressed in clothing she had not seen him wear since the last great feast-day. She watched their progress along the far aisle with a mixture of astonishment and anxiety. He bent his head to listen attentively as Lady Nearra spoke, and laughed at something she said. They had the air of a couple who had spent some time in each other's company.

Where had they come from to walk down the far aisle? Not from the bowers, surely, and they were at the wrong end of the hall for the stairs leading from the chambers above. Dena followed the aisle back along the wall to where it joined the wide passage from the main doors of the hall to the kitchen.

The kitchen. Dena's heart leapt. Had they demanded entry to the store Mildthryth had made her own? Had they been to gloat over Rhodri, or to hurt him in some way? Dena peered through the smoky atmosphere, trying to see beyond the kitchen archway, but from where she sat she could see neither the work-benches nor the entrance to the store.

What could she do? It was too late to leave the table now. The Lady Nearra was settling herself in her central place.

'May I join you, ladies?'

Wybert's voice boomed like a death-knell in Dena's ear, and every muscle in her body tightened as she sat staring rigidly in front of her.

'Certainly,' Ethelin answered brightly. 'I am sure we can make room for you. Dena?'

What could she say? Ethelin shuffled a little to her right and motioned for Dena to do the same. Like the lumbering bear he was, Wybert slotted himself into the space and sat on the bench beside her. No matter how Dena tried to keep her distance, their shoulders rubbed each time either of them moved.

Boys hurried along the table leaving a square wooden plate and a heavy pottery mug before each person. Large bowls full of fine-crystalled grey salt were placed at intervals. It seemed there was going to be plenty of meat.

A priest rose to his feet and everyone fell silent to listen to the chant of thankfulness. The hubbub of conversation rose again as the people waited for the food to be brought in, and boys too young for their task sloshed ale from over-filled buckets all along the aisles.

The whetstone travelled slowly up the table as they all in turn attended to the edges of their eating-knives, and spoons appeared from belt-pouches and chains round their necks.

Dena tried to rid her mind of memories of the day: the horror of seeing Rhodri's wounds, the seething hate she had directed at Wybert. Wybert now sat next to her with all the piety and gentleness of a member of a holy order. Diplomacy, she told herself as her blood surged in her ears. She was not there to cast judgment or cause arguments, but to listen and to watch.

The whetstone passed to Wybert, and he made a great show of sharpening his knife. Dena could not avert her eyes. His deft movements of wrist and fingers held a hypnotic fascination, and when he held out the whetstone to her, it was like being pushed further into a nightmare.

As though her hands were not her own, she took it from him. It felt strangely warm for stone, and heavy, like a dying heart. The palm which held her knife oozed with chilling sweat. She sat there with tools of torture in either hand, and a voice she knew to be Rhodri's screamed inside her head.

'Allow me to help you, Dena.'

Wybert's large hands engulfed her own, and suddenly she held nothing. As quick as lightning, the blade danced along the stone, and with a flourish he handed back the knife. Forced by the Devil, she looked into his face and found him smiling down at her, his eyes glinting like the newly-sharpened edge.

'I can do it so much better than you!'

A hard, expanding bubble burst inside Dena's chest, and churning nausea thrust its way up her constricted throat. A hand to her mouth, she rose from the bench, almost falling over it in her haste to be gone from that place. She turned to the left, but her way was blocked by boys bringing platters of roasted meat, freshly cut from the spit, blistered and glistening like Rhodri's skin.

With an unuttered cry she shut her eyes to it and changed her direction, hurrying along the rear aisle and through the maze of central tables towards the towering doors of the hall.

Outside, the cold evening air hit her like an icy blast. She leant against the unyielding stone of the wall, gulping down lungfuls of the sweet-tasting atmosphere.

'Beware', Mildthryth had warned her. 'Beware of Wybert.' But how was she to know he could change so much? How was she to know he could take such delight in hurting Rhodri, in hurting her? What had happened to that kind, grey-haired man who had walked with her along the defences of Edwulf's estate, who had shown her how to handle a hawk, who had taken her to see the first blossoms of the spring? He was a monster. A monster!

CHAPTER
NINE

'WHAT AILED you this time?' Ethelin demanded when she entered their bedchamber.

When she saw the coverlets drawn up to her neck, Dena had hoped that Ethelin might not start any conversation. It was in her mind to feign sleep, but her anxious thoughts were far too active for her to have carried the deception with any mark of success.

'I felt ill.'

'So Wybert said.'

Dena wondered what else Wybert had said, but she could not bring herself to ask, fearing the inquisition which she knew would follow.

Ethelin climbed into the opposite side of the bed and settled herself down with an irritated rattle of the throat. Dena kept well to her own side, not wanting to give her aunt any excuse for chastising her further. She had had enough torments for one night. All she wanted was to sleep, but although it came quickly for Ethelin, Dena was not allowed the same comfort.

Hour after hour she lay, watching patterns of light from the night torch flicker across the wall, listening to the eerie silence of the great hall, tensing fearfully at the occasional sound of footsteps beyond the door.

It was not Wybert, Dena kept telling herself, he was not hunting her; but she could not forget the look in his eye, like a man wagering heavily on a bull-baiting, caught in the frenzied madness of the blood-lust. Madness. Mildthryth had told her Wybert had a madness.

What form would it take? What was it likely to make him do? He would try to hurt Rhodri again, she was certain. No matter what Mildthryth believed, Dena knew it would only be a matter of time before he sought Rhodri's life. He wanted revenge, she was sure of it, revenge for being forced to flee Edwulf's hall, for losing Edwulf his lands and his people at the tun.

No one had spoken of the people at the tun, not even Ethelin. Perhaps no one yet knew of their fate. What would happen to Rhodri when news arrived? Wybert would be given a free hand to do anything he wanted —anything.

She tried to close her mind to the pictures filling her head, to Mildthryth's voice saying 'All night I heard him', to the sight of Rhodri slumped against the wall, to the sound of his screams. The horrors of wakefulness turned into the nightmares of sleep without her knowing, but still the pictures came, more insistent, more vivid, until she awoke with a cry and sat upright in the bed, staring into the wide eyes of Elma.

'My lady . . .'

Dena looked about the chamber, half expecting to see the visitations of the night standing starkly against the walls. She dragged each breath into her aching lungs and pushed her fingers through her hair. It was flat to her head, wet with perspiration.

'Where is Ethelin?' she panted.

'She rose before it was light and went to warm herself by the fire in the hall. She could not sleep for your tossing and turning. You kept crying out. You have a fever, my lady. The bed is soaked with your sweat.'

Dena shook her head. 'Nightmares, only nightmares.' Or had it been something else? Had those weird shadows of the future she had seen on the hovel wall taken a shape she could understand? Had what they foretold already happened? Was Rhodri already dead? She had to know.

'Get me another smock.' She sprang out of the bed and pulled the soiled one over her tousled hair.

Elma sighed and shook her head, but took a clean smock from the chest. She spoke very quietly, as if expecting to be rounded on. 'The Lady Ethelin does not wish you to leave the chamber. She believes you are too ill.'

Dena felt sorry for her, always caught between her aunt and herself, but she was not going to be dissuaded.

'I have to go, Elma.'

'I do not understand why you are so fretful about that Welshman.'

Dena stopped dressing and stared into Elma's serious face.

'Everyone is talking about you, even the lowliest kitchen-boy. There is no need to wonder why the Lady Ethelin is so angry.'

Dena felt her stomach twist. 'What have they said? What do they know of him?'

Elma shuffled and cast down her eyes, not wanting to repeat the scandals she had heard. 'Everyone knows you had him taken to the store by the kitchen. I cannot see why. Nobody wants him in the hall, prince or no prince. He is a Welshman.'

'Has . . . Has anyone tried to move him?'

Elma looked at her in astonishment. 'No one would be so foolish as to try. Mildthryth sits with him, chanting incantations to the Devil! She has painted magical signs on the doorway. Anyone trying to enter is shrivelled to the size of a pea!'

'Elma . . .!'

The girl hung her head and shrugged her shoulders. 'It is true,' she warned. 'I think she has put a spell on you, too. Please, Lady Dena, go to the priest and have it removed before it is too late!'

Dena waved her away. 'Do not be so childish, Elma. No one can put spells on other people, not even Mildthryth.'

'Oh, she can, my lady, she can! I have seen it. She is a witch!'

'Enough!' Dena cried in alarm. She had no idea how witches were looked upon on Lord Baldric's estate. Edwulf had a great tolerance for the old teachings, but Lady Nearra had a Christian priest for a confidant, and Dena had heard of such men burning witches without a trial.

'She is not a witch, she merely . . .' Dena hesitated. Mildthryth was obviously keeping unwanted visitors away through superstition. If Dena were to dispel those fears, she might do more harm than good.

'Oh, away with you. I have no time for this.'

In the corridor, everyone was awake and up. The bedding-pallets had been upturned against the wall to make more room for the constant passage of scurrying servants. No matter what the dilemma facing them, it seemed that the gathered noblewomen did not wish to be without the luxuries of their own halls, or at least to be seen without them. Gossip and rumour were rife among the ordinary people, and Dena knew it would be no different for the nobility, who had nothing better to do but parade before each other like pheasants in a mating dance. There was too little for *anyone* to do. The expected siege by the Welsh had come to nothing. Perhaps the Lady Nearra might listen to her with a little more patience the next time they spoke.

There was a great deal of noise coming from the hall, and Dena faltered at the bottom of the steps, wondering if she were doing the right thing. Mildthryth had been very specific about her bringing attention to the storeroom, but if everyone already knew where Rhodri was, what harm could a short visit do?

She pulled aside the curtain and stepped on to the soft rushes covering the stone flags. There seemed to be more people crowded into the hall than there had been the previous evening. The smoky atmosphere had not been relieved, and a new fire was adding to the stuffy air. The sour smell of drying clothing assailed her nostrils, and Dena realised that the people were taking shelter from the autumn rain. She made her way down the aisle, pleased to be part of a gathering so intent on its own deprivations that she could remain anonymous. She reached the kitchen arch without one person bidding her good-day.

To her relief, she found the door to Rhodri's cell as plain as it had always been, devoid of any magical inscriptions, no matter what Elma had been led to believe. When she peeped round the kitchen wall to see who might be there, everyone was busy preparing food, and there seemed to be no guard. She was looking for excuses not to enter the store, she told herself sternly. She had to go inside. She had to see for herself that Rhodri had not been harmed.

But what if he had? What if he had?

She took a deep breath to catch her runaway fears, and boldly walked up to the door. The latch lifted with a loud click, and without looking behind to see if anyone had noticed her, she quickly passed inside and closed the door behind her.

She gasped at the sight which met her eyes, gasped

and held her breath to capture the moment and hold every detail of it.

'Rhodri, you are well!' she breathed. The relief and the thankfulness burst in her chest to fill her whole body with warmth and contentment.

'Told you he was strong, I did, but you did not believe me,' Mildthryth chuntered.

Dena took a step forward, her shins nudging the edge of the pallet. She wanted to get closer to him, to sit by his side and hold his hand, to throw her arms round him, but there was no room except to stand and stare.

Propped against the wall, his chest and arms sticky with the salves and potions Mildthryth had applied to his wounds, Rhodri's sunken eyes could only survey her coldly. Curtained by his lank, dark hair which fell in matted locks to his shoulders, his face still looked very pale. For Dena, he was a joy to see, and she clasped her hands before her, wanting to tell him so, but not knowing how to bring the words to her lips.

'Tell this witch of yours to stop calling me "my prince". I am not a prince. I have never been a prince.'

He was in pain and he was angry, and his words were designed to hurt, but they only made Dena's smile the broader.

'He is an ungrateful cur,' Mildthryth snarled. 'Bites the hand that heals.' As if to prove it, she extended her hand to touch him, only to have it knocked aside.

'I am not your doll!'

'But I can make one,' Mildthryth retorted, 'to stick *pins* into!'

Dena's smile faded. 'Stop this! The door is thin enough. Do you want the kitchen workers to hear you?'

Mildthryth grunted and shuffled her body further along the wall. Dena turned to Rhodri.

'Have you any idea how close to death you are? Everyone out there howls for your blood. Up and down the valleys the people have fled from their homes to take shelter here. They are expecting to be laid siege to, to be massacred as they sleep. There is no lock on this door. It is only Mildthryth who is keeping them at bay.'

He raised one leg and scratched lazily at his braies below the knee. Dena could not believe his contempt.

'She is risking her life to help you!'

'And you? Are you risking your life, or is this just a way of cleansing your conscience?'

'I did not betray you!'

Rhodri threw his head back and scoffed. 'You talked so fast that it is a wonder you did not spit your teeth out in the rush!'

'I saved your life.'

'For what? So that I could be dragged here and tortured?'

Dena shook her head in anguish. 'I did not know . . .'

'Know? You know nothing! What have you saved me for, this time? To be paraded in chains for your entertainment? Or are you waiting for my eyes to be put out and for me to be gelded? That is what happens to prisoners who cannot be ransomed, and no one will pay for my release, no matter how many of you call me "prince".'

Dena's shoulders hit the stone wall and she could back away no further. She was trying hard to keep down the knot of emotion forcing its way up her throat. She bit back the tears which stung her eyes, determined that he would not see her cry.

'You hate-filled oaf! All I have ever done is to try to help you. You deserve none of it!'

'I never asked for it. I do not want it.'

'Then you will get it no longer!'

In a flurry of temper and humiliation, she lifted the latch, pulled open the door and slammed it behind her. She turned on her heel to pass beneath the kitchen archway, but her legs had lost all sense of movement. Quietly leaning against the stone pillar was the massive bulk of Wybert. Dena felt her colour drain as they gazed at each other. He had been listening, she knew he had.

Wybert pushed himself off the wall and began to walk past her into the kitchen, but he paused, turning his head towards her and looking at her with sad, haunted eyes.

'He never was worth it, my lady. Truly, I am sorry.'

Dena watched him shamble away like a beggar. There were no blazing eyes, no sadistic delight, only . . . Only what? Dena shook her head, too confused to make sense of anything any more.

Dejectedly, she walked into the hall and along the aisle, pausing at the open doorway to rest her head on the iron bindings. The rain had stopped. People were tending their animals, stirring kettles over licking flames, talking, laughing. Somewhere a harp was being played. Someone was singing an accompaniment, but it was not a happy song. It was slow, and sad, and it touched Dena's heart and made it ache. She could not go back to Ethelin's bedchamber, or to the ladies' bower, or even sit by the fire in the hall. She wanted to be alone, but there were too many people. Everywhere there were too many people. She gazed at them all crowded in the courtyard, huddled round their open fires, beneath their makeshift shelters, all too afraid to venture beyond the gate in case they were set upon by the Welsh hordes.

Dena raised her head from the heavy door and gazed out above the heads of the people to the open gateway and the beckoning fields beyond. There were no Welsh hordes. It had been no more than a diversionary rumour set about by Wybert, she was certain. There lay her peace, her solitude—out among the harvested fields.

Like a light in the darkness, she followed the stone-laid cart route down from the hall to the defence wall without seeing anyone on either side of her. Men, tired of their constant vigilance, lounged by glowing braziers at the gate, but no one called a halt as she walked outside.

The sense of space was overwhelming. The view was unhindered across the cropped land, right up to the edge of the dark green forest. A bird called above her, and she raised her eyes to watch a pair of buzzards wheel away to her right and disappear into the low grey cloud. To be so free . . .

An old woman, bent with age and endless toil, crossed her path with a basket of roots, but she did not speak. Dena carried on round the outer defence ditch, wanting to find somewhere quiet to sit and think, but the noise of the courtyard kept invading her mind, making her restless. She walked on, skirting the defences, paying no attention to her sodden feet or the mud clinging to the bottom of her kirtle. She might have kept walking all the way round to the second gateway, had she not met a small girl picking flowers.

It seemed inconceivable that one so young should be on her own beyond the safety of the fortifications, but there was no one else in sight, not even an older sibling.

'What are you doing here?'

The girl raised her head, and her tiny heart-shaped face burst with a smile.

'Picking flowers.' She held them up towards Dena's face, and she bent to smell their perfume.

'They are very colourful,' she said. 'Are you picking them for your mother?'

The girl shrugged and picked another tall-stemmed daisy to add to the bunch in her hand. 'I would like you to have them.'

Dena was taken aback by the girl's gift, but accepted the crushed stems and raised them to her face again. 'Thank you! But will your mother not be angry that you are giving away your beautiful flowers?'

'No, she likes you.'

Dena looked at the girl with new eyes. There was a certain amount of recognition, but she could not put a name to the child. She crouched down so that they were almost at the same level.

'Are you one of the Lord Edwulf's people?'

The girl nodded, and Dena smiled at her. 'Where are you all living? I have not been able to find any of you.'

'By the little bridge during the day. We sleep by the dog runs at night, but the dogs do not like us. They think we are the Welsh, and they bark at us.'

The girl thought that was funny and Dena laughed with her, but all the time her mind was in a whirl. Edwulf's people were living beyond the fortifications while it was light, no doubt on Wybert's instructions. If that did not make a lie of Wybert's fear of a Welsh uprising, Dena did not know what would. She stifled her indignation. Edwulf's people had lost all they owned at the hall, and although she knew that they had not suffered at Gwylan's hands, there were other dangers in the forest. She decided to see for herself that they were all safe, and offered the girl her hand.

'I think it might be best if we take you back to your mother. What is her name?'

'Bette.'

Dena stared at her in astonishment. 'You live at the tun?'

The girl nodded brightly. 'I like living there. I can play where I like.'

Dena held her tiny shoulders, desperately wanting to ask a hundred different questions. The girl looked up at her expectantly, but without any sign of alarm. The Welsh had attacked the tun. Dena had seen the flames, passed the open gateway. Could it be possible that they had all escaped? Taking a firm grip of the child's hand, she began to steer her towards the rear of the defence ditch.

'Come, let us find your mother.'

Bette was cleaning a fresh deerskin, and, like the other people, looked perturbed to find her daughter hand in hand with a lady, but Dena quickly put the gathering at their ease and was soon sitting by a fire sharing a bowl of broth, listening to their adventures.

'The Welsh surprised us, it is true. They walked through the gate with swords drawn.'

Dena shuddered. 'You must have been terrified!'

Another took up the story. 'We thought we were dead, but they herded us all together, and their leader told us who he was and that he was taking back his lands.' He laughed a little. 'He even asked if we would be willing to work the land under his lordship instead of Lord Edwulf's.'

A titter of irony swept round the circle, and Dena could not help smiling at the bravado they showed now which she knew would have been lacking in the face of Gwylan.

'What did you say in return?'

'We told him we were no mewing heathens. We were

loyal to the Lord Edwulf, and if he wanted our lord's lands, he could work them himself!'

Everyone guffawed and added their own asides to bring more sparkle to the story.

'How did you escape?'

'Drove us out, they did, like sheep to pasture.'

'Then you all escaped unharmed?'

The jokes, the laughter, all slowly subsided.

'It was old Wain. You know how he was, my lady, always living in the past, telling us how good a soldier he had been. He cursed us for leaving without a fight, said he could not live with the shame of it. He said Wybert had to be warned. Before we knew, he had gone back. We could not wait for him in case he brought the wrath of the Welsh down upon our families. We hoped he would catch us. We have been hoping that he would walk in out of the forest.' The man spread his hands in a hopeless gesture, and hung his head.

Events began to fall into place in Dena's mind. Gwylan had insisted that Rhodri guard her well, not because his men would necessarily violate her, but because he did not wish her to have a chance to set light to the thatch as Wain had done.

She gazed at the sorrowful group sitting about the fire. 'You could have done no other. Your first loyalty is to the well-being of your families. The tun can be replaced; you cannot. Wain will be well remembered by Lord Edwulf. The smoke was seen. Everyone escaped from the hall before the Welsh arrived.'

'We heard you were captured.'

Dena felt herself blush slightly. 'Yes, but I was treated well. I was held as a hostage so that the Welsh could gain better terms with my uncle.'

The raising of eyebrows was slight, but still notice-

able. It seemed that the people had their own ideas
about her treatment.

'Is that why you are taking such an interest in the
welfare of this Welshman that was captured?'

Dena found herself nodding furiously. 'Hostages
always take a prominent part in talks.'

It was true—they did—but that had been the last
thing on her mind when she had thrown herself on top of
Rhodri in an effort to save his life.

Her return to the hall was made with a much lighter step.
She entered the fortifications over a narrow bridge slung
between the deep defence ditches, and was welcomed by
more of Edwulf's people who had heard a dozen different tales about her capture. Everyone seemed in fine
spirits, considering what had happened to them, and she
spent most of the afternoon listening to the stories they
had to tell.

It was almost time for the evening meal when she
entered the hall. The tables and benches had already
been set out, and a marvellous rich aroma of roasting
meat hung in the air, setting her taste-buds alight.

She glanced along the wall to the kitchen archway, but
the door to the store was hidden by the stonework. Her
exasperation with Rhodri had subsided. She should
never have let it rise. She had wanted him to show
appreciation of what she had done for him, there was no
denying it, but she should have seen his position from his
point of view, not her own. He had been in pain, he had
been resentful, but most of all he had been fearful for his
life, a fear he had tried to mask with his anger, just as she
had tried to mask hers when she had been taken captive
by Gwylan's men. Rhodri desperately needed to be able
to rely on someone, to have hope for his situation, but

Dena realised now that he dared not give his trust in case that, too, was taken from him, and he was left with nothing.

In the morning, before the ladies broke their fast in the bower, she would visit him again and make her peace with him. He would know by then that he could put his trust in her, that he was safe while Mildthryth tended him. It might not be enough, but at least it was a beginning.

Ethelin was preparing to leave their bedchamber as Dena opened the door, with Elma making final adjustments to the pleats in her headcloth.

'Where have you been? You can never be found when you are wanted!'

Elma began to blush, and quickly averted her eyes. Dena knew that the girl had been at the receiving end of Ethelin's spite again, but she held her tongue. Making an issue of it in front of Elma would not help the girl at all.

Ethelin turned to say more, but stepped back in exaggerated horror when she set eyes on her niece.

'Dena! The meal is ready, and you stand there looking like a field-worker! What have you been doing?'

'Talking to your people, Ethelin. Have you been to see them since you arrived?'

The question took Ethelin by surprise, but she soon regained her composure. 'I doubt if their spirits would be lifted by the sight of me covered in mud.'

Dena had to smile. She doubted it also.

'I am not waiting for you,' Ethelin announced airily. 'You can come down in your own time, but do not leave it too late or you will find yourself sitting on the floor with the dogs.'

She flicked back her head, making the edge of her

headcloth dance round her shoulders, and left the chamber in a flurry of skirts.

Dena turned to Elma. 'Has she been screaming for me long?'

'Since noon, but I did not look for you too hard.' An impish light lit in her eyes, and the two women shared an illicit chuckle at Ethelin's expense.

By the time Dena descended the flight of steps and entered the main chamber of the hall, it was well full of people and there were few seats available on the benches. She managed to squeeze on to the edge of one of the higher trestle tables at the far end, but she could feel no warmth from the central fire there, only a draught from the high windows which made her shiver and wish she had brought a cloak.

She listened as the priest chanted the prayer, and passed on the whetstone without sharpening her eating-knife. As she was far from the main party, a thick slice of stale bread had been put before her instead of a wooden plate. She had eaten off the same many times in her father's farmstead.

'Lady Dena?'

Dena turned to the touch on her shoulder, to find an old retainer standing there.

'The Lady Nearra wishes you to sit with her.'

Dena looked at him in surprise, wondering if he had got the message wrong.

'Oh, of course,' she stuttered, trying to swing her legs over the bench without bumping the person next to her.

She followed the bent old man along the aisle to the top table, glancing nervously at the other diners. It was indeed an honour to be asked to sit with Lady Nearra, and she wished she knew what she had done to deserve it. Perhaps, at last, Lady Nearra was beginning to have doubts about Wybert's insistence on a total Welsh uprising.

The thought brought an inner glow, and she straightened her shoulders and stood more erect, no longer feeling self-conscious. They passed Ethelin sitting four places from Lady Nearra, and Dena could hardly contain her smile as she saw her aunt's scowling face.

The Lady Nearra was deep in conversation with the noblewomen to her left when Dena was ushered into the seat next to her, so they did not speak at once. Beside the odd pleasantry, little was said during the meal, either, and Dena began to wonder whether the invitation had been made not with any serious intention, but merely to affront one of the other noblewomen who had displeased the Lady Nearra—Ethelin, perhaps. It would certainly be in keeping with the petty politics these women revelled in.

Dejectedly, Dena looked about her. Wybert was nowhere to be seen, and she did not know whether she should feel relieved or anxious. He had never been one to miss his meals as long as she had known him. He had often called a halt to their hawking parties so that they could be back at the hall in plenty of time. She hoped he was well away from the hall, foraging about in the forest again, but somehow it seemed too much to ask.

After the meal, a central place was cleared, and amid great excitement, people came to show their skill at tumbling. A man in a tunic of multicoloured rags came round the tables telling jokes and playing the fool. He brought much laughter, fighting imaginary foes with a child's wooden sword, but Lady Nearra's dogs thought it not a game at all and began to jump up and snarl at him, bringing even more laughter from the onlookers.

He was followed by a harp-player, but instead of

sustaining the merriment, he brought forth sad faces and damp eyes as people remembered and feared for their loved ones away fighting with the king. It made Dena think of Rhodri, too, sitting with Mildthryth in that cramped store under the kitchen archway. Perhaps this might be a good time to talk to the Lady Nearra about him. If she would publicly announce that he was to be treated as an honoured hostage, there would be no need for hiding in holes in the wall.

She waited until two riddle-givers had lifted the people's spirits with their guessing-games, and gently nudged Lady Nearra to catch her attention.

'May I speak of the Welsh nobleman, Rhodri ap Hywel, my lady?

'Certainly, Dena. It was with him in mind that I asked you here.'

All Dena's rehearsed words flew away as she tried to contain her joy, but Lady Nearra did not seem to notice.

'You are a quick-witted young woman, and were with these Welshmen long enough to gather a little insight into their aims. How far do you think they will push into English-held lands?'

'Only as far as Edwulf's estate, my lady. You must believe me when I say this, Lady Nearra. There is no Welsh uprising. My uncle took his lands from the Welsh, through force of arms, from a man called Gwylan. With Edwulf's estate now weakly defended, he is trying to regain them.'

The Lady Nearra hardly seemed to be listening to Dena. Her eyes were elsewhere across the smoky hall, and she raised her hand in some sort of gesture before turning to her in reply.

'Yes, my dear. I understand that. Most of the noble-women here are married to men who took their lands from the Welsh. It is the way of it. If what you say is true, and I will admit that there has been neither sight nor sign of any Welshmen since you were brought to this hall, tell me why a son of Gruffydd was fighting with a little-known Welsh landowner.'

Dena's breath caught in her lungs. Of all the questions she could have been asked, and could have replied to honestly, this was not one. She had no idea why Rhodri was fighting with Gwylan. There was a bond between them—she had seen it—but how could she explain that to the Lady Nearra when she did not understand it herself?

A sudden hush fell across the chamber, and then a roar of jeers and angry shouts. Dena looked up to see what was causing all the ridicule and derision, and her gaze followed those of the howling mob round her. Mortified, she watched with widening eyes as Rhodri shambled into the hall, Wybert at his side. He had been given no smock to hide his wounds, but chains at wrist and ankle which only allowed him to shuffle forward at Wybert's goad.

Dena clenched her fists, forcing her nails into the flesh of her palms, willing herself not to cry out loud.

'Merciful Lord, no,' she breathed, but the two men came closer to stand before the Lady Nearra—to stand before her.

Despite the heavy chains, despite the soreness of his body, Rhodri straightened his back, defiantly tossing his dark hair away from his face. Unseen, an apple-core sailed across the chamber and hit him on the shoulder. Dena saw him give a little shudder, but that was all. The people laughed relentlessly, and amid a hail of scrawny bones and uneaten food, the multicoloured fool came forward with his wooden sword and proceeded to play-fight Rhodri, prodding and poking and dancing round him to the delight of the feasters.

Dena closed her eyes to it, but she could not close her ears or her mind. Inside her body a twisting knot broke free and dissolved, leaving nothing but a numbing hollowness. Someone touched her arm, and she opened her eyes to find Lady Nearra bending her head towards her ear.

'I think your concern for his health was a little exaggerated. Look, he can stand without help. He is perfectly well.'

Dena's mouth fell open at the woman's callousness. She could not keep silent, she could not!

She looked up at Rhodri, determined to try to put a stop to this humiliation, but no words came to her lips. His stance was as before, but his head had tilted slightly. No longer were his eyes fixed on some imaginary place high above their heads, they were looking down, down at Dena. Hard and fierce in the paleness of his face, his dark eyes burnt the hatred he felt straight into her heart, a hatred not for the Saxon English who taunted him, but for her and her alone.

CHAPTER
TEN

DENA'S PRIVATE hell was more vivid, more horrifying,
than any priest could conjure from the holy scriptures.
Rhodri hated her, and he hated her with cause.

Each time they had spoken, he had prophesied tor-
tures and humiliations, and she had disregarded his fears
as she might the fancies of a child—but they were true.
Everything he had foretold was coming true! She had
only wanted to help him. From the beginning, his good
was all that had been in her mind. Her need to help him
had over-ridden every other consideration, blinded her
to the prejudices of those around her. He had spoken
from experience. Had he not told her of being sent to
King Edward's court as a token of goodwill, only to have
his trust betrayed by his own kin? His wish to die was a
wish to escape the fate he had already suffered once.
Why had it taken her so long to see that? Why was she so
naïve?

She sat on the bare boarded floor, her head in her
hands. Her cheeks were dry now. The tears which had
flowed with her grief were spent. She raised her head a
little and looked about the chamber. It seemed so cold
and cheerless in the glimmering light of the night torch.
Ethelin was stretched diagonally across the bed, Elma
curled up like a cat on her pallet. Both were still as heavy
with sleep as Dena had found them.

It had been a useless quest, to try to discover where
Rhodri had been taken when Wybert had dragged him
from the hall. The Lady Nearra did not know, or would

not tell her. She had been quite adamant that he would be well treated, just as adamant as she had been about his good health earlier that evening. Dena had finally herself gone in search, asking for sightings of Wybert or Mildthryth, but in the darkness no one had seen either of them, and the people had laughed at her, believing she was drunk on ale.

She was neither drunk, nor mad, though many would believe her so for caring for this Welshman as she did. Rhodri might wish for his release through death, but while she lived, she would fight for his life. She would need assistance, though; she knew that. Mildthryth must help her.

It was barely light when Dena opened the chamber door and stepped out into the passage. Most of the servants still slumbered, and she had to pick her way along the narrow gap by the wall to the steps. It was no different in the hall below. Wispy trails of smoke curled up towards the rafters from the ashes of the central fire. A few people were beginning to stir, rattling coughs disturbing the uncanny hush the hall knew only during the depths of night, but Wybert was not among them. Neither was Mildthryth.

Dena was beginning to worry about Mildthryth. 'My prince', that is what she called Rhodri, 'my prince', as though she were a devoted follower. She would never have given him up to Wybert without a struggle, nor let him be manacled hand and foot to be taunted before his enemies. Had Wybert beaten her until she was senseless?

As another, more sinister thought came to her, Dena shuddered. Perhaps Wybert had not ventured near Mildthryth at all. Perhaps he had spoken to Lady Nearra's priest, whispering of witchcraft and evil potions. The priest would not have feared Mildthryth. Protected by the holy water, he would have ignored the old woman's screams and curses. Perhaps she, too, was lying manacled in some dark hovel to await her trial. Dena was filled with a new urgency. Two lives, not one, depended on her actions.

Her steps faltered as she reached the archway to the kitchen. The door to the tiny storeroom was closed as before, but the barrier was not giving any sense of protection now. Dena reached out her fingertips to feel the rough, smoke-blackened wood. It was exuding a kind of menace, as though it were hiding some grisly find. The little hairs on Dena's neck rose in a fearful tingling anticipation that was hard to dispel. What would she find through that door? What had Wybert's madness made him do?

She held her breath as she lifted the latch, and jumped when the resultant click echoed loudly in her ears. The door swung open with a low moan, and she stood at the threshold, afraid to venture further. She chided her foolishness, and took a step forward.

If she had allowed her imagination to run riot, the reality which met her eyes was just as bewildering. The bedding-pallet had gone, Rhodri's cover, Mildthryth's bottles and pouches, even her faded rawhide bag. Barrels were now stacked along the narrow end wall, sacks of grain leaning against them. Huge cured meats hung from hooks in the beamed ceiling. One had not been prepared long enough, and slowly dripped its bloody juices into an ever-widening puddle on the floor. It was as though Rhodri and Mildthryth had never been there, had never existed outside a vividly remembered dream. Surely Wybert was not removing every trace of them from this earth! Were they already dead and in some shallow grave? Dear God . . . surely not!

Dena ran out of the storeroom and into the kitchen. She tried to think rationally. They had been taken to the dark hovel by the stables, of course they had. But what if the hovel were empty? She would search every building in the compound if she had to, every sleeping-chamber in the hall, but she would find them. She had to believe that she would find them.

'Dena?'

Recognition of the voice made her catch her breath, and she turned to find Wybert sitting on a barrel in the alcove by the archway, a still-steaming hunk of freshly baked bread in one hand, hard cheese in the other. Allowing her fears full rein, she hardly noticed his surprised expression before she launched herself at him.

'Where is Rhodri? What have you done with Mildthryth? You hate-filled devil! Where are they?'

If Wybert had not pushed himself to his feet to tower over her, Dena felt she would have easily careered straight into him like a ferocious bolting animal to pummel him with her fists until he spoke the truth; but he was a daunting bear of a man, and although he used always to show her a most quiet and courteous disposition, she was awed by his massive strength.

She caught her hands together in front of her, her voice whipped from her throat as she realised her vulnerability. She took a step backwards, watching Wybert's stunned expression change until his face was filled with hard lines as he narrowed his eyes and advanced upon her.

'That barbarian is well out of your reach, and you shall not seek him out! I will have you bringing the name of Edwulf into disrepute no longer. By the holy saints, woman! Have you no idea of what is being said behind your back? What songs are being sung about you round the evening fires outside these walls? Have you no shame at all?'

Dena found herself trembling as she looked up into the teeth of his anger, but it was not through fear for her own life.

'You have *killed* him!'

'Killed him?' Wybert looked astonished. 'I would not waste a sharpened blade on that miserable wretch. Word has been sent to Edwulf to tell him what has happened. As soon as he arrives, talks about a ransom will be started. Until then, I suggest, no, I *order* you to conduct yourself like the lady you are supposed to be. Not even the lowest Saxon whore would disport herself before a Welshman as you have been doing.'

Her cheeks begin to burn alarmingly, and she drew breath to utter some retaliatory remark, but none came. Wybert turned away in disgust.

'What have you done with Mildthryth?' she managed to ask.

He whirled about in fury. 'What are you accusing me of now? Murdering Mildthryth? Why should I wish to do anything with her?'

Dena took another step backwards, away from those wildly gesticulating arms.

'She . . . She would never have let you take Rhodri without a fight.'

Wybert's arms fell limply to his sides, his whiskery mouth hanging open in stunned incomprehension. He shook his head in bewilderment. 'It was Mildthryth who asked me to take him back into my custody.'

'I do not believe you! She would never have done such a thing.'

He thrust his hands to his hips, the menace seething

between his crooked teeth as he spoke. 'That is your
trouble, girl. Your mind is addled. You believe every
lying syllable that Welshman tells you, but never the
people who took you to their breasts and gave you
shelter! You listened to that rogue, Gwylan, as you
might to some kind of pure-in-heart holy man when he
spoke of atrocities your uncle was supposed to have
committed. You never stopped to question his motives:
the reason he, both of them, took you to their hearts so
readily . . .'

Wybert shook his head again, sorrowfully now, as
though he knew his words were lost to her, as though he
realised he was wasting both his breath and his time; but
the seed had been sown, and Dena's mind was clouding,
stilling her tongue, confusing her thoughts.

'I have little care, now, if you believe me or not,' he
added wearily. 'I did, once, but not now. If you think the
only truth comes from the mouth of that cackling witch,
Mildthryth, go and ask her for it. She has returned to
Edwulf's people by the narrow bridge.'

He lifted the remains of his meal to his lips, but instead
of eating, looked at it for a moment before tossing it
aside and slinking out under the kitchen archway to the
main chamber beyond.

Dena stared at the space he had occupied, her hands
still caught in front of her as though in silent prayer.
Pictures of remembered events danced in her head.
Half-forgotten conversations took on new, deeper
meanings, and all the time Ethelin kept laughing at her.

'You are so naïve in these matters. Men of that rank
often play with the affections of unworldly girls. It is
merely a diversion for them.' Her tinkling laughter
echoed again and again through Dena's head.

She was naïve in the affairs of men. She had no

knowledge of the workings of their minds. How was she supposed to be able to tell lies from truths when she had no criteria with which to compare?

Yes, she had believed Gwylan when he had cursed Edwulf for the manner in which his lands had been seized; and yes, she did believe that he would have killed her when the tide of battle changed against him, even though she had not heard it from his lips. Such a man was capable of lying to her—obviously he was. But had he? It had been Wybert who had sent her to the north tun in the first place, a plan schemed with Mildthryth and Edwulf, even before Edwulf had left to join the King. Gwylan's attack had been expected and planned for.

And Wybert asked why she did not believe him . . . How could she believe him? How could she believe any of them?

She had believed in Rhodri when he had held her close, when he had spoken words of undying love. Surely he had not been toying with her as Ethelin insisted? No, it could not be true. She had seen his hurt at Gwylan's rebuff. That was not part of some game.

Yet the doubt was still there, small, but niggling. If only Rhodri had remained constant in his manner towards her instead of . . . But he believed she had wilfully betrayed him, that she was gaining prestige from the taunts and trials he was having to endure.

Dena raised her hands to cover her face as the cacophony of sights and sounds of the previous evening's spectacle came stinging back to her. He believed it was all her doing, she knew he did. Mildthryth could not have given him to Wybert, not knowing what would happen to him! It was beyond reason.

She kept repeating this conviction as she hurried out of the kitchen into the wattle-fenced compound outside.

Few people slept now. Boys were squatting over smoking fire-pits, building the flames ready to heat the kettles bearing the first meal of the day. Letting herself out of the tied gate in the fencing, she picked her way along the pathways fouled by humans and animals alike, drawn by the sound of barking hounds caged too long without exercise.

Edwulf's people were suffering like all the others living without the shelter of a thatched roof. They were tired through lack of sleep. They ached through lying on hard, damp ground and they shivered with the cold. None of these deprivations seemed to have touched Mildthryth. Dena found her bending over a steaming pot, slowly stirring the pungent contents with a long-handled spoon. She faltered a few paces from the old woman, recognising her, but unable to accept that she had apparently come to no harm at Wybert's hands. Dena stumbled on, her heart sinking with every step she took.

'Mildthryth?'

The old woman inclined her head and grunted as she saw who stood before her. 'Thought you would be coming.' She returned her attention to the pot.

Dena shuffled uncertainly. Even if the knowledge was not to her liking, she had to know; she had to hear it from Mildthryth's lips.

'Wybert says it was you who asked him to take custody of Rhodri.'

'That is correct.'

Dena's heart exploded. 'How could you! Wybert tortured him . . . You know he did. It was you who healed him. How could you give him back to Wybert so that he could be paraded in chains like that?'

Mildthryth kept at her gentle stirring. 'Prisoners are

always paraded like that. They are the trophies of the victors. Where have you lived that you have never seen this before?'

'Only captured outlaws! Rhodri is a prince, you said so yourself. To let him be chained . . .'

'How else could he have been restrained?' Mildthryth suddenly straightened, and looked pointedly at Dena through narrowed eyes.

'He did need restraining,' she emphasised heavily. 'Getting cunning as well as stronger was that young fox. He wanted his wings, his freedom.' She spat her contempt. 'He would have been cut down before he had seen the sky. Even I need sleep, and he could be patient. Oh, I watched him. He could be patient.' Her wandering eyes flashed to Dena once again. 'Is that what you wanted? For him to be cut down in the great chamber? His blood to stain the floor stones red?'

Dena was shaking her head even before she spoke. 'No, of course not.'

Mildthryth dipped the spoon into the boiling liquid and brought it to her lips to taste. She added a handful of the shredded herbs that were lying at her feet.

Dena found her tongue again. 'But to give him to Wybert! Was there no other way? Could you not have put a spell on him to make him be still?'

She knew she had said wrong by the manner in which Mildthryth turned to look at her.

'Do not mock matters of which you have no understanding.'

It was a quietly-spoken phrase, hardly above a whisper, and as flat in tone as a death-knell. It made Dena shudder, and she averted her eyes, afraid to meet the old woman's gaze.

'He is safe, if that is your worry. Do you think I would

let him leave my side if I thought otherwise?' Dena
raised her head to find Mildthryth grinning at her. 'I cast
the fates for him,' she simpered. 'I know.'

Dena gazed open-mouthed at her. More rumours and
half-truths surrounded Mildthryth than the legends of
the sea, but did she know . . . know for certain?

'Where is he, Mildthryth? I must see him.'

'No!' she spat. She began waving the dripping spoon
at Dena in earnest. 'You must not seek him out. You
must not see him at all. Lord Edwulf will return, and
they will start to talk about his ransom.'

Dena shook her head, remembering Rhodri's words
of hopelessness.

'His kin will not ransom him. He told me. If there is no
ransom forthcoming, he will be killed. His wish to
escape is not born out of heroism.'

'There is more to a ransom than money. Edwulf wants
his hall back. Gwylan will give it to him in exchange for
Rhodri.'

Dena thought for a moment. Could it be as simple as
that? Pictures began to form in her imagination, and
they made her flesh creep.

'No,' she said. 'No, Rhodri believes he will be used as
bait to ensnare Gwylan. They will all be killed.'

Mildthryth inclined her head like a bird listening for
danger. 'Perhaps.'

'*Perhaps?* We cannot allow this to happen, Mildthryth!
We must free him.'

'No! We must let the fates turn. You must not see him.
Swear it.' She pointed the spoon at Dena's throat like
a knife—or something more deadly. Dena found difficulty in swallowing. She had no doubt that Mildthryth
had the power to do anything she wanted.

'I swear,' she murmured.

The old woman grunted and turned back to her pot, the conversation ended. Dena could not let it end. All she could think of was Rhodri. Alone somewhere, chained hand and foot, he would be harbouring thoughts of her betrayal, planning retribution.

'*You* could see him,' she whispered, 'and take him a message?'

'No messages. Do you think I am a lovers' go-between? She raised her head and cackled like a mad-woman, her eyes glinting with inner thoughts. 'Me, pouring words of love and affection down our prince's ears . . .' She laughed again, more uproariously than before.

'You could tell him that I did not betray him.'

'He would not believe me. He believes only what he wishes to believe, like all men. There will be no messages. Now go. Do you think I bend over this fire to help my aching back? They ask for potions because they are ill. What do they expect? Does a blackbird leave the foulings of its unfledged in the nest? Does a fox litter its own den? Too many people are trying to live here now. Men were never meant to live in such numbers. Already the arguments have started, and now there is sickness. Soon they will begin to die—and then who will they seek to blame?'

Dena backed away, leaving Mildthryth to her mutterings. Rhodri was alive and seemingly free from further harm, and the fates looked good for him. What else could she ask, except to be at his side and at peace with him; but that was like asking for the moon to hold!

Perhaps, when Edwulf returned to begin talks about his ransom, she might be allowed to see Rhodri then, to speak with him, even just for a little while. Perhaps there would be no trickery. Perhaps Edwulf and Gwylan would mend their differences. Perhaps she could have the moon to hold. It was a hope, at least. A hope to cling to.

CHAPTER
ELEVEN

WITH NOTHING to do but sit and dwell on the occurrences of the last few days, Dena began to notice how other people reacted to her. Wybert had been right. She did have a reputation no woman would envy, and sitting alone with her thoughts was not helping to allay what the gossip-mongers were saying. With Elma's help she took a bath, groomed herself, and gently edged her way into the lives of the other ladies. The Lady Nearra welcomed her quietly, and the other women took their role from her. Ethelin was pleased to share the work of embroidering the new banner for her lost hall, but wary in case Dena offered any more disturbing antics which could put her own standing in jeopardy. Dena remained the soul of discretion.

Life went on unhindered for the ladies; sewing, gossiping, airing their prejudices, nursing intrigue, parading their vanities, anything to mask their unending boredom. And it was boring, sitting there waiting for something to happen, knowing that back in their own halls they guided life over their entire estates. Anything was seized upon as a diversion. Anything.

Ethelin had been smirking all the way through the morning meal. She had a piece of information she was eager to share with the others—after they had begged and courted her enough. Dena knew the signs. It was irksome when the other women played these games, but when Ethelin did it, Dena's stomach twisted.

'You know something,' Corliss sang in a lilting voice.

'Do tell?' urged Fleotig.

The others took up the cry. They were so much less restrained when the Lady Nearra was not there to cast a wearisome eye over proceedings.

'It is nothing,' Ethelin remarked, making a casual gesture with her hand.

'It is nothing,' Hunig mimicked. 'Ignore her.'

The women resolutely turned their attention away, only the odd flicker of an eye betraying this for what it was, another turn in the game. All was silent for a while, until Ethelin, brimming with girlish excitement, could stand it no longer.

'It is a *nothing* which had to be bought with a ring.'

At once the women tugged on the bait.

'A ring!'

'You gave a ring in payment for a favour?'

'A sapphire ring,' goaded Ethelin gently.

'A *sapphire* ring?'

Corliss hushed them all. 'Your brain is addled. What possible favour is worth a sapphire ring here?'

'Ah,' intoned Ethelin knowingly. 'Wait and see.'

A new rush of excitement simmered round the circle.

'This favour your ring brings . . . It is coming here?'

'Soon.'

As if to some prearranged signal, there was a sharp knock on the door of the bower. A hush fell over the assembled women and hopeful eyes slowly turned towards Ethelin.

The door opened, and a small, bearded man with tiny hunted eyes stepped across the threshold. As well as the usual dagger, he carried a short sword contained in a sheath hanging from a leather strap worn diagonally across his body; this was odd for any man not taking his turn to guard the wall. Ethelin stood, and with a sweep of her hand, beckoned him to their circle. He smiled a little in return, nodded, and stepped outside again. The curious ladies could make nothing of it at all.

Queen of all she surveyed, Ethelin preened before them, basking in the glory she already felt was hers. When the man returned, the ladies' gasps of surprise and astonishment were matched only by the sickening lurch of Dena's heart.

'I give you Rhodri ap Hywel, son of Gruffydd, a prince of the Welsh!'

It was a triumph for Ethelin, a triumph none of the other noblewomen could come near matching, and she knew it. She accepted her praises like a victorious warrior returning from the battlefield, but it was all a blur to Dena, half heard and distant as if carried to her senses on the wind.

'What have you saved me for?' screamed a memory. 'I wanted to die . . . by the sword, to die like a man. You have condemned me to a life of torture, of hell, the plaything of women!'

As the other women rose around her, Dena began to shake her head in a daze, trying to blot out the reality of Rhodri's words. Already a tearful knot of emotion was filling her chest, surging up her throat. She could do nothing . . . nothing but look at him and feel herself dying inside.

He looked fitter than she had expected. A dark beard was forming thickly on his face. His colour had returned to normal, and his eyes no longer had that hollow look of the dying about them. He wore the same filthy braies he had been wearing when captured, but he had been given a short smock, if not a tunic, to wear over them. He was still manacled at the wrist, a short length of chain allowing him some movement, but, thankfully, the leg-chains had gone and he could walk normally, although barefoot like a slave.

'Ladies, please restrain yourselves.' Ethelin's voice taking command again awoke Dena as if from a dream. 'The guard reminds me that his time with us here is short . . .' There was a rustle of disappointment. 'We must abide by the guard's judgment, ladies. We have no wish for him to encounter the wrath of my steward. If you could all sit, we could, perhaps, ask the prince some poignant question or other.'

Amid a flurry of giggles and ribald remarks, the women returned to their stools.

'After all,' continued Ethelin, still on her feet and standing so close to Rhodri that she could almost rub shoulders with him, 'how often do we have a prince in our midst? We have hardly been able to see a glimpse of him,' she pouted. 'At least, the majority of us have not. Have we, Dena?'

Her eyes turned to Dena, crouched round-shouldered on her stool, and all the other women, too, gazed at her. Slowly, she raised her head, not to acknowledge their expectant looks, but to meet the stare of the only pair of eyes which mattered in that circular bower.

Rhodri stared down at her, contempt and hatred flaring in his dark eyes. The betrayal was complete, now. She could feel it. It was not of her making, and yet, in a way, it was. But she could not have watched him die. Even if she had known in the beginning what would happen to him, she could not have stood in the misty greenness of that glade and watched his life be taken from him. She loved him.

Looking up at him as she did, she knew there was no mistake. No infatuation, no pity or compassion could taste as bitter as this. She loved him with all her heart, though she could never tell him so again. She could not bear for him to believe that her professed love was only another—a final—betrayal.

'How many men have died at your hands?'

Hunig's coyly asked question hit Dena like a lash across her back, but Rhodri did not take his eyes from her, or alter a muscle of his stance.

'Oh, do answer, prince,' teased Ethelin. 'Do not be modest.'

There was a flurry of giggles. Rhodri remained unmoved.

Ethelin crossed behind him to stand at his other shoulder, her eyes sweeping lasciviously up his form.

'I would not say you were particularly striking . . .' She drew a long-nailed finger down his arm from the shoulder to the elbow. 'But there must be something about you that makes you so appealing.'

'Perhaps we should ask Dena that question?'

The gasps of delight echoed loudly in her head, and then it was filling, filling with anger and resentment, filling to the point of bursting.

'Come, prince, let us all see what she finds so beguiling. Take off the smock.'

'No!'

Dena was on her feet, her fists clenched tightly by her side in an attempt to stop herself from shaking with the pent-up fury raging inside her.

'Enough! There has been enough!' She searched for some understanding in their sullen faces, but they gave back only belligerence for her having interrupted their frivolity.

'What kind of women are you to do this?'

'Pay no heed to her.'

Every head turned to stare at Rhodri, everyone silenced by his drawling tone. With his audience captivated, he slowly turned a pair of shining dark eyes on Ethelin at his side, and gave her a smile that would have stopped any woman's heart.

'She is merely jealous that another woman should find me . . . shall we say . . . appealing.'

His words hung in the air for everyone to savour, for everyone to interpret in their own way: the same way.

The nervous guard stepped forwards to grip Rhodri's arm, but before he had a chance to drag him backwards, Ethelin raised a hand and motioned him aside. Dena watched in disbelief as Ethelin lifted her face to Rhodri's, the corners of her mouth curling in a blatantly tantalising smile.

'And how are you . . . appealing?'

There was a dull clinking as Rhodri lifted his manacled hands and traced his fingertips down her headcloth.

'Surely you can guess?'

The noblewomen held their breath, as if the slightest sound might break the charged enchantment leaping between the two. Dena could only stand transfixed.

'Guess?' prompted Ethelin, her eyes as large as a maid's on her first courting.

Rhodri passed behind her, catching her shoulders with his hands, delicately massaging her skin through the fine cloth of her kirtle. Ethelin responded with desire to every sensual move he made.

'Look at her,' Rhodri urged, dropping his face so that it appeared just over Ethelin's shoulder. 'She stands there so pale, as silent as a mouse . . .'

Dena felt herself begin to blush, as all eyes turned to her.

'Who would believe that such as she would claw at my chest, begging me for more . . .'

The cry of strangled glee which erupted in the bower was short-lived, but hid Rhodri's movement long enough to take everyone except Dena unawares. Her lips opened to shout a warning, but no sound came from them, and she watched, mesmerised, as he thrust Ethelin into the guard, sending them both sprawling to the floor.

Dena raised her hands to her mouth in horror as she saw Rhodri draw the man's sword, but the screams of terror ringing in her ears did not come from her constricted throat.

Amid the flailing limbs of the unbalanced couple, Rhodri hacked down with the swinging blade, sending a shower of hot blood across the closed door. Ethelin rolled clear of the guard to sit dazed and uncomprehending; until she saw the sticky mass of red glistening on her kirtle and her hands. Her face creased in lines of terror, and she scampered on her hands and knees across the floor to try to lose herself amongst the other cowering women.

Rhodri turned on them all, his teeth gritted, his eyes wide and wild, as Mildthryth's words came streaming back to Dena.

'You will never reach the wall, Rhodri! You will be cut down!'

The chains clinked at his wrist as he swung the sword about, its bloody point pressing against Dena's chest.

'Out of the way!' he screamed at her.

In that moment she knew his goal was not the wall and the freedom of the forest. This was his death fight, his last attack on every Saxon who had ever tortured and taunted him. He would die, but he would die in a pool of blood of his own making.

'No! Rhodri, you cannot! I beg you!'

Her cries for his mercy were in vain, and she knew it. As he bobbed to go round her, she moved too, always keeping her own breast to the point of the sword, keeping herself between him and his intended victims.

'They are the same as the whores in Edward's court. Move, Dena!'

'No! If you wish to kill, then kill *me*! Let my body be the first to fall.'

It was like listening to a tree crack open in the forest. Oblivious to the screams around them, their hard stares were only for each other. Dena could hear each laboured breath as Rhodri dragged it between his teeth. She could see the rise and fall of his chest beneath the coarse cloth of the cream-coloured smock, and taste the shining perspiration rising on his skin.

He turned the sword in his hand. The point dripped blood at her feet. The door thudded into the limp body of the dead guard, and he whirled about, ready to meet his attackers, a new intensity rippling across his taut muscles. The heavy corpse did not move, and the door held fast.

The bower shook as if the very earth was moving. Grit and dust fell in a shower from the thatching. Dena watched a tapestry rise and fall as the wattle wall behind it was smitten from the outside. Men were hacking their way in.

She turned to Rhodri, the panic rising in her throat, but his attention was caught by a renewed attack on the door. Under the concerted weight of those pushing behind it, the dead guard was slowly being moved aside. Bit by bit the door was opening.

Again the bower shook as the giant blade of a battle-axe tore through splintered wood and embroidered cloth alike to hang there a moment, like an animal sensing its prey, before being pulled free, ready to strike again.

Tears of despair rose to blind Dena's eyes as she saw Rhodri's hunted look changed to one of futility.

'Oh, Rhodri . . .' she breathed.

He turned to her, but he could see only the cowering, screaming women at her back. Her heart twisted as she saw the burning light of hatred rekindle in his eyes. They both moved at the same time, he with his sword-arm raised in vengeance, she to intercept his thrust.

'No, Rhodri, no!'

She pushed her hands flat against his chest, straining as she laid her weight against him, but it was like trying to hold a falling cliff.

'Dena, get away . . .'

She heard the clink of his wrist-chain as it draped behind her head, felt it tighten and be drawn rigid down her headcloth to her shoulders. She was being pushed back, bent backwards by the sheer weight of him. Her body arched beneath his onslaught, and she gasped as his teeth gnawed feverishly at the side of her neck. Then his lips were upon hers, devouring her, his darting tongue searching for every crevice in her mouth.

Dena dug her fingers into his chest as if she would never let him go. The smock was moulded to his body like a second skin, soaked in his sweat. She could feel every muscle, the stretching of every sinew, the hardness of his ribs in that slender body she ached for, clung to.

The blow sent them both reeling. Dena struck her head on the hard-packed earthen floor and her senses flew. She felt Rhodri's weight upon her, heard the chink of his wrist-chain as she was extricated from his manacled arms. His weight was lifted from her, and a desperate voice screamed in panic in her head. She rolled over, pushing at the floor with her hands, trying to gain her feet, but she could not get up. When she raised her head to look for Rhodri, she saw him through a forest of legs being pummelled unceasingly with the hilt of hand-held weapons.

'No!' she screamed. 'No!' They did not stop their death-dealing blows, and she could not be sure if her words had been real or imagined.

She reached out to him, but the forest of legs moved, and he was dragged through the door, the clinging smock oozing crimson across his chest. With a choking sob, Dena closed her eyes.

'My lady? My lady?'

Dena could hear voices, women's voices. There was crying, too, and an occasional heartrending wail. She became aware of a cold wet pad across the back of her neck. The water was trickling down the body of her kirtle. Aches began to make themselves felt, aches and bruises and a hammering in her head. She tried to rise, and found herself being helped.

'Are you well, my lady?'

Dena nodded to relieve Elma's anxiety, but she soon wished she had not. With the pain returned the memory, the fear and the horror. She clasped Elma by the shoulders, staring wildly into the girl's face.

'Where have they taken him? What have they done to him?'

Elma's expression changed from that of surprise to one of resigned irritation. The violence that Rhodri had felt now surged through Dena's veins. She tightened her grip on the maid and shook her, her voice almost reaching screaming pitch.

'Where *is* he, Elma?'

The girl turned pale and moistened her lips, looking at Dena as though she had lost her senses.

'The pillory-stake,' she stammered. 'He has been taken to the pillory-stake before the main doors of the hall.'

Dena flung her backwards and struggled to her feet. She thrust through the milling people helping to restore calm to the noblewomen, and darted out of the bower and along the cobbled walkway to the corner of the hall.

Every person who had taken refuge within the defensive walls of Lord Baldric's dwelling seemed to be thronging the space in front of the hall. They stood shoulder to shoulder, shouting and cursing, screaming for the death of every Welshman who had ever lived. Dena called for a passage through, but none was made for her, and she had to push and prise herself past each man and woman in turn.

Without warning, the crowd parted, and Dena stumbled forward to find herself facing Wybert. The colour of his face told of the rage he felt, his white, staring eyes the madness Mildthryth had warned against.

'You! I told you not to seek him out! Not to go near him!'

Dena felt the power drain from her limbs. She shook her head, trying to back away. The crowd pushed forward. There was nowhere to escape to.

'I did not.' She lifted her arms to protect herself as he lunged towards her. 'Believe me, I did not!'

Instead of the expected blow, Wybert lifted her bodily off the ground, took hold of her round the waist and tucked her like a squealing pig beneath his huge arm.

It was an ungainly ride, suspended there, and she would have fought him, however uselessly, had it not been for the unexpected reaction of the heaving throng. Someone hit her on her rump, another across one arm. Blows began to rain down on her from every side, and the hate issuing from their lips astounded her.

Then she was free from them, if not from their voices. Bewildered, she watched as her hands were tied. She was tossed on to the back of a horse, and the trailing thongs of her restraint fastened to the saddle.

She looked about her for someone to call for help, and saw Rhodri hanging half-senseless by his wrist-chain looped over the top of the pillory-stake. Dena felt as though a knife-blade was twisting in her chest.

'Rhodri . . .' she screamed. 'Oh, Rhodri!'

Heads moved across her line of vision. A man stepped up, carrying a bundle of dry brush across his back. He tipped his load at Rhodri's feet. Dena's breath froze.

'No!' she shrieked. She tried to pull herself free from the horse, but her writhing only made the animal skittish. She turned to Wybert.

'No, please, I beg of you!' Tears were streaming down her cheeks now, her head rolling on her neck in her anguish. 'You cannot do this!'

Wybert ignored her. 'Take her away before I burn her with him.'

The horse began to move forward, away from Wybert, away from Rhodri. Dena turned in the saddle as far as her tied hands would allow. Rhodri was regaining consciousness; she could tell that by the movement of his head. Someone threw water into his face to quicken his recovery. The pile of sticks at his feet grew larger.

'Rhodri!' she shouted. If he should have to die, let their gaze meet one last time. Let him know how much she loved him!

'Rhodri!'

He never raised his head towards her. Her voice was drowned by the unanimous call for vengeance. Clods of earth and excrement sailed through the air to hit her on the back, on the head, in the face. She bowed over the saddle, trying to escape the tirade, looking ahead past the guard leading her horse to the yawning gateway and the forest beyond.

Then she saw a figure standing alone by the wall. It was Mildthryth, waiting there for her to pass.

Dena's head shot up, her own pain forgotten. 'Mildthryth! Do something! Anything!'

The old woman's eyes turned up to meet Dena's, and slowly she shook her head.

'It is the scheme of things.'

'But the fates . . .' she pleaded, turning in her saddle to keep Mildthryth in view as the horse walked on.

'Ay, the fates.' She shook her head again. 'You saw him, Dena. You saw him.'

CHAPTER
TWELVE

DENA'S ESCORT did not follow the main track into the forest, but turned abruptly right as soon as her horse was clear of the gate, to lead round the perimeter of the outer defence ditch. She could only look back helplessly.

Rhodri . . . So close and yet so far.

The grey stone wall which towered beyond the ditch stood unyielding, shielding her eyes from the horror within, from the tormented souls who chanted hatred in the same voice in which they chanted the Christian Mass. Even the watchers had deserted their positions on the wall.

Rhodri . . .

Dena dragged her eyes from what she could not see, and stared at the rawhide thongs which bound her hands to the front of the saddle. She pulled and strained, trying to stretch the ties enough to work her slim hands free, but she only succeeded in tightening them further, tightening them until the rough edges of the narrow bindings grew sharp and chafed her wrists.

The guard turned his horse across the harvested fields and Dena's mount obediently followed, caring more for the tug on its lead rein than the squirming rider on its back. The cultivated land was narrow here, the forest close, a deeply-cut stream-bed acting as the natural border between them. The guard led the horses down into the shallow gurgling water and up the further bank. The yellowing trees swallowed them with hardly a stir.

Dena worked harder, faster, knowing all the while it

was to no avail. She worked in a frenzy, ignoring the pain, ignoring the blood. It was no hope at all, but she had to cling to it, had to use it to keep Mildthryth's judgment at bay.

'You saw him, Dena. You saw him.'

'No! I did not seek him out. I did not! The fates could not be so cruel . . .'

The single rise of exultation came muffled to her ears, but it came. It penetrated her mind, stilling her thoughts, smothering her anguish.

She listened. She held her breath and she listened, but no more cries reached her from the hall. There was no need of any more. Slowly, she began to breathe again. She could not believe what her mind was telling her. She would not believe it. She turned in her saddle to look up at the skyline, to prove that she was wrong . . . but her sight never rose above the first limbs of the swaying birch-trees. She could not bear to look higher, to see the smoke rising to the heavens. She could not bear it.

She hunched over the saddle until her forehead touched the raggy mane of the horse, her grief leaving her in huge, racking sobs.

Rhodri was dead. She prayed, begged, that, by now, Rhodri was dead.

Like the journey to Lord Baldric's hall taken only a few days previously, Dena knew little of the ride. The trees dappled their autumnal colours above her head, about her face, under the steady plodding of the horses' hooves, but to her there was no beauty in it, only a death-like finality which heralded the coming of a never-ending winter. They did not stop except once, just briefly, to let the horses rest.

Dena looked down at the guard's face so close to hers,

knowing that he had spoken to her, but having no memory of his words. She had not realised that the horses had stopped walking, that her escort had dismounted. She found it difficult to accept that such a simple action could have occurred without her knowledge, but it had. He stood there, looking up at her, staring up into her face, seeing . . . seeing what? What could he see that she could no longer feel? She tried to speak to him, to ask him, but the words would not come, and then they were moving again, and he was not standing before her eyes any longer, but riding the horse in front, as if he had been plucked from her side by magic, as if a spell had been cast on him, or her . . . Perhaps the spell had been cast on her . . .

Darkness came like a rising tide, carried on the silent beating of a bat's wing. An eerie screech of an owl was echoed again and again through the trees. Far away a wolf sang its chilling song to the moon.

Dena thought she saw its eyes shining through the trees, bright, yellow, flickering, but the knowledge brought no fear to her heart, which she found strange until she reasoned that it could not have been a wolf but more likely another being of the night, perhaps even Mildthryth in a changed form watching her, stalking her, ill-wishing her for laying her eyes, her hands, her curse upon Rhodri.

Dena watched the yellow eye grow, a single eye, a guttering eye, an omnipresent eye shedding light to the four corners of the world. She lifted her head to bathe her face in its glory. It reached out its wind-whipped flames for her eyes, to blind her, to engulf her, to make her a part of its eye, a golden fleck in its raging iris.

The eye grew dim with shadow, the shadow of a man's head, her guard's head, looking up at her, cutting her bonds, lifting her from the horse's back. He had no limbs, no body, only a head encircled by the searing yellow light of the eye behind him. A cup came to her lips, a wooden bowl, a bitter liquid forcing itself between her lips. He peered at her, the guard's head, peered at her with shining yellow eyes, lighted eyes, sons of the omnipresent eye which glowed about his head. And she drank. She drank.

It was a cave. Dena had lain there for some time, looking at the rock above her head, tracing her sight over its sharp contours, over its green and purple lichen. It was a cave. There was no other explanation. It had to be a cave. Where was she?

She tensed as the light grew dim and then bright again. It was as though someone had paused in front of a window, paused and then passed by. There were no windows in caves, only entrances, guarded entrances. The man was close. He was humming, trying to sing some half-remembered song.

'Yes, you are awake at last. That is good. Yes.'

Dena shuddered and turned her head to face the man. He was not her escort at all, but much older. His weatherbeaten head had shrunk with age and looked like a child's on top of wide, bent shoulders. He had no hair, except for a few spiky whiskers clinging to his chin. He kept nodding and smiling as he approached, which made him appear all the more grotesque. She tried to back away, but his movements belied his age, and she flinched as a gnarled hand shot out from a sleeve of his dusty brown robe to touch her forehead.

'Yes, there is no fever. That is good. Yes.' He kept nodding and smiling, as if he could do no other.

Dena struggled to a sitting position, pulling the filthy,

worn cloak which had been her cover in front of her
hunched knees. It could offer no protection, but it was
all she had. She peered over the man's shoulder to the
mouth of the shallow cave. Beyond, she could see an
oak, its low-hung branches dancing in the wind, its russet
leaves being scattered like giant coloured snowflakes. Of
her escort, there was no sign.

'Do you have a memory? Yes, do you remember?'

She remembered Rhodri. Her chest heaved as she
remembered Rhodri, but the journey . . . The journey
was indistinct, hazy, like a dream.

'I do not remember coming here,' she said slowly. 'I
remember a lighted eye, and a . . .' A floating head, but
that could not be right.

'Do you know why you are here? Yes.'

All puzzling thoughts of the journey flew from Dena's
mind. She stared at the old man, a cold clamminess
creeping up her spine.

'No,' she whispered hoarsely.

'I know not, either,' he conceded, still nodding. 'A
nunnery is the place for you, not a hermitage. Yes, not a
hermitage.'

Dena looked at him in surprise. She altered her
position a little to give her a better view of all the walls of
the cave, and there, in a natural alcove, was carved a
cross bearing the Saviour in the most delicate relief. She
saw the old man with different eyes. The robes he wore
were like a monk's. His feet were as bare as his head.

'You are a holy man?' It was hardly a question which
needed answering now, but she felt she had to ask it.

'Some say yes, some say no. I serve the Lord, and all
mankind who wish to cross the marsh. Yes. In safety I
take them across the marsh.'

'Is my escort still here? The horses.'

The hermit nodded.

'No horses. No one here but ourselves and our Lord.'

She had been left. She felt strangely puzzled about her fate. What had been in Wybert's mind when he had despatched her to this place?

Wybert . . . The very name brought the blood rushing through her veins. He had taken Rhodri and tortured him, kept him in chains like a baited bear and humiliated him, dragged him into the courtyard, and . . .

'They burned him, burned him to death!'

All the anguish, all the horror, came hurtling back, and she held her head in her hands and sobbed.

'Was he a good man?'

She stared at the hermit through her blurring tears. It was not a question she had expected. She had never thought of Rhodri in terms of good or bad. He was just a man, but like no other she had met, like no other she could ever hope to meet. She had felt fear in his company, but also protection, trust and, most of all, love.

Oh, what pain that love could bring, what wonders. She had barely known them, but it had been enough. In the violence of that bower his touch had unleashed a surging passion, the power of which she would never know again; but it was enough, enough to know that he loved her as she loved him.

She nodded her head in an unconscious imitation of the old hermit. 'Yes,' she murmured. 'He was a good man. Will you pray for him?'

'I shall pray for you. You can pray for him. Yes; but not here. In the sleeping-hall. Yes, in the sleeping-hall.'

The hermitage did not consist merely of the old man's cave. It was a large rectangular place bordered by a stream on one side and ditched, but not palisaded, on the other, boundaries leading into the face of a rocky outcrop that contained the cave. It sat directly across the narrow track, rather like an inn, but Dena could not tell which way led back to Lord Baldric's hall and which to the marsh the old man had spoken of.

Even though Dena had never heard of the place, travellers seemed to use the hermitage regularly, for there was stabling and a good supply of hay to hand. The grass was short underfoot, as if well cropped, and in some places worn away completely. The sleeping-hall was large compared with the cave, and could easily have held twenty people or more. A wooden cross, almost a replica of the one carved in stone on the cave wall, hung from a beam, and it was here, in quiet contemplation, that Dena spent most of her time.

When visitors did arrive, she was not eager to welcome them. She looked at the young man before her, and at the other two who had dismounted behind him. She could not recollect seeing them at Lord Baldric's hall, but there had been so many people crowded in that small space that it would have been difficult to remember every face. He had said his name was Bemere, which she had no reason to doubt, and he had called her 'my lady' and bowed slightly, something she found incongruous under the circumstances.

'I have no wish to return with you,' she said at last. 'I have lain my head upon the warm, sweet grass and slept here three nights. There is no malice here. There is no greed. Until the hermit bids me to leave, I shall stay.'

Bemere let his eyes fall for a moment before returning to meet her gaze. 'This is no request. It is an order.'

The bitterness Dena had vowed to keep in check rose like bile in her throat.

'Return to the steward Wybert and tell him that I . . .'

'Your uncle sends us on this errand. It is *his* order we carry.'

Bemere's simple statement snatched all force from her words.

'Edwulf has returned?'

'Yes, my lady, in great victory, with packhorses laden with booty from the battlefield.'

It seemed unbelievable that her uncle should ever return: he seemed to have been away for so long. Dena shook her head dismally. Why could he not have returned three days before?

'It is true, my lady. Lord Baldric, too. They rode hard when news of the Welsh uprising reached them.'

'There never was an uprising,' she murmured. She had said those words so often. When would someone believe her?

Bemere carried on as if he had not heard her at all. 'They do not stay long, my lady. They have to regain the king's company as soon as they can. Do you hear me, Lady Dena? We have to return at once.'

She looked into his earnest face and saw the eagerness to please his lord caught in the gentleness of the youth's hazel eyes. What use was there to try and fight against the will of men? Perhaps Edwulf would listen to her. Perhaps she could gain some little recompense for Rhodri against Wybert, but she doubted it. She doubted whether anything at all would have changed.

She turned to the old man, hovering quietly at the back of her.

'I thank you for giving me shelter, hermit. I hope I shall be allowed to return, if only for a short visit.'

'Yes, yes. You return. I shall guide you across the marsh.'

Dena smiled at him. She wondered if he ever listened

to what people said. Across the marsh lay the lands of the Welsh.

The journey was as any journey along a narrow forest track. Often it was easier to walk than to ride. The occasional open glade, with its views of distant blue mountains, became a source of welcome relief from the monotony of the endlessly twisting path they followed.

They rode together in a bunch: a lead, Dena, Bemere, and the last youth bringing up the rear. The young men spoke rarely and looked back often. Dena began to take notice only as a release from her encroaching boredom.

They were a youthful trio, only Bemere being of her age. Apart from the customary knives, one carried a cudgel, the other two swords. There was not a shield between them, or any other sort of arms, much less a protective cap or thick leather jerkin such as Gwylan's men had worn. And yet there was a likeness, in the eyes. A hunted look she had seen but fleetingly in Gwylan.

'Are we being followed?' she asked.

Bemere was quick to grasp her words. 'Why do you say that? Have you heard something?'

She shook her head, surprised at the panic in his voice. 'I thought I heard a horse whinny a while ago.' He gazed back along the trail. 'It is difficult to be sure when the wind blows at the tree tops.'

'I heard nothing,' said one of his companions.

Bemere was not put at his ease. 'One of us should go back along the path.'

There were no volunteers.

'Clif, go quietly. Call if all is well. Ride like the wind if it is not.'

Dena watched the youth turn his horse and ride away. It seemed ridiculous to split so small a group, but she did

not speak of it. Her fears were fixed more on who it was
who followed. Bemere believed it was the Welsh, she
could see it in his eyes, but she was returning to Edwulf
to tell her version of past events. There was no denying
that it would be a different story from that told him by
Wybert.

She stole searching glances at her guards as they
carried on up the path. An escort of three sounded
substantial if they were seasoned fighting men, but
gawky youths with hardly a show of stubble between
them? Perhaps this was why they had been sent to collect
her. Their hacked remains would be ascribed to Welsh
vengeance, no matter who had held the sword.

They plodded along the track without a word.
Bemere's eyes turned more to the rear than to the front,
but there was no sign of Clif. Dena did not think they
would ever see him again. There was a fluttering in her
chest which grew worse until it hurt to breathe. Nervous
perspiration oozed from every pore, making her kirtle
stick uncomfortably to her back and the reins slip in her
hands.

'Bemere!'

Instinctively they held in their horses and looked back
along the path.

'Bemere! It is well!'

Their relief was short-lived. The trickery was evident
as soon as the first man turned the curve. Bemere
grasped the reins to Dena's horse in an effort to make a
fast escape, but as the track filled with armed men on
both sides, they could do little except stand and watch
them approach. Bemere drew his sword. His companion
held his cudgel close, but to fight was useless, the
numbers too many.

Clif lived. He was still astride his horse, his hands

clasped behind his back. Beside him rode the familiar figure of Gwylan, to Dena's knowledge the only one of his band who could speak the Saxon tongue. She smiled in her relief. Whatever Lord Gwylan had in mind, she was pleased it was not Wybert.

She turned to Bemere. 'Lay down your weapons.'

The youth seemed to be in two minds.

'Do you want to be cut down where you stand? Lay down your weapons! I know this man. Let me speak with him.'

Looking heavenwards for aid, Bemere let his sword slip from his hand to land on the stony ground at his horse's hooves. His companion's cudgel quickly followed. Dena sat straight-backed on her horse and tried to look more confident than she felt.

'Greetings, Lord Gwylan.'

'Good-day to you, Lady Dena! It warms my heart that we should be able to travel the same path again so soon.' He grinned at her, his dark eyes twinkling with delight.

'Are you saying that you, too, are riding to Lord Baldric's hall?'

'Yes, to make some sort of peace with your uncle. I still hold that hall he built on my land, but I feel I have a much firmer hand now that, once again, I hold his niece as well.'

So that was it. Dena could not keep her chuckle of irony to herself. 'I always seem to be a hostage in your hands.'

Gwylan shrugged and turned his fingers with a flourish in the air before him. 'It is the way of things.'

It seemed to Dena that Gwylan was in a very affable mood. She glanced at the dispirited Clif on the horse beside him. The youth's tunic and smock had been torn down the front to expose his chest, the cloth at his waist

dyed red with blood from a wound hidden by the edge of
his smock.

'Have no worries about his health,' Gwylan told her.
'He is more ashamed than hurt.'

'Was there any need to harm him at all?'

'I had to know if you were meeting anyone along the
way. He would not say, and did not believe me when I
threatened to disembowel him.' He tossed his head in
Clif's direction. 'He changed his mind when he saw the
colour of his own blood.'

Dena found it hard to control her distaste. 'The word
about you is correct, my lord. You *are* barbaric.'

Gwylan merely chuckled. 'But of course, my lady. Of
course.'

'May he be freed now, or do you intend to bind us all
hand and foot?'

He turned and muttered something in his own tongue.
It took no time at all to cut Clif's bonds. The youth
massaged his wrists a little and inspected his chest, but
even Dena could see that the wound had been made only
for show. The blood had already clotted, the gash
knitting without any help from a herbalist. Bemere
caught his attention, and Clif bade his horse walk forward until he reached his two companions.

Gwylan eyed them critically. 'They make a puny
escort.'

Dena sighed. 'I believe they were chosen for that
reason. I fear I am to be murdered along this route.'

Gwylan's eyes widened until the white shone all round
the dark iris. She did not think he could have shown such
surprise at anything.

'Who plans this?'

'The steward Wybert. To explain would be to relate a
story full of twists and turns. It is easier to say that

Wybert would rather not have me speaking to my uncle.'

Gwylan clamped his mouth shut until it was lost in the curly wool of his beard. His grunt of indignation was missed by no one.

'Wybert be cursed! This is Edwulf's treachery. He knew this would be the route we would take. There is no need to wonder why he stipulated our arrival on the morrow!'

He slapped a clenched fist into his open palm, the sharp retort startling the horses. He looked at her with fierce, narrowed eyes.

'It seems you are not so much another hostage as another sacrifice, young Dena. You are taking it very calmly.'

She could do little but agree. 'I have lived years in these last few days. I cannot rekindle the zest in my heart.'

The anger seeped away as he looked at her. He seemed tired himself.

'It saddens me to hear that.'

For some reason she felt embarrassed by his concern. She shuffled in her saddle, looking down the length of the track to his men crowded there.

'I find it strange that you should be so willing to venture into Edwulf's hands.'

Gwylan snorted. 'A man cannot always load the dice in his favour. While he holds Rhodri, there is little I can do to call the terms.' Dena felt the colour drain from her face, but Gwylan was too busy shaking his head to notice. 'I thought I might foil any trap he could lay by arriving a day early, but with all this treachery afoot . . .'

'There is more than you imagined,' Dena stated flatly. 'Rhodri was burned to death three days ago.'

Gwylan turned ashen. It was Bemere who spoke.

'My lady, no! You speak of plots to murder you . . . Do you want these Welshmen to gut us all as we stand here? I beg you, please, tell the truth.'

Dena bowed her head over her horse's neck. She could hardly speak for the tide of emotion rising swiftly up her throat. 'It is the truth.'

Bemere turned directly to Gwylan, the pleading in his voice bordering on anguish.

'No, believe me, my lord. The nobleman Rhodri lives. It was he who instructed Lord Edwulf that the Lady Dena should return.'

Dena shook her head as she cried, her words drowned by waves of horrifying memories.

'It is true,' Bemere insisted.

Gwylan drew his lips into a thin line and leant heavily on the pommel of his saddle.

'She does not believe so. Dena, stop that wailing. We do not travel another step until this matter is decided.'

She had cried the first day at the hermitage, slept little the first night for her grief, but had not wept since. She had believed that her heart and mind had accepted Rhodri's death. It seemed she had only tricked herself into burying her pain in a grave as shallow as his.

'Now,' Gwylan continued, 'let us have the truth of this.' He pointed to Dena to begin.

'Rhodri was brought to the ladies' bower. My aunt had bribed his guard. They wanted to liven their boredom by teasing him, like a game, baiting some animal . . . He killed the guard and would have killed the women, too, but . . . He was overpowered, and dragged to the pillory-stake, and everyone was shouting, and throwing things, and . . . and they piled sticks at his feet.'

The sobs were coming again—Dena could not stop them. Everything she spoke of so vaguely she could see in vivid detail as though she were reliving it.

Bemere took up the story. 'You saw no more. Wybert tied you to a horse and had you taken to the hermitage.'

'Why?' Gwylan's simple question took them both by surprise.

Bemere shrugged uneasily. 'The people were angry. They might have burned the Lady Dena along with the Welshman. Nobody likes a woman who whores with an enemy, especially a noblewoman.'

Dena's head shot up, her eyes wide and fierce. 'I did not whore with him!'

Bemere snorted derisively. 'It was clear to us all.'

'Then I curse you for your blindness!'

'Quiet!' Gwylan commanded. He turned to Dena. 'Did you see him burn?'

'No,' she conceded. 'But I heard the roar of the people.'

'A roar, perhaps, but it was not because he burned.' More confident now, Bemere looked at her as he might at a misguided child.

'The Lady Nearra sent a group of armed men to beat back the mob, and the Welshman was taken to her chamber. The steward Wybert went, too. No one knows what was said there, but rumour had it that his temper was not to be tested.' He paused momentarily, as if weighing matters in his mind.

'There were other rumours, too, of intrigue and plots.' He glanced cautiously at Dena. 'There were so many rumours that nobody gave much truth to any. Our lords arrived the next day with horses loaded with booty. The fyrd has been returning ever since with tales from the battlefield. It seems it was a great victory.'

Gwylan moved his weight in his saddle. 'Well, Dena? Could Lord Baldric's wife have taken such a step? What reason would she have had?'

Dena felt she was floating in a dream. To speak would be to destroy the softness encompassing her.

Rhodri was alive? It did not seem possible, too improbable for even a hope, yet she wanted to hope. Her whole being was flooding with new hope. Rhodri was alive!

'Dena, could this have happened?'

'It might. Wybert kept insisting that the Welsh people were rising in arms all along the border. Again and again I told Lady Nearra that this was false. I think, in the end, she began to believe me. At least, she had doubts about the truth of Wybert's allegation.'

Gwylan pursed his lips and nodded in comprehension. 'Now I understand why there were so many groups of men patrolling the paths. The fox!' He turned to Bemere. 'The fyrd that returns . . . how many were lost? Half? A quarter?'

Bemere scoffed. 'Hardly a man from Lord Baldric's estate.'

Gwylan let out a long, tired sigh and rubbed his face with an open palm. Dena feared they were both thinking the same thing.

'Do you believe Edwulf will have an army waiting for you?'

'I would, if I were in his position.'

Dena looked down the track at the groups of Welshmen taking their ease. Some stood watching, some sat sharing a joke, others tended their horses, inspected their arms, cast dice to pass the time. They were as any Saxon men, loyal to their lord, loyal unto death.

Dena shook her head. 'You cannot go, Gwylan. You

cannot lead them into such a trap.'

'It may not exist.'

'It does. Believe me, it does! Rhodri knew he would be used as the bait to ensnare you.'

'And Rhodri? Should I leave him to his fate?'

'I can go. I can speak to the Lady Nearra, to Lord Baldric.'

'And your murderers along the route?'

Dena groaned. She had forgotten them. 'Give me some of your men as escort . . .'

Gwylan shook his head. 'You clutch at straws, Dena, and you have lost all sight of what we are fighting for. It is the land, Dena. Not Rhodri's life, not my life or the lives of my men. It is the land.'

He tossed back his head, his eyes shining with inner emotion as he looked at the trees about him, looked at them as if he knew them, as if they had once been his friends—once, long ago.

Dena felt her heart go out to him. Now, perhaps for the first time, she began to understand the reason for all the fighting, for all the treachery.

'Are you sure that all these lives are worth it?'

Gwylan looked at her dispassionately, a man feeling his wounds, feeling his years. 'Without the land, there is no life for any of us, only slavery.'

He sat tall in the saddle, calling his men to make ready. 'We go on, young Dena. I have crossed the marsh once this day. I do not cross it twice . . .' He grinned at her, his eyes twinkling with renewed vitality. 'Not unless I have been raiding Lord Baldric's cattle.'

At any other time she might have found amusement in his remark, but not then. His show of bravado sounded like a heavy door bolted shut before her face; a slab of roughly-hewn stone turned to seal a grave.

CHAPTER THIRTEEN

DENA AND her youthful Saxon escort rode in the centre of the body of Welshmen, the place Gwylan had decided would be the most safe if they were attacked, but if enemies were waiting along the route, they did not show themselves. Dena did not know whether to feel relieved or embarrassed. After all, she had no proof of anyone's ill intent, and from the cold attitude of her disarmed company it was clear that they believed her fears to be merely wanderings of her fevered imagination.

Everyone grew quiet as they neared Lord Baldric's hall. Had a man swung a sword, Dena would have not been surprised to see the tension fall in solid blocks on each side of the narrow track. No man bade his horse move forward without first peering through the under-growth. She kept her eyes to the front, firmly fixed on the heavy leather jerkin of the man on the horse before her. This was a trap—she knew it was. Her wildly beating heart kept telling her so, but what form would it take? When would it come?

Why was all so quiet? They were close enough to the defensive walls of Lord Baldric's hall to have been able to hear the people going about their everyday tasks. There should have been some noise, the calls of the animals, something . . .

It had been quiet like this when the Saxons had attacked them in that misty glade, when Rhodri had first been taken prisoner. Rhodri . . . was he truly alive—or was he dead? Dena was not certain any more. Had her

small escort been picked because they would offer no
resistance to the enemy, or had they been selected
because they could lie so convincingly? They had fallen
so easily to Gwylan, given information so readily. Had
there been a victory over the Norwegians, or was that a
lie, too? Hundreds of men fell during a battle. Could it
be possible that hardly a one had been lost from Lord
Baldric's estate? Was Gwylan's belief real or feigned?
What *was* Gwylan planning to do?

If only she could calm her imagination, but she was
looking for answers, looking for exits where there were
none. Her horse stopped without her giving a touch to its
reins. All the horses had stopped. The cold grey stone of
Lord Baldric's defences rose, unconquerable, across the
narrow field. They had arrived.

Dena raised herself as high as she could to see over the
heads of the Welshmen. In the field, to the right of the
track, opposite the open gateway to the hall, a long
trestle table had been set with food and jugs. Men stood
at the further side of it: her uncle, Lord Baldric, a line of
armed men a little behind, but there was no sign of
Wybert, or of Rhodri. Gwylan, accompanied by a small
group of his own retainers, had left his horse and was
walking over to them. He stopped. Dena watched him
remove his helmet and unbuckle his sword-belt. Leaving
his arms with one of his men, he continued alone to stand
a little way from the table.

Lord Baldric raised his arm in welcome, but Dena
could not hear what was being said. They were too far
away; the breeze was snatching their words and hurling
them in the other direction. She had to be able to hear
them. She had to know what was happening.

She clutched at the horse's mane and slipped from the
saddle. The Welshman beside her pointed and hissed

some unintelligible words, but even if she had been able to understand him she would have ignored his plea. She bobbed between the horses and ducked into the open woodland, running along the bank of the stream until she passed the line of Gwylan's waiting bodyguard, and was close to the talking noblemen. Crouching in the bracken behind a birch-tree so that she would not be noticed, she fought to bring her breathing under control in order to hear what was being said.

'Of course we had guards posted for sight of your arrival. It was Edwulf who said you might come a day early. Because we await you with a laden table, there is no reason to suspect treachery on our part.'

Gwylan's snort of derision was loud enough to be heard clear across to the ranks of his own men. Lord Baldric opened his arms expansively, choosing to ignore the blatant questioning of his honour.

'I stand before you, not as a Saxon, but as a man born of a royal house who acts as an intermediary between two landowners. I look upon each without favour to the other.'

Gwylan threw back his head and laughed. 'Now I know there is treachery afoot!'

Lord Baldric folded his arms across his substantial stomach and eyed him in a more confidential manner. 'I do not know how good your information is, but it is in all our interests, especially mine, to get this dispute settled as soon as possible—by nightfall at the latest. King Harold led a great victory against the Norwegians by a bridge at Stam's ford. The waters ran red with the blood of those who would treacherously assert their right to wear the English crown. Now another usurper sets his greedy eyes upon this land, William of Normandy. His ships are already beached on the southern coast, his army making ready. King Harold flies on the fleetest horse for London. At first light, Edwulf and I shall follow to be by his side on a new battlefield. This tawdry dispute *will* be settled before nightfall.'

Dena shuddered at the coldness of his tone. The threat was there, plain for all to hear, and Gwylan's men, ignorant of the English tongue, looked on in blissful innocence.

She turned to Edwulf to see where his intentions lay, but her uncle's face was as stony as the defensive wall behind him. He would not let his hall, his thegndom, slip through his fingers so easily. He had gained favours by fighting with the king, which was why he had been so eager to leave his hall, his people, to the threat of Gwylan's attack. Any man who would risk so much would not stand idly by and let a decision fall another's way.

She shut her eyes in an attempt to bite back her rising fears. Could there never be an end to this warring?

The men were talking again, talking of Rhodri.

'If you hold him, show him.'

'He is safe.'

Gwylan turned to Edwulf like a snarling dog. 'Safely buried in a grave somewhere?'

Edwulf stepped to the table, and leant his weight heavily on stiffened arms. 'You hold my niece.'

He almost spat the words, the vehemence reverberating between the stone fortifications and the wood where Dena hid. Instinctively she clasped her hands to her head, ready to shut out rumours she had been told of, and had told herself, but had barely believed could be true.

'And who informs you of this?' sneered Gwylan.

'Lord Baldric's posted guard, or your cut-throats sent to murder her?'

It was difficult to know who said what in the fury that followed. When order was restored and explanations called for, Gwylan was only too eager to build on his advantage.

'Not once, but twice, has this brigand delivered his kinswoman for the slaughter . . .'

'Lies! You would listen to this Welshman . . .'

'Yes, Edwulf,' Baldric cut him short with a glare that would have iced a boiling lake. 'I will listen to a Welshman's words, just as I have listened to yours. Time is short. Should you wish to loosen your tongue again, I shall speak to Lord Gwylan privately and give you no chance to hear what is said between us.'

Rage rippled through Edwulf's burning face, but he said nothing further. Dena believed that had her uncle had his sword to hand, he would have struck Gwylan a killing blow without thought to the consequences. She had always known that he could be brusque, and at times, unapproachable, but the hatred he now exuded . . . It was a madness, Wybert's madness!

'Believe it, Lord Baldric, this nubile maiden, daughter of his dead brother, given to the hands of an advancing army, an army whose blood-lust was risen for the battle . . .'

Edwulf turned away in disgust, but kept his mouth shut. Gwylan was in his element. It seemed to Dena that he would have made as good a story-teller as he did a leader of vengeful men.

'Had it not been for the young nobleman Rhodri ap Hywel, the Lady Dena's fate would have been sealed. It was with the honour of his forefathers that he took it upon himself to be her protector. Did he not stay by her side when your own men encircled them?'

Dena could not stop herself from blushing as she listened to Gwylan's story. She could only be amazed at how he contorted the truth to suit his own ends. No wonder he had not wanted her to attend him at this meeting!

'The lady has an agile mind, Lord Baldric, and a keen sense of justice. She is not a maid to sit with her embroidery and close her mind to what goes on around her. Do you think it was coincidence that she was taken from your roof before your return? Taken to the old hermitage by the marsh, left unguarded there, a route well used by outlaws and Welshmen alike? I tell you, Lord Baldric, it was the lady herself who told me she would be murdered upon the path here. I ask you in plain truth—would you have showed such favour to me standing here before you, had her hacked body been brought here for your eyes to feast upon? There is a stink of treachery in the air. You know it! False tales of Welsh uprisings filled your people's hearts with fear, but it served Edwulf well.' He paused, and looked at his adversary.

'No, Lord Baldric, I will not give this thegn his niece. Though I risk all I have fought for, she stays safely in my hands, lest she mysteriously take to her death-bed before the sun has a chance to rise again.'

With a flourish that could have graced any royal court, Gwylan stepped back from the table to await the next move.

Edwulf was not so patient, and turned to Lord Baldric. 'May I speak now?'

'No.'

'But it is all lies!'

'All of it? Even these tales of a Welsh uprising along the length of this land?'

The two men looked at one another. Edwulf spoke so quietly that Dena could hardly hear him.

'That was not my doing. I was at your side in the service of King Harold.'

Lord Baldric lifted an eyebrow in a most disconcerting manner.

'A dog cannot be blamed for the trick its master teaches it!'

There was another, significant, pause in the talking. Dena could almost feel the heavy atmosphere enshrouding the table. It seemed certain, now, that words had already passed between Lord Baldric and Edwulf. The Lady Nearra had, finally, believed her. Perhaps Bemere had not lied, after all? Perhaps Rhodri was alive!

Her chest filled to bursting as her hopes rose. When was she going to see him? Where was he? Why was he not there?

He was there, walking out through the gateway, taking long majestic strides into the field, but slowly, lazily, so that all might see him and know who he was.

The manacles were gone, the spoilt and dirty clothing. His dark shoulder-length hair, once so greasy and full of tangles, had been groomed until it shone. The narrow temple braids he had worn when she had first set eyes upon him delicately brushed his cheeks as he moved his head. An embroidered tunic of the deepest purple hid his scarred, maltreated body, and at his wrists the soft cloth was caught, not by chains, but by golden bracelets which glinted in the dwindling sunlight.

Dena pushed her knuckles into her mouth and bit down on them to stop herself from crying out in her joy, but there was no need. Had she called his name, none at the table would have heard her for the tremendous cheer that erupted from the Welsh ranks. She smiled, laughed even, as she watched him meet Gwylan, and the two men embraced.

What happiness she felt! Could she, dared she, run out from her hiding-place and take him in her arms?

It was a sore temptation, but one left in thought too long. The noisy welcome subsided, Gwylan and Rhodri parted, and once again the oppressive quiet returned to the field as the men eyed each other ominously across the table of untouched food.

Dena crouched low in the bracken, mindful of Gwylan's words. It was the land he was fighting for—not Rhodri's life, and certainly not her own, no matter how eloquently he defended her to Lord Baldric. Everyone was secondary, and more than likely could be sacrificed, to his goal. He would be none too pleased if, by being seen, she was to jeopardise the strength of his hand in any way. Much better that she should lie still and merely listen. She watched as Lord Baldric opened his arms.

'Our faith is good, that you cannot deny. It would be well if, as an act of your good faith, you discharge the Lady Dena into my hands. I willingly pledge her my protection.'

Gwylan showed little enthusiasm. Lord Baldric continued.

'She must be sorely tired after the strain of the last few days. The old hermitage makes for poor hospitality even with a full quota of retainers, and the lady has been in the saddle for many long hours. I think she would be grateful for rest and refreshment while we go about this business.'

Rhodri moved towards the table and filled a handsome glass goblet for himself from a jug. 'There would be little advantage for her to take refreshment in your chambers, my lord, however sumptuous they may be compared with the hermitage. She rides into the wild depths of Welsh-held lands with us this night.'

Dena stared at him as he nonchalantly quenched his thirst. She had craved his company, longed to be by his side, but put so bluntly . . . Could he not have stolen a moment to ask her? She sighed. Sweet words were as alien to this place as an undying friendship between Gwylan and Edwulf.

Lord Baldric was laughing. 'It is good that a little jesting should alleviate the seriousness of this matter.'

Rhodri slapped the goblet down on the coarse surface of the table. 'I do not jest. The Lady Dena is not part of any conditions to be agreed here, or any compensation. She is *mine*.'

The awkward silence only served to highlight Dena's growing disquiet.

'*Yours?* Like a horse is yours, or a cow?'

Rhodri straightened his back and slipped his fingers into the wide belt about his waist. 'Yes.'

Dena caught her breath. What was he saying? How could he be so tactless? After all the things Gwylan had said about her . . . She looked to Gwylan, hoping that he would say something in defence of her honour, but he had taken a step back and was watching the exchange with cool interest. Could this be part of some ruse they were playing?

Lord Baldric was not laughing now. His expression had turned decidedly fierce.

'I thought Welshmen stole only cattle. Have you taken to stealing our women now?'

Rhodri sneered his contempt. 'We have always stolen

your women. Perhaps you never noticed, because they were not of noble stock?'

'Edwulf told me you had demanded her to your bed.'

Rhodri turned his back on Lord Baldric, enabling Dena to see his face. She could not believe the mockery flitting tauntingly across his handsome features.

'But of course,' he said, waving a jewelled wrist in the air. 'Of course.'

Hiding her face in her hands, Dena sat mortified as her heart sank heavily. Edwulf's resentful voice drifted across to her.

'Well, Lord Baldric. Am I to be silent *now*?'

She did not listen further. She had been warned . . . She could not say that she had not been warned. Ethelin's tinkling laughter haunted the dark recesses of her mind. 'A prince? Is that what you think you have caught yourself, Dena? A prince?'

How could she have been so foolish? Like some silly maid of thirteen years, she had deluded herself. The animosity, the belligerence—it was his true self she had seen, not a covering for some softer emotions he dared not show.

When had he ever shown her any gentleness? Only the once, in that glade, and now that she looked back on it, his devotion had held a much less virtuous edge to it. And she had thrilled to his touch! How could she have done? There had been nothing but lust in his mind in that bower: pure, uncurbed lust.

She shuddered, suddenly feeling unclean. No wonder bawdy songs had been sung about her round the evening fires. Her reputation was in shreds, her honour—an ironic chuckle escaped her lips. What honour? By night-fall Edwulf would be only too pleased to let Rhodri take her into the wild hills of Wales. She would not go! For too long she had been tossed from hand to hand like some plaything. She was tired of their intrigue and their power-plays, of forever being used as a sacrifice or a hostage. She would show them! She would show them all!

Like a watching spirit, she rose from the bracken and swung herself round the birch to the lip of the deep-cut stream. She slithered down its earthen bank without thought of damaging her long kirtle, and strode through the ankle-deep water as though it did not exist. She scrambled up the further bank, the storm growing in her chest, and marched across the open field towards the objects of her anger.

Rhodri was leaning with one thigh upon the edge of the table, his attention fixed firmly on Lord Baldric. The others watched her approach in utter disbelief, but he did not turn until she was almost level with him. His expression was as incredulous as that of the rest. He slipped his leg off the table and made a move towards her, his lips curving into a lying smile of welcome.

'Do not say a word,' she warned, 'less I lose my self-control and strike you across the face before your men.' She turned to address the others, too.

'I am here to make plain my position. I am not the possession of any man, and will not be treated as such for the benefit of your talks.' She turned back to Rhodri, her erupting rage making it difficult to speak the words she needed.

'As for joining you in your bed . . . I would rather enter a nunnery!'

Her fists held rigidly by her sides, she turned, flinging her uncovered hair into his face, and strode towards the open gateway in the high defensive walls.

'Dena . . .'

It was Rhodri's voice, not her uncle's or Gwylan's . . . but Rhodri's.

Oh, that it had not been! She had wanted to hate him, to blame him for the deception of her own mind, but her anger was dissipating even as she crossed the threshold of the gateway, changing into the bubbling tears of misery.

All the people were crowded there, people from the many estates in the area, silently watching, silently listening to the bargaining of their noblemen, waiting nervously to hear if the outcome would lead to peace or the bloody warfare they feared. She could see them through her brimming tears. They looked at her with guarded eyes, drew their children close, moved aside to let her pass unheeded.

Dena quickened her pace, not wanting to be near them, not wanting to be near anyone. Why was she feeling like this? She had expected to experience elation after giving voice to her condemnation as she had; to feel avenged. All she knew was desolation.

'Dena!'

His cry hit her like an arrow in the back. Dearest Lord! Was he following her? *Please*, she prayed. *Spare me that, I beg of you!*

CHAPTER
FOURTEEN

DENA RACED up to the open doors of the hall, jostling aside anyone who impeded her way. She climbed the stone steps, almost tripping in her haste to mount them, and ran down the empty passage until she reached the sanctuary of the sleeping-chamber she had shared with Ethelin. Thankfully, Ethelin was not inside. Dena was alone in the room.

Resting her back against the heavy oak door, she closed her eyes, waiting for her heart to quieten its drum-like beating. She was safe there, safe from the unwelcome, prying eyes of the people, safe from Rhodri. He would not follow her here. He would not be allowed to follow her here.

She bent and pulled off her sodden slippers, dropping them by the door. Her breathing had calmed, the heat of her humiliation had subsided, but it had left her uncomfortably sticky. Her heart was still pounding. She walked over to the chest by the wall, but found no reason to be there. She walked back, trying to calm herself, trying to put everything that had happened behind her.

It was over, she told herself; there was no more to be done or said. The seed had grown, flowered, withered and died. The circle was complete. She had been shown her mistake, and had accepted it. It was time, now, to begin afresh. She clasped her hands together, still fighting to regain her composure, her self-esteem, and began to walk again, pacing the bare-boarded floor like a caged animal desperate for freedom.

The latch clicked loudly as it was lifted, and Dena turned quickly, afraid to discover who was entering. It could be a dozen people she had no wish to see. It could be Rhodri.

She was so relieved to find Elma, that she stepped across with a welcoming smile and took the girl by the hands.

'Oh, Elma, how good it is to see you!'

The maid looked taken aback. 'You—You are not angry with me?'

Dena did not understand. 'Why should I be angry with you?'

Elma blushed a little and averted her eyes. 'You were angry with me in the ladies' bower.'

The memory came flooding back: Elma's wide, frightened eyes, her own ferocious voice as she had shaken the girl mercilessly.

'I can only apologise to you, Elma, and say how sorry I am for the way I treated you. I was wrong, and I hope you can find it in your heart to forgive me.'

For a moment, Elma was too amazed to even speak. Dena doubted if anybody had ever apologised to her before. She seemed too embarrassed to think of a suitable reply.

'Have you come with a message?' Dena asked, to draw the conversation gently in another direction.

'Oh, yes! The Lady Nearra wishes you to join her at the evening meal. Lady Ethelin has sent me to help in your dressing. Would you like a tub to bathe?'

'A pail will do. Have you any idea why the Lady Nearra wishes to see me?'

Elma shook her head and began to help Dena out of her wet kirtle.

'No, my lady, but there has been much to-ing and

fro-ing from her chambers these last few days. You would not believe what has been happening. When Lord Baldric and Lord Edwulf returned, I heard that the arguments went on all night . . .' She glanced awkwardly at Dena. 'Of course, it is only rumours that I heard.'

'Yes,' Dena whispered. 'You must always be very wary of rumours. They can so easily be started to discredit people: rumours and straightforward lies.'

Elma did not answer. Dena wished that she had. The silence hung about her shoulders like a sodden wrap.

It was as though something had snapped inside her. She wanted to cry again, to let the misery and the hurt leave her body, leave it for good. She did not want Elma fussing round her. She wanted to be alone. She pushed wispy strands of hair from her face in irritation and turned to her, trying to keep her voice as steady as she could manage.

'I will bathe. I am sorry to change my mind, Elma, but I think it will ease the pains of the ride. Do you think you could find a tub?'

'Of course, my lady. I shall be as quick as I can.'

Dena sat on the smoke-darkened chest with her back against the cold stone of the wall. She could feel the rough, hand-hewn rock through the thinness of her woollen smock, the sharp, gritty protrusions forcing themselves into her skin. She had no wish to move.

The tears had come and gone, though she could not say why she had shed them. She had hoped for some sort of release, but instead had been left with a lassitude that threatened to overwhelm her. She was cold, too. The light entering the small window was fading, the shadows growing longer. It would soon be nightfall. Rhodri would be riding away, riding away for ever.

She cursed her feeble mind. She knew what he was, how he spoke of her to other men. What was this longing? Why did she not feel defiant?

The latch clicked its warning, and she hastily wiped her eyes and rubbed some colour into her stained cheeks. She did not want to foster any more rumours in Elma's mind; but it was not Elma. It was Wybert.

She watched him hold the latch as he pushed the heavy door closed. He was muffling its metallic sound, trying to be as quiet as he could. He had entered her chamber unobserved. He wanted to keep his presence secret.

Her stomach gave a sickening lurch. The intrigue, the arguments, the power-plays—they all came rushing back to her. Had she been correct about Wybert? Did he not want her to speak to Edwulf? Had he come to *kill* her?

She drew breath to let out a scream, but he turned to face her, and the cry lodged in her throat and would not move. She looked on in revulsion as his eyes swept up her slim frame, only hidden from his gaze by the thinness of her smock.

'I seem to have chosen a poor moment,' he murmured. 'I apologise for this disturbance, but I had to speak with you before you saw your uncle.'

Dena took a step backwards, her worst fears realised, but Wybert did not advance upon her. He seemed embarrassed at being there.

'I have not much time to speak to you. I do not know what words to use . . .' He grimaced, emphasising the lines about his eyes and the corners of his mouth.

'The rumours, the reputation you have gained, it makes no difference . . .' He paused again, shaking his head. 'No, it does make a difference. It gives me hope.'

He looked at her in earnest, his moist eyes full of pleading.

'I have always been fond of you, Dena, ever since that day you arrived in the snow. You were blue with the cold, such large, frightened eyes . . . I—I wanted to take you in my arms then, and give you the security you so desperately needed. Later, I asked Edwulf for your hand, but he had his eyes set on a courtly suitor for you.'

His voice trailed off to nothing. Dena saw him wince, as though he was biting back emotions he did not wish to put into words, emotions she hardly dared to guess.

'That will not be, now,' he added quickly. 'The King has promised Edwulf lands east of York. His thegndom is guaranteed, a place in the royal court. You will be an embarrassment to him there, perhaps even stop him being appointed to a position of authority. He will not take you with him, Dena. He will send you to a nunnery.'

Wybert nervously clasped his great hands together and tried to smile, but it did not put Dena at her ease. She felt strangely odd, being so baldly shown this side to his nature. Although she had lived under the same roof as him for nigh on three seasons, she had never had an inkling that it could have possibly existed. She listened with an unreal fascination, all the while expecting him to laugh and explain it as some savage jokery.

'I know you have no love for me. I do not ask for it. I would be a good husband to you, Dena. We could raise strong sons. You would be mistress of the hall. Edwulf might visit his lands here only once in a year. The rest of the time it would be ours to enjoy as we pleased. If you spoke to Edwulf, and told him you were willing for this union, I might be able to persuade him to agree.'

'I am not willing, Wybert.'

The sound of her own voice had a strange, awakening

effect on her senses. How could this man, who had taken such delight in sharpening an eating-knife like a tool of torture, stand before her and profess his—his love? How dared he stand there as meekly as a mouse and offer her marriage as an escape from life in a nunnery? It was beyond belief!

'I am not at all willing,' she reiterated more strongly. She could feel herself trembling, trembling with the tension and the anger building inside her.

'You tried to kill me, Wybert! You sent me to the north tun, knowing I would fall into the hands of the Welsh. You sacrificed me!'

Wybert paled, his lined face taking on the iron-grey colouring of his hair.

'No,' he breathed. 'No, you must believe me, Dena. I did not sacrifice you to the Welsh. I would rather have died than do that to you. I thought you would be safe there. I thought Gwylan would cross the marsh, and come by way of the old hermitage to the south of the hall. Radford saw them at the waterfall. It is to the south, Dena, believe me. I thought you would have been safe at the tun. Mildthryth told me she had seen them coming from the south, seen them with her mind. I believed her. I believed her!'

Dena held her breath. Wybert was crying. Like a child, he was crying. Tears were rolling down his cheeks, and he did not care. He did not even try to brush them aside. It was as though he did not know they were there.

He was waiting for an answer. She could tell by the plaintive look upon his face that he was waiting for her judgment of him. She was not sure whether she believed him or not, but she feared the reaction she might provoke if she spoke harshly.

'I believe you, Wybert.'

It was like pulling an arrow from a wounded animal. He moved from side to side in his joy, trying to speak words that would not come, his eyes shining in his excitement. He started towards her, but pulled himself short just as Dena began to back away. It was as if he remembered himself, remembered where he was, what state of dress Dena was in. He retreated towards the door.

'You will talk to Edwulf?' he prompted.

Dena did not know what to say. It was a foregone conclusion in Wybert's mind that she would agree to be his wife. She could not bring herself to accede to his wish, not even to rid herself of his company, but he was waiting, waiting for an answer that would satisfy him.

'I must think on it,' she began. Wybert turned peculiarly quiet, looking at her sidelong. 'It was in my mind to enter a nunnery,' she added quickly, 'as an act of repentance for my sins, to give my life to doing good instead of mischief . . .' What was she saying? She was babbling like a brook after a rainstorm. She placed her hands together and hoped that the Lord would forgive her blasphemy. 'I must pray, and take God's guidance.'

Wybert was nodding. 'Yes, it is the best way. I pray often, asking for guidance. The Lord never deserts a true believer. I shall go to the chapel and pray for you. We shall both pray.'

With a short nod of his head, he turned and lifted the latch to let himself out of the chamber.

Dena stared at the dark wood of the heavy door, hardly daring to believe that he had gone. Mildthryth had been correct. Wybert did have a madness. There was no doubt, now.

Much to Elma's unspoken consternation, after all her

efforts to bring the heavy tub, Dena was hardly in it long
enough to wet her skin. She could do little except
apologise and entreat the maid to hurry and braid her
hair. The sooner she spoke to someone about Wybert's
behaviour, the safer she would feel.

She had thought of seeking out Edwulf, but then felt
that such a hasty act might not be entirely wise. She was
still dubious about many of his motives. If he thought it
might serve his interests, he could well insist upon the
marriage, whether or not Wybert was mad.

The Lady Nearra would be the one to confide in, as
she had already discovered Wybert's lies about a mass
Welsh uprising. She knew Dena had been speaking the
truth from the beginning. Surely she would be sym-
pathetic, and Lord Baldric had offered his protection of
her, before witnesses, too. This might be a fortuitous
time to make sure that she received it. No matter what
she had told Rhodri in a spate of anger, she did not relish
spending her remaining days in the strict confines of a
nunnery.

The main chamber of Lord Baldric's hall was not as
crowded as Dena had expected. In fact, in comparison
with the usual bustle of an evening meal, it was almost
half empty. The setting of the tables had been rede-
signed to afford plenty of space in the aisles. Beside the
stone steps where she had faltered, the tables had been
arranged in the usual lines, but beyond the central fire,
towards the kitchen, they had been laid in a narrow
rectangle with a vast area behind, that was empty except
for two long benches.

Dena noticed Lady Nearra's old retainer walking
towards her and went out to meet him.

'I am to be seated next to the Lady Nearra, on her
instructions.'

The old man nodded, obviously already having been told, and turned to lead the way. Many of the ladies were already seated along one side of the rectangle. Dena's gaze was drawn to Ethelin, but whether by design or accident, she was too intent in her conversation to notice her niece.

The retainer indicated Dena's allotted cushion on the bench, and politely stood aside to wait until she was seated. She took time to settle herself, all the while glancing up and down the table, not at the waiting ladies, but at the plates set before them. The usual square wooden platters had all been replaced by metal ones: some of silver; those towards the centre of the table, of pure gold. She touched the rim of hers with a fingertip. A pure gold plate. She had never seen one before. She studied the empty table opposite. It was set in the same way: gold plates to the centre, silver plates to the edges. The standing goblets were exquisite too; coloured glass, engraved metals. In the centre, at the edge of the table, standing on its own plinth, was a beautifully worked chalice, the precious stones round its rim glittering darkly in the dancing firelight. This was no normal meal.

Dena motioned to the elderly retainer, who dutifully stooped to listen. 'What celebration is this? The return of the fyrd? The king's victory?'

'No, my lady. It is in honour of the Welsh noblemen.'

Dena stared at the deserted table. The Welsh. Gwylan had not left. He was being honoured with a feast.

Her mind focused on the seating arrangements. Of course, the women at this side, the men at that. Lord Baldric and Lady Nearra would be seated at the centre of the tables, with the other nobles and guests on either side of them.

She caught her breath. She would be looking directly

into the eyes of Rhodri! No, she could not sit and endure his gaze. She had been subjected to enough humiliation. As she began to rise, she thought better of it. She had to speak to the Lady Nearra, and she might not get another chance. Besides, would it not be better to sit and talk gaily with others, ignoring Rhodri completely? He would see her empty place as a kind of victory for his insults, but to be ignored, to show that she had no care . . .

The hollow bravado of her thoughts crowded in on the reality of her feelings. She did care. She cared for Rhodri, and had mistakenly believed that he cared for her. His mocking duplicity had hurt her deeply, and it was a hurt she could not hide.

She slipped her legs over the bench and rose to leave, but found her way barred by the Lady Nearra.

'Sit, Dena, sit. I must speak to you.'

Lady Nearra made herself comfortable, and Dena sat heavily on her cushion, pulled between obedience and her need to leave.

'My lady, I have no wish to join in this cel-ebration . . .'

'What celebration? Men—they can never agree over the simplest discussions! There is no celebration. Gwylan will not set foot within these walls, nor will he allow his men to eat food taken out to them in case it has been poisoned. The man is cautious beyond belief. He sees treachery at every turn.'

Dena let the Lady Nearra parade her annoyance without interruption. She glanced at the empty table opposite, at the place which would have been Rhodri's. She could see him sitting there, in a ghostly kind of way, his narrow braids dancing alongside his sun-burnished cheeks, the flash of his dark eyes as he laughed. He had

laughed with her in the intimacy of that glade. He had
put his hand over hers and smiled in his contentment
—or so she had believed. No arrow could have hurt
more than the shaft of truth which had buried itself in her
heart as she hid among the bracken at the edge of the
wood.

'Dena, do you listen to me?'

Dena shook herself from her reverie and looked into
the Lady Nearra's anxious face.

'I tell you there is plotting within our own ranks. I do
not trust your uncle. His eyes are set far above his
station, and he has a hungriness about him that bodes ill
for anyone who stands in his way. I have little respect for
that Welshman, Gwylan, but I hear that he stood before
my husband and demanded your protection, believing
your life to be in danger from your own kin.'

Dena wearily dropped her eyes. 'He was trying to gain
an advantage over Edwulf.'

'Perhaps, but that does not mean there was no truth in
what he said. I put little faith in a man who would risk the
safety of his lands and his family simply in order to gain
favour with a new king. And that tale he had Wybert tell!
He threw the stability of the whole area into chaos
merely to guarantee that those fighting men who could
be rallied would protect his property in his absence. The
man is despicable!'

Dena glanced at her in concern. She had always
thought of the Lady Nearra as being quiet and unassum-
ing, content to run her hall and leave politics to the men,
but to hear her now . . .

'Wybert has a madness.'

For a moment the Lady Nearra was silent. 'It surprises
me little,' she said. 'There was an unaccountable wild-
ness about him after I had stopped him burning that

Welsh prince. He was incensed that I should have interfered.'

'He wishes me to wed him.'

'After all he has done to you? The man *is* mad.'

'I fear his anger if I refuse. In plain words, I fear that I might not be allowed the choice. He says that Edwulf would be only too pleased to be rid of me, and I believe him. Lady Nearra, I need the protection of your husband.'

She placed her hand on top of Dena's, and squeezed it reassuringly. 'I will ensure that you have it. Do you have other relatives you can go to?'

Dena shook her head, too close to tears to speak.

'And you do not wish to enter a nunnery?'

She could not hide her look of surprise. It seemed that the discussions had been relayed to the Lady Nearra in every detail.

'I thought not.' A little smile played across her lips. 'Many an untrue word is spoken in anger. You fought for that young man so long, Dena. Why do you not make your peace with him before he leaves?'

Dena lowered her eyes, not wishing to speak of Rhodri. 'I was not the one to betray faith. He spoke of me as though I were a whore. I was never his.'

'Not in body, perhaps, but even I could see you were in mind. You had no other reason to fight for him as you did. A woman does not always give her heart to the one her family would choose for her.'

'He degraded my name before other men, and laughed while he was doing it.'

'The ways of men are many, and never more confusing than when they stand with a sword in their hands.' Lady Nearra shook her head sadly. 'I can only say that he did not speak thus of you when he was under my protection.'

An inexplicable turmoil raged within Dena. Her pride demanded that she shun all mention of him, while her heart ached to find reasons, excuses for his deception.

'Rhodri spoke of me?'

Lady Nearra raised her eyebrows guardedly. 'He spoke of little. He had no trust, but he was genuinely fearful for your safety.' She sucked her lip thoughtfully. 'If I were you, and I wanted to know what was truly in his heart, I would ask the old woman, Mildthryth.'

'Mildthryth?'

'Yes. There is a link between those two. She knows Rhodri of old.'

'I do not think so. She spoke of seeing his father once.'

'Gruffydd? He was killed three years ago,' Lady Nearra said in surprise.

Dena nodded. 'She told me.'

They were interrupted by the elderly retainer, who whispered a message into Lady Nearra's ear. She nodded to him and made to leave the table.

'It seems that a settlement is at hand. My husband asks for me. I shall speak to him about your guardianship at the first opportunity. Remember what I said: see Mildthryth.'

Dena watched her make her way down the aisle, the skirt of her embroidered kirtle trailing along the rush-strewn floor. Did she need to know what truly lay in Rhodri's heart? Did it matter any more?

She stared at the empty table opposite, at the chalice standing unused, the chalice of faith. Every man would have drunk from it: Rhodri, Gwylan, Edwulf, Baldric. Each would have taken it in turn and drunk as a mark of faith, but each believed in treachery and would not be the first to raise the cup.

It did matter, to know what Rhodri held secret in his

heart. Perhaps Ethelin had been right. Perhaps, from the very start, he had played with her affections, gained amusement from watching her react to his whim. Yet, all that filled Dena's mind now was his look of desperation as she had let her anger have its head at the table in the field. He had called her name as she had run from that place, and followed her to the very gates of the hall, calling her name again and again. If she had only stopped to listen to what he had to say. Like the warring lords, she had had no faith.

Go to Mildthryth. Yes, she would seek out Mildthryth, not to learn what was truly in Rhodri's heart, but to tell what was truly in hers. Mildthryth would find a way to speak to him. Mildthryth could see more than mortal eyes could show. She would know how to reach him.

CHAPTER
FIFTEEN

OUTSIDE, IN the cold, clear air, the dark cloak of night was chasing the last yellow streaks of daylight to the furthermost reaches of the western horizon. There was a gentle breeze, but it was not strong enough to blow what few clouds there were across the face of the quarter moon. Dena was grateful for its light, however pale and shadowy. She had no wish to walk past Mildthryth without recognising her.

It was a gamble, going to the area by the dog-pens, Edwulf might have moved his people, or got Wybert to do it for him, but with Gwylan's men still beyond the wall, Dena reasoned that it was a gamble weighted heavily in her favour. It was one, luckily, in which she succeeded.

'Why have you come?' Mildthryth demanded.

Dena recoiled at the old woman's angry tone. 'I came to speak with you of Rhodri. I hoped you could tell me where he was, or take a message to him.'

Mildthryth growled in the shadow of her hooded wrap. 'Did you think of this yourself, or did someone send you?' A bony finger darted out and prodded her forcefully in the chest. 'Speak truthfully, now.'

Dena took a step backward, peering anxiously at the old woman in the gloom. She sounded different . . . almost fearful.

'The words are mine alone, but I came on the prompting of the Lady Nearra.'

'Nearra!' Mildthryth threw off her hood and gazed

about. 'The woman knows,' she hissed. She grasped Dena's arm and began to drag her away behind the huts.

Dena tried to pull herself free, but the old woman's grip was like iron. Mildthryth paused in the heavy shadow of overhanging thatch, and stared back along the path. There were people shuffling about, trying to find somewhere warm and dry to spend the night. Nothing seemed out of place.

'What is wrong?' she whispered.

Mildthryth pulled her on a little further. 'I am discovered. I knew that woman suspected something when she called me to her chamber. She wanted me to attend to Rhodri's wounds, or so she said. But I knew she had guessed. 'I *knew*.'

'Guessed what?'

Mildthryth looked at her and chuckled. 'So trusting a child! How could you have ever suspected me of being Gwylan's eyes, Gwylan's ears? No one did, especially not Edwulf.'

Dena could not believe what she was hearing. 'You spied on your lord for Gwylan?'

'Edwulf was never my lord. My allegiance has always been with Gwylan. It was of my ancestors and shall be of my descendants.'

'You are Welsh,' Dena gasped, 'but you speak our language so distinctly!'

'And Gaelic and French, too. It changes nothing. How did Gwylan know to attack the hall? Did a raven tell him?'

'You poisoned the ale, Mildthryth. Those men nearly died.'

'I warned Gwylan there would be treachery. I sent him a sign, but the foolish man misread it.'

'A sign? What sign?'

Mildthryth cackled in that haunting way she had. 'You!'

Dena rocked back on her heels.

'I knew the men sighted to the south were merely a feint, that Gwylan was coming from the north, so I got Wybert to send you to the tun to meet him.'

Dena was struck by an awesome thought. 'Edwulf knew nothing of the plan?'

'How could he? He was riding to the King.'

Dena shuddered, the bile rising in her throat. All this time she had been convinced that Edwulf and Wybert had been plotting against her, using her for their own selfish ends. It had been Mildthryth, the one person she had trusted.

'They could have *killed* me, Mildthryth.'

The old woman tilted up her head to look at her, the moonlight clearly showing the defiance in her face.

'Your life is not sacred. The power is in the land. Only the land endures.' She shook her head sadly. 'Even Gwylan does not see that.'

Dena turned away, biting back tears of frustration and anger. She cared nothing for the land.

'And Rhodri?' she spat acidly. 'What part did he have to play in this charade?'

'I was as innocent of the mischief as you.'

The sound of a man's voice in the darkness startled the two women. Dena jumped back in alarm. It was Mildthryth who drew the knife.

'Put up your weapon, old woman. It is truly Rhodri ap Hywel!' He stepped out of the shadows to show himself in the moonlight. 'I shall do you no harm, though I fear there are many here who would.'

Mildthryth grudgingly thrust the knife back into the depths of her clothing.

'You are a fool to come within these walls again,' she rasped.

'Perhaps, but you are a bigger fool to stay.'

Mildthryth stumbled by him. 'I do not stay. I cross the bridge to stand with my true lord. I would advise you to do the same.'

Rhodri merely nodded. Mildthryth paused to see if he was going to follow her. When he made no attempt to do so, she turned and melted into the darkness.

Dena clasped her hands together in a vain effort to stop herself from trembling. He was standing before her, Rhodri, as she had envisaged. His dark hair blended with the shadows, making it almost invisible to her eyes, but his face was flooded with moonlight, revealing his cheekbones, the curve of his chin, in a starkly chiselled form.

'I knew nothing, Dena, only that you fell into my hands—and into my heart.'

There was a fluttering in her breast that she could not readily identify, but it excited her. There were no words to tell him how she felt.

'You stand in the shadows,' he whispered. 'I cannot see you.'

The shadows were like a shield, protecting her. She was vulnerable, afraid that this moment might dissolve in some hideous nightmare and leave her with nothing.

She stood, silently, the night breeze pulling playfully at her clothing, until her courage returned. She stepped on to the lighted path, curling her fingers round his hands that were outstretched to meet hers. It was a tentative joining, one full of promise, full of apprehension.

'I truly believed you had betrayed me, Dena. It gave me more pain than any wounding of the flesh. I was angry, resentful, ashamed that I could be so easily deceived. The belief ate into my mind, smothering all else. I could not see that it was only you who were constant in such a maelstrom of deception.'

She heard him draw breath and hold it in his lungs. His fingers curled tighter about her hands. His skin was warm, wet even, perspiring like her own.

'Those words you heard me speak before Baldric and Edwulf—they were never meant for your ears, never meant to harm you. It was not until the Lady Nearra took me into her protection that I realised what rumours you had endured. Even the wagging of the vilest tongue was believed. I asked if you were safe. They would not say. I demanded to see you. I was laughed at; but when Baldric returned, there was a change. He was anxious to restore peace to the land. Through me, he believed he could placate Gwylan. I was given food, a chamber, clothing, anything I wanted, but when I asked for you, all I received was excuses.'

He stepped towards her, drawing her hands to his face, holding them to his cheeks, brushing her fingers with his lips.

'Dena, I thought you were dead.'

She quivered at his touch, at the strength of emotion in his voice. How often had she longed for him to respond to her in this way! She wanted to hold him close, to tell him she loved him with all her heart, to tell him that the past did not matter, the future was all . . . But there was a need within him, she could feel it, a need to rid himself of the guilt he bore. She had to let him speak, let him cleanse his soul, if that was what it took to calm his fevered mind.

'My joy knew no bounds when I heard you rode with Gwylan, but the fear came rushing back. Saxon, Welsh

—both would use you to gain their own advantage, just as they used me.'

He dropped her hands to clutch her shoulders, bringing her closer to him as he looked into her face with an urgency bordering on desperation.

'I have seen this before, Dena, and felt its consequences when I was left in King Edward's court. Had Edwulf offered Gwylan a quarter of his lost lands, he would have handed you to him without a qualm. I would never have seen you again. I had to see that you were eliminated from the talks. I was willing to try anything, even to degrade your worth.' He shook his head dejectedly. 'But you were never meant to hear. Never.'

Dena could bear no more. She lifted her hands to his face and cradled his cheeks in the softness of her palms.

'Rhodri, my love . . .'

His breath escaped his body like a tremulous wind rushing free. She felt it on her lips, moist and yearning, felt his arms slip round her shoulders, supporting her back. Softly, tentatively, his mouth came down on hers. Arching her neck, she closed her eyes, letting her temporal existence fuse with the immortality of her desire.

She gasped as his lips whipped away so savagely. His arms, no longer gentle, forced her from him with a power that rippled fearfully through her limbs. Her eyes snapped open. She did not believe the change in him, begged him to deny it.

The reason was in his face, his eyes narrowed against the glaring torchlight. She reeled about to find its source held high in the air. Encouraged by the night breeze, its dancing flames licked at the thatching above their heads. Beneath it, almost silhouetted in the glare, was a burly giant of a man who could be none other than Wybert!

'Now the truth is plain, indeed! Talk of nunneries and a life devoted . . . You would cuckold me and laugh!'

Dena had not seen him draw his sword, and the sight of the rising blade glinting in the torchlight filled her with terror. She stepped back against Rhodri, pushing him away with all the force she could muster.

'Go! For mercy's sake, be gone!'

Instead of turning away, Rhodri put his arms round her and they tumbled beneath the overhanging roof to fall against the wattle wall of the little hut. There was a dull crunching as Wybert's sword cut into the brittle thatch and jammed there. Rhodri threw Dena to one side to give him room to draw both sword and dagger.

'It is your head he wants! Follow Mildthryth. Run to Gwylan!'

There was no fond smile, no meaningful look to say what a thousand chosen words could not. The lover's cloak had been thrown off. With teeth bared and blood high, Rhodri was a fighting man once more, all the instincts of his boyhood training to the fore.

He jumped into the narrow passage between the huts, his sword raised in defence, as Wybert bore down on him with a roar of bear-like rage. The clash of forged weapons shattered the eerie silence of the night, and Dena jumped as if her own body had sustained the blow.

She struggled to her feet, slipping on the foulings of man and beast alike, and backed along the fragile wall to the edge of the low-roofed hut. The spectacle of the fight held a terrifying fascination which threatened to immobilise her. Rhodri was the younger man, slimmer, more agile in his movements, but it was the massive bulk of Wybert which held the stronger arm.

Rhodri shuddered as he held and deflected the power of his assailant's two-handed blow. Again Wybert came on, the sword whirling like a demented threshing-flail. His face was contorted beyond recognition, his eyes wide and wild as the demon writhed inside him. The madness drove him now. Dena could see it in the light of the discarded torch. He attacked without thought for his own defence, for the protection of his own life. Hate fed on hate, multiplying his strength beyond normal bounds. Rhodri would not defeat him. The realisation screamed in Dena's mind. Rhodri could not defeat him!

She stood a moment, fighting down the panic. Perhaps he did not intend to defeat him. Perhaps he was merely stalling Wybert, giving herself time to escape over the bridge. Rhodri was the fleeter of foot, and could easily outrun Wybert. Yes, that had to be the plan—but she had not run. Rhodri had fallen into Saxon hands in the glade because she had not run on his command, because he had altered his flight to come to her side. Dearest Lord, if he should falter a second time!

The vision of Wybert's sword slicing down on to Rhodri's defenceless back made her turn at once. She gathered the skirt of her kirtle and ran for her life, for his.

As the bridge came into sight, Dena hesitated, dodging behind the last small hut. Bathed in the dim, silvery moonlight she could see a man leaning on its guard-rail —a sentry. He was not looking in her direction. Should she try to run straight by him? Would it be better to walk sedately? She dithered. Mildthryth must have crossed safely, she told herself. By what other way had Rhodri been able to enter? Her stomach heaved in uncertainty.

There was a fizzing noise, like that sometimes made by ale during the brewing, only louder, and the whole scene, the bridge, the defensive wall, the sheer sides of the ditch—everything—was flooded with a brilliant light. The guard turned to look, and Dena turned with him. Flames were rising above the roofs of the huts, bright red sparks being carried up into the night sky on a pall of grey smoke.

'Rhodri!'

Her cry came unbidden, but was lost in the cacophony of screams and shouts and the barking of the dogs in their pen. Fire! The fear of man and beast alike. Wybert's discarded torch had set a hut aflame.

Dena did not think. Her decision was instant. She raced back the way she had come.

The light was so bright, the heat so intense, that she thought at first she was seeing spectres in the smoke. Wybert and Rhodri had parted and were standing a little distance from each other, Rhodri almost wedged beneath the overhanging roof of the hut next to the fire. In a semicircle, behind Wybert, a group of armed men were moving closer.

'You *dare* to burn my estate!'

Dena was surprised to hear Lord Baldric's voice above the crackling of the flames, and then she realised what he thought had happened. She flung herself forward.

'No! There is no treachery. It was Wybert's torch.'

The men were taken aback by Dena's sudden appearance, but not Wybert. He unleashed himself with a scream that froze her in her stride. She saw his face twisting in a frenzy as he loomed before her, bearing down on her with his sword raised high. She could do nothing. She stood as if transfixed, her eyes widening to accept each awful detail as the glinting blade swept down.

There was an ear-splitting clash above her head, and

she flinched to see Rhodri forcing Wybert's sword aside with his own. Without warning, without a cry, Wybert shuddered and then went limp. His legs buckled beneath him and he fell to his knees. He seemed to hang there a moment, the hate-filled madness draining from his whiskery face, before the sword slipped from his hand and his body slumped on top of it. Dena stared at the bloody pool stretching itself across the back of his tunic. She stared, but she could not accept that Wybert was dead.

'It is better that my sword strike him down.'

Dena raised her eyes at the sound of Lord Baldric's voice. He was standing so close that it seemed impossible for her not to have noticed him before. She shuddered at the sight of his bloodied sword held rigidly in his hand, held ready for defence or attack.

The tense atmosphere began to permeate her senses. Rhodri still had his sword-arm across the line of her body. The two men were watching each other, both distrustful, both waiting for that sudden convulsive movement which would send them into combat. She saw Rhodri tighten his hand round the hilt of his weapon, and sent up a silent prayer.

'I will have nothing mar this peace I have forged between Edwulf and Gwylan. He swore he would keep you on a leash!' Baldric bared his teeth in his anger, and drew his lips down in a thin line. He stepped back and turned to his men.

'Pull that hut down before it fires my hall. Pull all these huts down!'

He looked back at Rhodri with eyes smarting from the smoke. 'Be gone, Welshman. I have not seen you here.' He motioned to the prostrate figure of Wybert. 'All this is Saxon business. Get back to the safety of your uncle's side, and stay there.' He curled his mouth in a mocking smile of derision.

'Yes, I know of your kinship with Gwylan, that his sister was bedded by Gruffydd during a drunken feast. There is no secret that Gwylan would not disclose if the price were right. He and Edwulf would make fine kin themselves. Be gone, bastard prince, before I change my mind.'

Dena laid a hand on Rhodri's arm. He shook her off, stepping between her and Baldric's men. He flexed his sword-arm menacingly.

'Your words do not shame me! I live by the sword in my own name, and I will die by it here.'

Baldric looked astounded. 'I kill you here, and every son from Gruffydd's loins will rise against me in a blood-feud!'

'It is your choice. You are the one riding to the south to fight beside your king. Dena goes with me, or my body falls here.'

The fired hut crumpled behind Baldric, momentarily catching his attention. As the other huts began to fall around them, Baldric's men stamped wildly on the smouldering thatch.

'Decide!' snapped Rhodri.

Baldric let his sword dangle limply by his leg. He looked from Dena to Rhodri, and back to Dena again.

'Is this your wish, or is there some duress I know nothing of?'

Dena stepped forward to stand beside Rhodri. Her heart felt so full that she thought the words would never come.

'It is my wish, my lord. I hope you will give us your blessing.'

'Blessing? You go with him, and there will be no

return, not even in widowhood. You cannot speak the language. Whatever you are to him, you will be a Saxon to his people, niece of Edwulf who sent the pestilence which killed their children. You will always be resented, and shunned for what you are. Do you still wish to go with him?'

Rhodri lowered his sword and turned to look at her. His dark eyes were haunted with concern.

'He speaks the truth, Dena. I can love you for the rest of my life, but I cannot make others love you.'

If they had been alone, she would have shown him her answer without the need for words, but the prying eyes stilled her. She looked to Lord Baldric.

'My heart, my love, my life; they all belong to Rhodri ap Hywel.'

Lord Baldric shook his head wearily. 'Be gone! Be gone! I have to smooth enough ruffled feathers without having Edwulf standing here with his sword in his hand.'

Dena felt Rhodri's fingers curl about her wrist, and she turned to him, hardly able to restrain her relief, her excitement. He had time for neither. He pulled her behind him, away from the remnants of the burning hut, along the path, past Baldric's silently watching men. They did not stop even when they reached the bridge. No guard stood sentry now, and they ran across, their feet thundering on the undulating boards, the sound echoing back to their ears from the depths of the defence ditch below.

The grass was damp in the meadow beyond. Dena could feel it soaking through her slippers, catching on the hem of her kirtle, but still Rhodri made her run, run though her lungs were bursting, run to the shelter of the forest edge.

Hidden from the moon's silver glow, they drew to a

halt. Dena sank on to the bracken, her chest heaving for breath. She wiped the sticky perspiration from her brow and looked up at Rhodri. He was panting, too, one arm leaning against the trunk of a birch-tree, but his eyes were fixed on the bridge, scanning the clearing between them and the defence ditch.

'Have you still no trust?'

Rhodri leaned over and pulled her to her feet.

'Never trust a Saxon!' he stressed. His stern face broke into a warm smile and he gathered her up into his arms. 'They wait until your back is turned, and then they steal your heart!'

Dena laughed. It seemed to be the first time she had laughed in a long, long time. She slipped her arms round his neck and raised her lips to meet his. Such a sweet embrace she could never have imagined. They held each other tightly, their bodies moulding into one. They parted, each with a sigh of unsatisfied desire.

'I think,' Rhodri murmured into her hair, 'that I will have to take you to wife faster than I thought. I can feel my father's blood raging in my veins.'

Dena smiled teasingly. 'The lover, or the fighter?'

He slid an arm about her shoulders, and began to lead her along the edge of the trees to where he knew Gwylan waited with the horses.

'Both,' Rhodri decided. 'It will always be both.'

EPILOGUE

RHODRI AND Dena were wed in the little wooden chapel adjoining Gwylan's hall. Dena made it her foremost task to learn the language and customs of Rhodri's people, and before the birth of her first child she could speak the language fluently.

As Mildthryth had foretold, King Harold did not live to see the winter through. He died on Senlac ridge on the 14th of October, only eleven days after Rhodri had won Dena for his bride. Many brave men died with him, including Edwulf and Lord Baldric.

When news of the defeat reached the Saxon estates straddling the Welsh border, the evacuation was immediate. With the fyrd very much reduced and the thegns dead, no one wished to spend a winter under the threat of Welsh incursions. Ethelin took her husband's people to her ancestral home in Mercia. No Welshman stopped them. By the first melting of the winter snows, Gwylan had repossessed all his lost lands without a drop of Welsh blood being spilled; but within a year he was fighting to retain them against an influx of Norman lords who had been granted whole areas of the borderland by the new King William. Slowly, inevitably, the Welsh had to retreat before the Norman onslaught.

Rhodri, as he had forsworn, never again sought out the kin of his father's blood, but stayed with his mother's family and fought alongside Gwylan in every battle that ensued. Dena, underterred by the adversities which beset them, remained steadfastly beside her husband,